A self-described bantersexual – make her laugh and she'll be eating out of the palm of your hand – Elizabeth McKenzie has written several screenplays for feature films, with her projects placing in top international screenwriting contests including Screencraft, Final Draft, and the Austin Film Festival. Her newsletter, Delusional, reaches more than 10,000 readers each week. Elizabeth lives in Melbourne, Australia, with her husband, their son, and their dog, who is the goodest girl.

BED CHEMISTRY

ELIZABETH McKENZIE

PENGUIN BOOKS

TRANSWORLD PUBLISHERS

UK | USA | Canada | Ireland | Australia
India | New Zealand | South Africa

Transworld is part of the Penguin Random House group of companies
whose addresses can be found at global.penguinrandomhouse.com.

Penguin Random House UK, One Embassy Gardens,
8 Viaduct Gardens, London SW11 7BW

penguin.co.uk

Penguin
Random House
UK

First published in the United States by Alcove Press,
an imprint of The Quick Brown Fox & Company LLC

First published in Great Britain in 2026 by Penguin Books
an imprint of Transworld Publishers

001

Printed and bound in Great Britain by Clays Ltd, Elcograf S.p.A.

The authorized representative in the EEA is Penguin Random House Ireland,
Morrison Chambers, 32 Nassau Street, Dublin D02 YH68.

A CIP catalogue record for this book is available from the British Library

ISBN: 9781804998625

Penguin Random House is committed to a sustainable future
for our business, our readers and our planet. This book is
made from Forest Stewardship Council® certified paper.

MIX
Paper | Supporting
responsible forestry
FSC® C018179

Dedicated to Harry Styles's hair.
None of this would exist without you.

And to those who ache to rake their fingers
through perfect curls—I see you. I am you.

CHAPTER ONE

"Ashleigh Hutchinson, please report to the principal's office."

The voice summoning me over the intercom crackles through the dull murmur of the chemistry lab. Students abandon their Bunsen burners and beakers—some clear, others filled with orange bubbling liquid, a couple with radioactive green—in favor of staring at me.

One beaker goes up in smoke. That'll be fun to clean up later. Or should I say, throw out? Not even acetone can save that beaker. And I refuse to use beakers that have been compromised by organic matter in my classroom. I do have standards.

The air is so thick with bitter smoke that I cough. The entire room smells like the burned coffee you get from the hole-in-the-wall coffee shop near the Metro station, the kind you know only makes a profit because caffeine is an addiction and a severe hangover can make you pay five dollars for a cup of literal garbage that's been baking on the sidewalk during a record heat wave in summer. Which I did, coincidentally, just this morning.

"Oooooohhh, what'd you do, Miss Ash?" Jonah calls out from the back of the class, setting off a chain of gossipy whispers. Other teachers have dubbed him the "class clown"—his mission, to disrupt the class. But the way I see it, he's a natural leader. And funny as fuck, too, though I'll never tell him that—he can figure it out when he inevitably becomes the CEO of a start-up in Silicon Valley.

I touch my nose and point at Jonah, implying I know what I did to get sent to the principal's office and I'm not telling. The truth is, I have no idea why I'm being summoned right now. Then I direct my attention to the entire class. "Turn off your burners, bottle up your concoctions, and finish your lab reports."

I launch myself out of the chair and crack a window to diffuse the smell. "Aaron, you're in charge," I say to the smartest thirteen-and-a-half-year-old I've ever met. "And don't forget to label your bottles. I need your name, today's date, and your blend." I close the door behind me.

The truth is, the lab report means nothing. It's the last day of school. They all passed with flying colors. But why waste one final opportunity to practice? Plus, I now have ten bottles of simple syrup just in time for the summer break. Okay, make that nine. They can't all be winners.

This year I went for a combination of orange-infused, lime-infused, and straight-up sugar water. I can't wait to try Aaron's tonight, hair of the dog and all. Which appears to be the only way to cure the kind of pounding headache I currently have. Believe me, I've tried everything else.

I turn the corner and nearly bump into Miss Clare, Sherman Oaks Private School's biology teacher and my personal hype woman.

"Ash," she says, placing her hand gently on my arm as we do the hallway tango of walking around each other while fitting in as much interaction as we possibly can before our feet take us our separate ways. She tilts her head toward the intercom in the hall with a smile. "Promotion?"

"On the last day of school? Hardly," I say, laughing. *I wish*. But maybe someday. Principal Holland will need to retire sooner or later, and I know I'm the right person to replace him.

"Another award, then," she says, getting excited.

"Maybe," I say, a little coy, like it's nothing when in fact, every award I win is another step closer to proving I'm capable of running the school.

I resume my march toward the office, but not before clamping down on the smile that's creeping across my face. Shit, maybe I *am* getting promoted.

Connie, the school administration manager, waves me through without looking up from her extremely loud and ASMR-porn worthy keyboard. She's always typing. I don't think I've ever seen her *not* type. Which is weird, right? Like how many school newsletters can she send out in a week? And how many times can she ask the parents for more money for even more "state-of-the-art" facilities?

I have a theory that Connie is secretly like Allison Janney's character in *10 Things I Hate About You*—an erotica author who goes by a pen name, something like Mike Hunt, and she writes all day about his "throbbing member" entering her "slit."

Now Connie gives me a small nod of permission and I head into Principal Holland's office. I'm immediately assaulted by a barrage of participation awards hanging from the walls. You know, "Best Dressed School of 1984" and "Healthiest Lunch

3

Menu in the County." I search for the "Biggest Asshole" certificate for Principal Holland but come up short. I don't even know how he gets these awards. Is there a principal awards night where sad people go to feel validated?

Don't get me wrong. I love teaching. I love my students. But I loathe Principal Holland. If I were to profile him like I was on *Criminal Minds*, my binge-watching show of choice, he'd be a serial killer, no question. Male, midforties, mother issues—which is why he obviously hates strong women. He thinks the world owes him.

Hearing me, the man himself swivels around on his vintage oxblood leather chesterfield chair and gestures for me to sit. "Ashleigh," he says in such a slimy way I almost vomit in my mouth. How can someone make you hate the sound of your own name? "Do you know the reason I've called you out of your class today?"

Guess we're skipping the small talk. Thank God.

I'm about to straight-up ask where my latest award is but decide to play it cool.

"Is it about the simple syrup? Brilliant, right? The kids love learning about hydrolysis," I say, explaining how lessons in chemistry can double as lessons in useful life skills.

He shakes his head. "We've had complaints."

Wait, what? *Complaints?* That's unexpected. I care for my students. I take them from flailing preteens who can't even tell you that hydrogen is the first element on the periodic table to having the top grades in the state. *And* they can whip up a mean simple syrup.

"What are you talking about? If I'm not mistaken, one of those awards on your wall states I'm the best chemistry teacher in the state." I point to the wall where, in fact, a plaque with my name on it is displayed. Granted the school's name is even bigger. And Principal Hollandfuck's name is on it too. But still, it's there. Proof.

The smallest smirk rests in the corner of Principal Holland's mouth. He's totally getting off on this. The *Criminal Minds* profile stands. I wouldn't be surprised if he had a basement full of body parts. Wheels up in twenty.

"It is not about your classroom, Ashleigh." Again, with the name. I shiver. "I've had numerous reports about your out-of-school activities," he goes on, emphasizing the *out-of-school* part so forcefully I can smell the stale tobacco from the not-so-secret cigarette he smokes at lunch. "Our reputation is important, and your . . . *promiscuous* behavior is leaving a bad taste in the mouth of the parents, the faculty, and the school community."

And suddenly, I know exactly where this is going.

Mrs. Kelly. The fucking PE teacher. She ratted me out.

Okay, here's the deal. Not that I need to justify myself to anyone, but this is what I know to be true.

There's oxytocin. That's the love drug. And then there's lust. That's the pure sex hormone. And they are polar opposites. I'm talking smokin' hot and frigid cold. Pleasure and pain in the ass. Soaking wet and very, *very* dry. Love and sex: never the two shall meet. You can fall in love, or you can have great sex. But love and chemistry can't coexist.

That's why the Bone It app was invented.

No dating. No love. Just hookups. For one night only.

Now imagine, if you will, the kind of men who use said app.

Yep. Those kind of men. Which, admittedly, makes meeting one of them after work an oversight on my part. But after two duds in a row, the horny inside was desperate.

Last week, app in hand, I found a dude who lived around the corner. I swiped right on my lunch break. He insisted he meet me at the end of my workday and walk me back to his place. Add in the handful of my ass he grabbed as I barely crossed the school gates, and to be honest, I'm lucky only Mrs. Kelly saw.

The man in question? I don't remember his name, but I remember he had a curve to it. And he reached places not even my vibrator could.

I *was* content with my rule. It *hadn't* failed me.

Until now.

Principal Holland's corner smirk has grown into a full-blown one. I want to punch it off his face. Instead, I take a breath. He's waiting for my response.

There are two ways this can go down from here. The first: he'll try to control my private life and, in that case, blessed be the fucking fruit. Or: he'll use this as grounds to fire me.

I note his smug expression. *Holy shit.* He's going to fire me. No. No way. Impossible.

But apparently, it is quite possible.

"We're letting you go, effective immediately," he says, looking oh-so-very-pleased with himself, as if he gets off on ruining a person's life. Which, let's be honest, he probably does.

I pick my jaw up off my floor. I can't believe this is happening. A part of my brain is questioning the legality of this—can he actually fire me for my social behavior? What will happen to my students who are taking advanced chem with me next year? Who's going to make sure the supply cupboard is properly labeled? I glance at my watch. It's 3:11 PM. The bell is about to ring.

"What the f—?" I stop myself, knowing if I let out one little *fuck*, I'm gone for sure. I clear my throat. "You can't fire me over the people I date." I use the term loosely because there is nothing date-like about my one-night stands. He doesn't need to know that, though.

He stands, making himself look bigger. A move I'm sure he read in *How to Lose Friends and Intimidate People.* I think we all know from experience that the kind of man—scratch that, the kind of asshat—that needs to make himself look bigger is lacking in the pants department. I vomit in my mouth a little for thinking about his crotchal region.

He bares his nicotine-stained teeth, like a junkyard dog going in for the kill. "As you *may* recall," he says, his voice oozing, "your contract has an ethics clause which states that no sexual interactions may occur on school premises. You violated that last week."

And just like that, the first wave feminists roll over in their grave. I do some quick arithmetic. Can I sue the school for wrongful termination? Nope. This school has one of the top lawyers in the state on retainer, thanks to the sense of entitlement these rich kids have inherited. There's no way I'd be able to afford to sue them and win.

"You already filled my position for next year?" I say, hating how soft and sad my voice sounds even to myself. These kids are my world. I may pretend to be tough and snarky, but I really do love that I help them love chemistry.

And now I can't do that anymore. Not here, at least. And maybe not anywhere close.

All the open teaching gigs for the following school year have probably been taken at this point. This is a sadistic blow. He could have told me a week ago when all the new positions were being filled. And, coincidentally, when Mrs. Kelly saw my ass being manhandled.

"Do you understand what 'effective immediately' means?" he says.

The bell rings.

My stomach bottoms out as reality crashes down.

Holy shit. I just got fired for being the best chemistry teacher in the state who also happens to have a healthy sex life.

What the actual fuck?

CHAPTER TWO

Sunlight pierces through the slats of my wooden blinds. My head pounds like a jackhammer listening to Metallica on speed. Emotional hangovers are more brutal than any alcohol-based malaise. Closing my eyes to the annoying happy rays, it all comes flooding back.

I got fired. I'm not going back. I can't pay rent this month.

Emily, my best friend, is lying facedown next to me, her long brown hair blanketing out the world. She came over yesterday after wrapping up her last class of the day at Sherman Oaks Private and asked whether I was in problem-solving or wallowing mode. I obviously chose wallow. And wallow we did.

"Bacon," she says, groaning as she flips on her back, reminding me that we can't handle hangovers like we used to.

"Bacon is always a good idea," I say, struggling into a sitting position. That's when I notice the bottle of tequila on her side of the bed, empty.

"What did you do last night?" I say, tilting my head to the scene in question.

"You were snoring so loud I had to drink myself to sleep," she says, rolling her eyes, like I'm responsible for her hangover.

"As if I snore," I say, throwing my pillow at her.

"You've been snoring since I've known you," she says, taking my pillow and adding it to her pile. I see she's wearing my old Rams sleeping T-shirt and I'm reminded that she let me snot on her shirt. The least I can do is get her some bacon.

"I don't have any bacon," I say, getting up. "Want to go to Hot Poppy?"

I don't have to ask twice.

A few minutes later, we're sitting in the corner booth of our favorite café nursing large coffees while we wait for our eggs and bacon. It's one of those tiny cafés with one corner booth inside and a single communal table that makes you question the business decision to open a café in such a tiny space, but it makes up for it with tables and chairs cramming the sidewalk and alley. The smell of freshly ground coffee wafting through the air dulls the whirl of the machine working double-time for fellow early breakfast goers.

"I wonder if Reseda is still looking for a chemistry teacher?" I say. I haven't said much since we got here, lost in my own thoughts. And Em hasn't pushed . . . yet.

The plan last night was to drown my sorrows from the fact I got fired. And to ignore the repercussions it'll have on my record. There isn't a school in the country who'd want a teacher, let alone a principal, who was caught being fondled in front of the children. To say I have no future is not an understatement. I do not fall into the category of "those who can, do; those who can't, teach." A career in education is "it" for me. But now I need a new plan.

"They're not," Em says definitively. Of course she knows. This English teacher is connected. She knows every principal within a ten-mile radius. Actually, scratch that. Every principal within a ten-mile radius knows her. Of course they're not still looking. No one is.

"What's even more fucked up is not only have I lost my job, my students, and my sense of purpose, but the cherry on this crap sundae is that I can't pay rent this month. What am I going to do?" I say, finally ready to figure out a solution. Because no, I don't have an emergency fund with six months of salary saved up. In this economy, who does?

Em's face is scrunched up like she's about to ask if it was me who farted. It wasn't.

"You're sure you can't you ask your mom for money?"

I bore my eyes into her face. *NO. FUCKING. WAY.*

"Your dad?" she says, almost wincing, but still willing to explore all options.

"You *know* I would rather prostitute myself out than ask either of those people for money," I fire back. "Serious options only." One benefit of over a decade of friendship is I don't have to explain why I don't want my parents' help. She knows the trauma they've inflicted. So she lets it slide.

But now Em's not looking at me. She's looking behind me. I follow her eyeline and see a notice board. On it is a bright red convertible for sale.

"I'm not old enough for a midlife crisis car," I say. "And I certainly can't afford it."

"What kind of car do you get someone who's in constant crisis?" Em says, and before I can react dramatically that I am *not* in a crisis while flailing my hands in the air like one of those wacky inflatable arm men you see in the parking lots of car washes, further proving her point, Em stands, walks over to the board, and rips a brightly colored piece of paper off it.

"Get paid to sleep," she reads, shoving the paper in my face.

"What?"

My emotionally hungover brain is in no mood for riddles. She's in the mood for a relaxing sofa session watching deranged psychopaths.

But since we're five miles from the sofa, I scan the paper instead. It's advertising a four-week sleep study program. They want to study insomniacs but need solid sleepers as their control group.

"You're perfect," Em says, when I look at her. "You snored all through the night and never once woke yourself up. You're as solid as they get."

"Let strangers watch me sleep?" I raise an eyebrow. "That's something straight out of a *Criminal Minds* episode, man. You know, the part where the ominous music plays as the victim gets murdered." I throw the paper on the table and sip the last of my coffee. The waiter walks past, and I gesture to the empty cup. "Another, please."

Em picks up the paper and points to some small font at the bottom my tired eyes didn't have the energy to read. "Yeah, but you get paid eight thousand dollars to do it."

I snap my attention back to her. "Are you for real?"

She nods. "It's perfect. You spend four weeks at the sleep study, we'll have the rest of our summer, *and* you get paid better than a summer school teacher's salary."

Only in America would someone in a clinical trial get paid better than someone who's in charge of shaping the minds of the next generation.

Em gets out her phone and starts typing.

"What are you doing?"

"Signing you up," she says.

"I didn't say yes," I say, without a hint of conviction. I mean, the money *would* be enough to pay my rent until fall with a little left over to keep our summer traditions alive. I, for one, am looking forward to learning the latest TikTok dance of the summer, drinking booze out of brown paper bags at the beach with salt in our hair and sand between our toes, and planning our elaborate Halloween party. Hell, maybe we'll even take up tennis.

"That coffee will hit your synapses in about three minutes, and you'll be thanking me because you know it'll be stupid to knock back this opportunity."

"There," Em says with a final tap of her phone. "You've got an interview next Friday." She puts it down just as the waiter brings our breakfast. "That solves the rent issue," she says, like it was nothing. "And gives us twelve weeks to figure out how to get your job back." She takes a bite of her bacon.

I raise an eyebrow. "I wouldn't bet on it. I went through the options when Holland was firing me. With the lawyers they have on retainer, it's not going to happen," I say with more bitterness than I intended.

"You'll be walking in with me on the first day of school, like we always do. Just you wait and see," Em says, smiling.

Emily's always had the knack of spinning shit to gold. And I want to buy it. I really do. I hear gold is always a good investment.

But to invest in gold, you need money.

I take a bite of my eggs, considering my current options. Looks like I'm going to that interview after all.

* * *

One midmorning sofa nap later, I'm showered and sitting in the garden of an upscale café I would never patronize by choice. It's the kind with white tablecloths and waiters who never let your water dip below a quarter full. If there was an Olympic sport in keeping their patrons hydrated, they'd win gold.

I'm waiting for my mother, Hillary Hutchinson, whose bio reads world-renowned relationship expert, *New York Times* bestselling author of *Dating, Mating, and Masturbating*, esteemed professor at UCLA, host of Netflix's number one series *Swipe Right with Dr. Hutchinson,* and most importantly, ageless beauty. If I had a dollar for every time someone told my mother there was "no way she could have a thirty-year-old daughter," I wouldn't need to do the stupid sleep study. She's an eye roll, but she's my mom. And I love her. Which is why I agree to these monthly brunches at places where people go not to eat, but to be seen.

I look up at the entrance from my seat—a huge comfy chair that would be more at home in a living room than on the patio of a café—and realize I'm going to be here a while, so I wave down a waiter and order two flutes of champagne. That's the level of fancy. *Flutes.* Of *champagne.* And so begins the waiting ritual.

If Mom makes it before I finish the first glass, the second is all hers. If not, dibs.

My phone vibrates on the white tablecloth and I pick it up. It's the Bone It app. I just matched with a Morgan.

Free tonight?

When I swipe open the message to investigate further, a gym selfie accompanies said message. Morgan's body takes up the entire photo frame. My eyes are immediately drawn to his white T-shirt straining against his abs. Abs that seem to draw the eye down, down . . . down. Abs that make me notice he's wearing gray sweatpants. Gray sweatpants that make me well aware he isn't planning on coming over to talk. Which works out perfect, because I don't intend on listening.

I use two fingers on the photo to zoom in, studying my potential hookup for tonight. Morgan is your classic kind of hot. His clean, short sandy-blond hair is styled into a side part.

I bet he gets eye-banged by every woman he walks past. Most men, too. And he'd deserve it. It's obvious he works for it. I can only imagine the stamina.

I bang out a quick *yes* as I polish off the second glass, the bubbles carbonating my blood and making me feel light and happy, like the summers of old when I used to enjoy knowing I was getting paid and there was a new class of eager students waiting for me on the other side. That done, I look up just as Mom materializes at the entrance, wearing a T-shirt dress with sneakers. Stealing the show is her untamed curly hair and signature CHA-NEL earrings. You know those ones that spell CHA in one ear and NEL in the other and are so fucking obvious that everyone's a bit like, *Yeah, we get the message loud and clear. You're wearing Chanel.* But damn, she looks so at home in herself. I make a mental note to replicate this ensemble when I get home, minus the thousand-dollar earrings.

I watch as she's stopped by someone equally as confident as Mom, the owner maybe, and her whole demeanor changes. There's an overly enthusiastic hello. There's a one-two cheek kiss. There's a lot of arm holding. And then the arm holder lets go and fishes Mom's book out of her bag.

Mom pulls out a pen, cracks open the cover, and signs the first page. When she finally sees me, she begrudgingly removes herself from her fan, who is obviously a better companion than her only daughter.

She must catch the involuntary sigh because as she approaches our table, she says, "I'm here! I'm here!" like she deserves a medal for doing the bare minimum like turning up to the brunch she scheduled that I would have happily rain checked. I remind myself to take more than the recommended dosage of Tylenol before I attend these monthly catch-ups. As a preventive.

"*Hi*, Mom," I say, making a point to greet her as a waiter appears to pour her champagne before her butt cheeks hit the seat. I'm tempted to top myself up just to see if the waiter will have a stroke.

"Hello, Ashleigh, *how are you?*" she says in a low and slow register, reminding me why there's a morning show somewhere that always wants a soundbite. Her eyes are trained on me, and I immediately chide myself. She *is* a therapist, and she loves a good reason to therapize.

"Good," I say, pulling a stock standard smile that gives nothing away. And while she is a brilliant therapist, I am a brilliant therapist's daughter. "Hungover. You know how it is, end of school party and all. I'm a little slow today," I add, knowing a simple "good" is like catnip for her. I will give her exactly what she needs to hear today to make this as painless as possible.

Before she can respond, we're cut off by a commotion at the entrance as a man carrying a monstrous bunch of flowers the size of his head, plus five other heads combined, attempts to enter. A security guard steps in front of the flower delivery man, blocking him from fulfilling his contractual duties. How did I not notice this beef-hunk security man standing at the entrance when I arrived? I mean, his back alone is what *Men's Health* "body part of the month" dreams are made of. We're talking broad shoulders that taper into a V down to his waist. *Form an orderly queue for the pull-down machine, lads.*

"Please. I need to see her," Flower Dude says, pleading, and I realize we're witnessing some sort of romantic-gesture-slash-allergy-nightmare.

"I'm sorry, that's not happening," Beef Hunk says with a soothing tone that carries a hint of authority, and I can't help but wonder what he'd sound like in the bedroom saying, "Good girl."

While the tone would most definitely work on me, lovestruck Flower Boy isn't buying it. He doesn't leave. Instead he loiters, attempting to catch a glimpse of his beloved inside.

I look around the café and notice everyone has bailed on their conversations in favor of watching this episode of *Days of Our Lives* unfold. That's one way to get through brunch without having to engage with Mom. Thank you, one-night-stand-turned-sad-lover-boy.

But then the show takes a turn.

"I need to see Hillary now," Flower Boy says, as his eyes lock on my mother—and of course, he's talking about my mom.

Mom, to her credit, hasn't bothered to turn around at her name and instead takes a sip of her champagne. "Mom," I say with alarm, trying to get her to face up to the drama she's creating.

"It's being handled," she says, picking up the menu for a quick perusal, like nothing is happening.

"Is it?" I slide my eyes back to the entrance, and that's when I see Annie, her assistant, standing next to Flower Boy, like it's just another service provided by our friendly neighborhood Spider-Man. There's hushed conversation between them as Annie wraps her arms around him and guides him away. "I hope you're giving Annie a generous bonus this year," I say under my breath.

Mom looks at me, head tilted, and I question whether I've taken the smartass daughter schtick a little too far, insinuating that my mother doesn't pay her staff well when I damn sure know she does. But then her phone pings. Annie. No doubt briefing her on the Flower Boy development. Which I'm positive wasn't part of the job description when Annie agreed to work with my mother. Knowing this feels like a minor victory.

Mom flips the phone over and thinks twice about the lecture I'm pretty sure was on the tip of her tongue. "I've been meaning to give this to you," she says instead, reaching into her bag and pulling out an envelope. "It's from your father."

I take the envelope, not bothering to ask what it is. When it comes to Mom and Dad, and their marriage-turned-divorce-turned-friendship, I just ignore it.

"You can let him know tomorrow." Before I can ask what she's talking about my mind snags on the word *tomorrow*. She must see it written all over my face.

"Isn't tomorrow your Sunday lunch?" she asks.

My mouth goes dry. *Oh.* That lunch.

"Right. Of course." I point to my head and make a stupid "silly me" face. "Damn hangover," I repeat, trying to recover the fumble. I wouldn't want Mom thinking I haven't spoken to Dad in months.

It's not that I've been avoiding him. Or that he's been avoiding me. I don't think. I guess you just wake up one day—that day being today—and realize you haven't been invited over for Sunday lunch in months.

Mom looks at me with those trained therapist eyes for a long, hard moment. I'm not sure she's buying it, but then, with a shrug, she decides to let it go. Thank goodness for small favors.

"So, what's new?" Mom asks, taking a sip of her champagne as if this brunch hasn't provided enough talking points to get us through to the last bite.

I got fired. I'm not teaching next semester. I have no money.

Of course, I say none of that out loud. Instead, I say, "Not much," and this gives Mom the opening to launch into her latest hookup, who—surprise, surprise—wasn't actually Flower Boy.

None of this shocks me—where do you think I got the idea for one-night stands from?

CHAPTER THREE

I stand outside the nondescript building known as the Sleep Lab, my phone pressed against my ear. "I can't believe I'm prostituting my sleep for money," I say to Emily.

In the week since Em signed me up, I've swung between actively ignoring the fact I'm desperate enough to enroll myself into a sleep study—or at least apply—to secretly wishing and hoping a teaching job will materialize in front of me, to thinking and praying my rent will magically get paid. But nope. Here I am, about to peddle my sleep for money. Oh, how the teacher has fallen.

"Money, money, money," Em sings through the phone.

"Yeah, yeah. Must be funny in a rich man's world."

We hang up and I push through the doors, blinking at the sudden change in light. The walls of the room are blindingly white, and I momentarily wish I hadn't left my sunglasses in the car. When my eyes have finally adjusted, I notice two things—one, the limp indoor plant in the corner of the room is trying—and failing—to bring life to the place, and two, there are a surprising number of people in the room. And even though only minutes ago I was bitching to Em about being here, now faced with the prospect of losing out on getting paid to sleep, I realize I want this gig. Bad.

I straighten my shoulders and stand tall as I approach the reception desk. It's staffed by two people who are handing out clipboards and pens. Besides the noise they're making, the rest of the room is silent.

After I whisper my name to one of the receptionists, he hands me a name tag, points to the only empty chair along the corridor, and asks me to sit, fill out the form, and wait for my name to be called.

I take my seat and scan the room. There are about twenty people in the waiting room, and another ten crammed with me in the corridor. Turns out I'm not the only desperate soul in the San Fernando Valley.

I start answering the standard questions on my clipboard when the unmistakable sound of Cardi B singing about her wet-ass pussy blasts out of my phone, through the entire corridor and into the waiting room. Shit. Why did I have a drunk female empowerment moment last night and change my standard ring tone to an actual *song* like some geriatric millennial?

All eyes turn to me.

I try not to make eye contact, but there is nowhere to look except at the people looking at me.

That's when I see *him*. I try to convince myself that I'm wrong. That it's a hallucination caused by extreme embarrassment. But just when I think I'm imagining him, he runs his hand through his hair. His curls can't be tamed. They flop back in place.

Oh, yeah. It's him.

Xander Miller.

I feel like a freight train is barreling me back in time to Junior year at UCLA, where a chance meeting outside a frat party led to a friendship that ended in one night of pleasure. One night of extreme pleasure.

From his chair, Xander Miller's lips tip up at the ends. Fuck. That can only mean one thing—he's back in the memory with me.

Him, on top of me. His arms, caging me in. My teeth, scraping the skin of the small tattoo on his bicep. Later that night, I studied that tattoo in detail. A swallow.

Cute. Hot. Off the charts chemistry.

And now he's sitting in the same room as me, an eyewitness to my mortification.

Fuck my life.

"Please make it stop," says the woman sitting next to me, breaking into my trip down memory lane and reminding me that Cardi B is a certified freak and she isn't afraid of letting the entire sleep study know.

"I'm trying." Not hard enough, though, because I can't resist another glance at Xander Miller.

There's a huff from my seat neighbor before she gets up and leaves. As if sitting next to me is like admitting she's an accomplice in disturbing the peace.

I pull out my keys, my wallet, my tampons—creating a pile of all my personal things for the world to see. I scoop my phone up and shut it off, but not before seeing *MOM* flash on the screen. I drop everything on my lap onto the floor with a loud *clang*.

With my phone finally off and the room returning to its uncomfortable silence, I bend over and start picking up my belongings.

My tampons have rolled underneath the plastic white seat next to me, which is now vacant. I've got my head between my legs when I see a pair of men's black Chelsea boots step into my vision and turn on their heel, before taking the empty seat next to me. The space between us crackles, and I don't need to look up to know who's sitting next to me. The butterflies start to rally my entire body like a cheer squad shouting *S! E! X!* and unable to tell the difference between a memory *from eleven years ago* and reality. Get it together, Ash.

Without trying to draw any more attention to myself, I inch my body closer to Xander and his good taste in footwear, stretching my hand out in some geek attempt at trying to make inanimate objects move. The force is not with me.

"Here," Xander says, his hand coming into view. I can't help but notice how his actions have closed the distance between us. I can feel him all over me.

"Thanks," I breathe out as I take my tampons out of his hand. Our fingertips brush and my cells are vibrating at the direct contact. It sets off an unwanted chain reaction of wanting.

I look up and finally get to take him in. Up close and personal.

His well-controlled mop of naturally thick brown hair hasn't changed. There's a new half-moon scar underneath the bottom left corner of his lip. Lips that were dragged all over my body at one point in time.

Stop doing that, Ash.

I finally look him in his eyes. They're a sunburst hazel that glints with mischief. My whole body feels like shoddy electrical wiring. Him? Cool as a cucumber scent radiates from him.

"You're drooling," he says. Instinctively, my hand reaches for my lip like I've been caught giving my horny away. Of course my lips. There is no drool. Fucker. I walked right into that one.

We hold eye contact for a moment. Now that I'm not ogling quite as much, I notice bags under his red-rimmed eyes. I'm betting Xander isn't here as a control. He looks like he hasn't slept well in weeks. A small part of me acknowledges that observation *could* warrant some kindness on my part. But a larger part of me doesn't care. That's the rule. No dating. And definitely no feelings.

Then, he leans forward, lips so close to my ear, I reflexively shiver.

"We're at a sleep clinic, not a sleep 'with' clinic, Hutchinson," he whispers. Then, he pulls back and looks me directly in the eye, destroying my confidence in a three-word rejection: "Read the room."

Wow. Okay. I thought he'd been nice back then. Clearly, I was wrong.

Before I can conjure up a comeback, a woman in a lab coat comes out to the corridor. I sit up straight.

"Thank you all for your patience. At this point, we're only looking for couples to make up the remainder of the study," she says.

A quiet groan echoes throughout the room as people start getting up to leave. I look over to Xander, who hasn't moved. He's looking directly at me, as if trying to send a telepathic message. I'm not picking up on it.

Then, he gives me a blink-and-you-miss-it nod just as the woman in the lab coat comes up to us and says, "Are you two together?"

I'm about to shake my head and boldly announce, "Been there, done that, got the T-shirt," when Xander says, "Yes."

It's my turn to stare at him. He stares back, and I suddenly get it. He *needs* this.

And then I remember. I need this, too. I mean, I *really* fucking need this. Maybe for a different reason from whatever is going on with Xander, but it's a big one and if it means playing fake boyfriend/girlfriend for a month while we sleep together but actually don't sleep together, I can suck it up. I think. Even if he was just a royal asshat a minute ago.

"We are," I say, cementing my fate.

"Great. Please follow me, then," she says.

And just like that, we're in.

She turns on her heel and heads for the door beyond the waiting room. Xander does one of those "after you" hand gestures. I grab my bag and start to follow.

"Thank you," he says. I barely hear the whispered words over the whoosh of the door as we head to who knows where in this lab.

What? Now you're *nice*? As if.

* * *

The woman in the white lab coat introduces herself as Dr. Waitley. She's the director of the sleep study, and she'll be processing our admission into the sleep clinic today.

Okay, so this is happening. There's no job interview where they ask you to tell them about a time where something went wrong and required "teamwork" to fix, which is good since I'd have to tell her about when the copper sulfate went missing during the fall semester and how we all "banded together" to "save the day" when really it was Emily and me who'd "borrowed" the stock to make green fire for our *Wicked*-themed Halloween party. So at least that crisis is averted.

Now I just need to deal with the Xander-shaped one.

The man of the hour and I take a seat opposite Dr. Waitley. Her office is small and crammed with reams of research papers. It reminds me of my desk at school—just replace the papers with tests to grade. Most teachers grumble about grading papers, but I love seeing my students showcase their newly minted knowledge. The dull pang behind my ribcage surfaces, reminding me that I'm no longer a teacher. Currently, my status is ex-chemistry teacher turned fake girlfriend who's *thisclose* to begging to get paid to sleep. I catch the heavy sigh in my chest and remember that my landlord is going to resort to calling me soon. *Let's do this.*

I look over at Xander. He hasn't said a word since we sat down. His face is taut, as if he was carved in marble by Michelangelo himself, like some Renaissance man-hero. Holy shit, he's uncomfortable. Like deeply uncomfortable. About the lying? Has he never lied in his life? I'm not saying I'm a constant liar, but I mean, that's the genetic makeup of the guys I hook up with and their subsequent Bone It profile. Lying about your relationship status. Lying about your height. Lying about what you can bench press. I promise no girl in the entire world gives a flying fuck about what a guy can bench press.

And is that a green tinge to his skin? Is he going to be sick? I want to smirk at him, I really do. But I can't risk it. This admission process needs to go off without a hitch. I mentally bank this image of him to use should I need to bring him down a few notches.

"Thank you, Dr. Waitley. We're so grateful to be here," I say, reaching over and grabbing Xander's hand. Another memory materializes at the touch. *Hands that trail down my sternum, tracing lazy circles around my stomach as we lie on top of a pile of tangled sheets.* Nope. Stop.

It's time to play the sweet, dedicated, and worried girlfriend who is absolutely not here to get paid but instead, of course, is here out of the goodness of her heart because her boyfriend suffers from terrible insomnia.

"Isn't that right, sweetie?" I say to Xander. I'm suddenly determined to not only get paid but to also win an Oscar for my role as "model girlfriend."

He stares at me for a moment, expressionless. Indifferent almost. Okay, well, I guess we could attempt to pass ourselves off as one of those couples who've been together forever and secretly hate each other. It'll be a dark drama, but I can work with it.

There's a beat before the corners of his mouth twitch and he intertwines his fingers with mine, clasping his other hand over the top and turning to Dr. Waitley. I wasn't expecting that. I look down at his hands and beg my brain to not bring up another memory.

"We are," he says, that little twitch in the corner of his mouth releasing into a smile that's so sweet it's sickening. "Really, really happy to be here."

The formalities out of the way—and the awkwardness only just beginning—Dr. Waitley proceeds to tell us that the study will run for thirty consecutive nights. We'll sleep, in the same bed, at the clinic in one of their special sleep labs so we can be closely monitored. We're informed that the goal of the study is to have a natural night of sleep that is as uncomplicated and comfortable as possible.

Well, shit, looks like we've already failed because there is nothing natural, uncomplicated, or comfortable about this.

She checks that we're available every night for the next four weeks. We are. She asks if we're comfortable wearing a few wires and being recorded while we sleep, explaining the wires are about checking our brain activity, breathing, and body movements. We both agree.

I nod along with the enthusiasm I reserve for teaching my students how to break apart covalent bonds, hoping that coupled with my intense eye contact she knows I am, *we are*, the perfect couple to complete her study. What's really happening is I'm actively trying to avoid thinking about Xander's hands. Twisted around mine. Turning my hands into the epicenter of some sort of seismic event. My whole body is vibrating.

"Great. Now onto the fun stuff," Dr. Waitley says with the enthusiasm I assume she reserves for the human circadian rhythm. I'm excited, too, but for different reasons.

"The money?" I say, slipping out of character.

I see Xander out the corner of my eye trying to swallow his laugh and his entire body changes, from marble statute to real-life person.

"No," Dr. Waitley says, giving a strange laugh-slash-cackle that I can't really decipher. "Your history together."

History together? I shift in my seat. All I know is that Xander is a sexual magician. He's responsible for the first orgasm I didn't have to give myself. Our chemistry was off the charts hot. And I ghosted him the morning after we fucked our way out of a friendship and into a one-night stand, never to see him again until ten minutes ago.

Xander lets go of my hand and absentmindedly runs said hands through his hair. The curls flop forward, not agreeing with his actions. I never knew I could hate and simultaneously adore hair as much as I do until right now.

"How did you two get together?" Dr. Waitley says, venturing into new territory that's going to test how well we can both lie—and lie *together*—after knowing each other for a grand total of three weeks eleven years ago. "I love a good meet cute."

I remember when Em and I had to lie about the missing copper sulfate and how we kept it close to the truth, saying that we used it in a Halloween-themed experiment for the kids that was technically not "part of the curriculum" but well worth it when they aced the hardest question on the test about boric acid. The lesson here? Keep the lie as close as possible to the truth.

"We met in university when I stole a bottle of peach schnapps," I answer, pulling from our actual meeting. I slide my eyes to Xander and find a slow smile tugging at the corner of his mouth.

"She thought she was being stealth, stealing from the frat party. But I couldn't keep my eyes off her the moment she walked in," he says. This is the first time I'm hearing his side of the story. I raise an eyebrow at this admission. It honestly felt like I was invisible that night. Until he found me outside drowning my sorrows.

"He bought me a margarita. We bonded over a 'proper' drink," I say, adding in further details. Dr. Waitley smiles at our little tag team storytelling.

"Chemistry," he says, finishing off our meet cute. I snap my gaze to him. He remembered what I said when describing the sweet, sour, salty, bitter taste of the perfect margarita he introduced me to. His lip twitches into a half smile, his hazel eyes amused by my response. We both remember.

"That's so fun. And how long have you been together?" Dr. Waitley says, interrupting our staring contest. She seems satisfied with our answer, and not at all suspicious that we actually haven't seen each other in eleven years, up until ten minutes ago, outside her lab.

"Depends. Are you talking about when we first met? First kissed? First slept together?" I say, words just tumbling out of my mouth. Oh my god, what is wrong with me? Beside me, Xander tenses but I don't dare look at him for fear I'll give it all away.

"Yes, apologies. I should have clarified," Dr. Waitley says, making me feel slightly better. "How long have you been sleeping in the same bed together?"

"Eleven years," Xander says, giving me a chance to regain control over the Broca's area of my brain. That's the area that's found to be most active right before you speak. Supposedly. I believe mine might be malfunctioning.

Dr. Waitley takes note. My mind flashes with an image of Xander's naked torso lying in bed next to me. Well, it's official. I have no control over my speech, my thoughts, and brain activity. I swallow. At least my involuntary reflexes are working correctly.

"So, I see from the paperwork, Ashleigh, you're the solid sleeper, and Xander, you have insomnia," she says, reading from our clipboards.

"Yes," he replies, and even though I knew he had insomnia, there's something about his simple admission that makes me uncomfortable. I love sleep. And I'm so good at it. I'm the best at sleeping. Nothing keeps me awake. Which is also why I must live on the third floor of an apartment building because I would be a prime candidate for getting murdered in my sleep. If I don't get my eight hours, I can't function. And here Xander is, sitting next to me, confirming that he doesn't sleep. I give myself a moment to feel for him. One moment. Nothing more. And then it's back to objectifying him. And his hands. Tracing my thigh . . .

"How does Xander's insomnia affect you?" she says to me, pulling me back.

Well, it makes me tired just thinking about it, I almost say. But then I stop and try to give it thought. If Xander were my person, which he never, ever will be, how would I feel? Worried. Definitely. I start to answer but Xander beats me to it, and I wonder if he possesses the ability to read my thoughts, which wouldn't be the first time since seeing him today, because he says exactly what I've been thinking.

"She worries. But she sleeps through it," Xander says with cocky confidence.

"Understandable," she says, nodding solemnly.

"She looks blissfully cute when she sleeps, though," he says, eyes flicking toward me like the adoring boyfriend he's playing.

His ad lib catches me off guard, but I manage to recover. "Aw, honey," I say, unleashing my own version of a sickly sweet smile. We are really nailing this whole "perfect couple with sad affliction worthy of a place in your study" show. And it reminds me what else we've nailed together.

"How often do you have sex?" she says, as though reading my mind.

"Every night," I say before I can add a filter from my brain to my mouth. Oh, we're back to that, are we? Thanks, brain, for the heads-up.

Dr. Waitley looks at me like I've said something she's never heard before. I stare at her, committing to the lie, but before she returns to her page she says, "You'll have to pause that routine for the duration of the study."

"Of course."

I steal a glance at Xander and see a faint smirk on his face. He's so casual he should be lying down. How is it that he came

Elizabeth McKenzie

into this fake relationship on edge, and I was the calm, cool, collected one, and now here I am, feeling like an electric live wire, exposing myself?

The power I once held in this arrangement has shifted.

But it doesn't really matter, does it? Because we're in this together now.

CHAPTER FOUR

I slam shut the door of my dumpy Subaru Legacy, the car ranked as one of the Top 10 Safest Cars from 2009 to 2014. That's not the reason I own it, but it is the reason it's one of Mom's hand-me-downs. She moved onto her Mercedes phase when her agent landed her a seven-figure deal for the Netflix special and insisted I take it because the "shit box" I was driving "is going to kill you one day." Hey, I kept that "shit box" immaculate.

Before leaving the room, Xander and I finished up the questions, signed the contracts, and were instructed to report back to the clinic next Friday for our first sleep session. We officially made it. We're in.

And now I have to deal with the fallout.

I take out my phone, itching to call Emily. It's her fault I've gotten into this mess in the first place. I need to vent.

But a knock on my window startles me. Cursing under my breath and hoping to God that I'm not about to be mugged, I look up to see Xander's midriff. Definitely *not* a carjacker. But the view makes my pulse race all the same. The window frames all my favorite body parts. Lower part of the stomach behind a fitted T-shirt. Waistband of his jeans peeking out. And let's not forget about the forearms. So underrated. It's not always about biceps. I bite my bottom lip to distract myself from the other body part that my blood is now rushing to at the sight of him.

I toss my phone on the passenger seat and as I roll down the window, he bends so we're face to face. He really is annoyingly hot. There's something about his attractiveness that isn't all physical. It's attitude too. The way he holds himself. The way he interacts with his surroundings. The way he moves in time and space. You can't replicate that level of hotness in a static image. Or a memory.

"Hey, you rushed out of there so quick, I didn't get to say thanks," Xander says, now leaning his arms on the window frame, biceps popping, and sure, I was just complaining that biceps get all the attention, but what can I say? In this case they deserve it.

Without his jacket on, I can see his arm is covered in a sleeve tattoo. It looks like someone spilled color across his arm and just kept going. A kaleidoscope of chaos wrapped around muscle. Like it tells a story. It makes me wonder what other body parts he got inked since I last saw him naked. Is his back still bare and unblemished?

"For what?" I say, refocusing on his face, using his half-moon scar as my anchor. The only problem is, it's close to his lips.

"For helping get me into the sleep study," he says, examining me.

That's when I see his eyes grow darker, the sunburst hazel disappearing into the horizon like at sunset, replaced with sepia-glowing nightfall. He's serious. And that realization is just what I need to get my out-of-control imagination tightly reined in. For some reason, I don't want to let him down. My brain reminds me I shouldn't care. But Xander is somehow making the system glitch. I *really* need to call Emily and process all this before my brain overheats.

"You're welcome," I say. It's succinct. Sincere. And honest.

"I got the answer to your question," he says, his eyes back to sparkling like the sun. Life force flowing through every word.

"What question?" I ask, perplexed.

Not saying anything, he pushes himself off the window frame, and my eyes track him like I'm a bounty hunter as he walks around the car, opens the passenger door, and glides in.

He picks up my phone from the seat before sitting down and holds it. Just holds it. There's something so personal about someone holding your phone. It holds the secrets to your conversations with your best friends, your search history, your calendar, and how you fill your days.

Being in proximity, in such a confined space, makes me acutely aware that Xander smells like a mixture of something sweet and something fresh. I don't know exactly what. All I know is it feels like I'm hot boxing his scent. And I'm kinda getting high off it.

"Your payday just doubled," he says.

What? There's nothing like talking about money to bring you back down to Earth. Does he mean what I think he means? Is he giving me his share of the sleep study money? Why? Is he mega rich? I should be reacting verbally to him, insisting that he take his share. But if he gives it to me, I won't just have enough to pay the rent, I'll have enough to actually enjoy the rest of my summer.

"Why don't you want the money?" I say, instead of thank you.

"I don't need the money. I need to sleep," he says. It comes out harsh and judgmental, like he's implying only losers who desperately want to get paid would come to a sleep study. His tone makes me judge myself, my brain taking stock of every decision that led me to this moment.

He holds my phone in front of my face to unlock it. I really hope he hasn't done this before with an unconscious body.

"What are you doing?"

He types a number into my phone. And then his phone rings. And then my phone pings while it's in his hand. To my shock and horror, a wicked grin flashes across Xander's face. I have no doubt that text was the Bone It app. Please let it not be one of the more detailed, creative messages.

"You've got my number and I've got yours," he says, handing my phone back. "And someone from Bone It wants to know if you're up for some 'eggplant emoji peach emoji tonight?'" *Oh, no.* My soul shudders.

Xander gives me a look and I can practically see the single shred of respect he had for me leave his body. Before I decide how I want to play out this humiliation, Xander opens the car door and I watch him leave in one easy motion.

"See you Friday," I call out without a single drop of enthusiasm.

He waves without turning around. Sexy jerk.

A moment later, my phone pings again. It's Xander. There's a photo of him in a dark club with a Cardi B T-shirt sticking to his torso and his hair slicked back from sweat and . . . who's that in the background on the stage? Cardi fucking B.

Unbelievable.

"Who even are you, Xander Miller?" I say, studying the photo, but when I look up, he's gone.

I open my text messages, ignoring Travis from Bone It and his embarrassing use of emoji, and text Emily: Meet me at the mall in twenty minutes.

CHAPTER FIVE

I'm in the changing room at Victoria's Secret with about forty different types of sleepwear from summer flannel (my choice) to lacy negligee (Em's choice). You'd think they'd have mastered change room lighting in this place, you know, being the home of the angels and all. But no. It is severe.

I'm in nothing but my panties surrounded by three mirrors, which means there's no escaping my naked body. No matter where I turn, there I am. I'm getting a front row seat to the cellulite on the backs of my legs, which I've been blissfully unaware of until this very moment. Who can I call to get a lobotomy so I can leave the store with a shred of self-esteem? I vow to return to my late-night shopping from the safety of my sofa where the lamp in the corner of the room does not accentuate the dark circles under my eyes that I had, up until this moment, thought I'd kept under wraps with creams and serums and solid sleep.

Em's hand appears through the curtains, handing me three more options. I inspect a particularly lacy number that leaves nothing to the imagination. The product tag reads, *A sexy-sweet essential in lustrous satin with delicate sheer lace and eyelash trim.* Whatever *eyelash trim* means. Basically, it's exactly what I'd wear if I wanted it off my body in sixty seconds. Not what I'd wear to ward off old friends/flames/hookups/whatever. I sigh, resigned that I won't be escaping this change room anytime soon without trying it on.

I rallied Em into this shopping trip with promises of a dramatic retelling of the events of the afternoon. She is an English teacher, after all. It dawned on me as I texted Em that I was going to be sleeping next to Xander for the next four weeks and I don't own a piece of sleepwear that wasn't designed to be ripped off in the heat of horny. Em isn't helping, but she is making it fun.

"So let me get this straight," she says, her voice muffled through the curtain. I can tell she's still laughing. "They didn't need any more single sleepers, so you decided to sign up anyway and sleep with *Xander*—your 'guy friend' from university who you slept with then bailed on the next day without so much as a thanks for the orgasms, *plural*—for four weeks. In front of people!"

"God, Em. You make it sound like we're making porn," I say, twisting into the tight lace before bending over. To my surprise, my entire insides aren't on show. Impressive. I guess Victoria *can* manage to keep a Secret.

"*Sleepy Spits Not Swallows*," Em says, deadpan.

I burst out laughing. "*Sleeping Booty.*"

"What is this? PG13?" she says. "Does the guy that gave you your sexual awakening not deserve better?"

"*Cum and Cummer*," I say, going there. I hear a slow clap from behind the curtain.

"And that is why you're the queen of Bone It," she says, recalling when we first happened across the app many moons ago. We were hanging our bodies off the bar stools in the corner of the Retreat like bar flies. It's the kind of bar that opens at midday on a workday. Dark. Sticky floors. Leather-faced locals who serve as a warning sign of your future should you continue to consume alcohol in the afternoon on a Wednesday. It was also the bar that was closest to the school, and we decided we were in dire need of a recovery drink post-death-by-boredom staff meeting that should have been an email. The entertainment we coupled with our beers? Downloading the latest app that promised no dating.

And that's when I realized we'd hit the jackpot. Men upon men who're simple, fun, and in a committed relationship with *themselves*. Complete with their gym selfies and their V-neck T-shirts and their fedora hats. All the trappings of the perfect one-night stand. Plus, you could filter to within a five-mile radius. We finished our drinks. I swiped right on someone named Chet. Em left. And ten minutes later, Bone It became my app of choice.

"But serious question. Do you know how you sleep?"

"Like a champ?" I say as I peel back the curtain and step out into the main dressing room area.

Em is standing in front of the mirror covered in feather boas. I'm talking the rainbow. Red, orange, yellow, green, blue, indigo, and violet. I don't even know where she got them; I didn't see them when we were browsing the racks. But right now, she's wearing all seven. She looks like a Technicolor Big Bird. That's Em for you—always finding the fun in the most mundane. Which is why I've even entertained the idea of wearing *lustrous satin*.

"It's true. Not even your own fart can wake you," she says, twirling. I stop in my tracks. Oh shit, I didn't even think about sleep farting in front of Xander. Insomniac Xander. Xander who does not sleep. Xander who will hear every single bodily function I can't control when I'm in the depths of my slumber.

"I sleep fart?" I say, horrified. Em looks at up me with a smirk. If the answer is yes, it will haunt me for the rest of my days.

"Not that I know of," she says, her smirk turning into a "gotcha" smile. "But you're the big spoon. You can't stay on your side of the bed. You're all up in my space, body limbs constantly trying to play footsie with me, and you know I'm cool with it, obviously, but is he going to be cool with it? I mean, what if he thinks you want to do more than sleep with him?" Em says, and this realization is worse than sleep farting.

"Which is exactly why I cannot wear this," I say, refocusing on the reason we're here in the first place. "My nipples are showing."

I walk up toward the mirror and meet Em there. She does a power pose, like she's at the end of her own runway show before looking me up and down.

"You look hot. Now tell me, was *he* just as hot as you remember?"

His face flashes in my mind. The curls that can't be tamed. The newly acquired half-moon shaped scar underneath the bottom left corner of his lip.

What is it about scars? It's like they activate something in my DNA from my sixteenth-century ancestors when times were brash, fencing was all the rage, and scars were a sign of bravery—and hence something to get all hot and bothered about.

My silence speaks the kind of volume you get from a Harry Styles concert where fifty thousand hot and horny screaming fans sing along to every single word of every single song.

"He looked good," I say, trying to cool my body down—it's heated up a couple of degrees just thinking about him.

"That hot, huh?" Em says, reminding me that while I pulled off the performance of a lifetime as Xander's girlfriend of eleven years, I cannot pull one over on my best friend. I ignore that comment as I make my way back to the change room. "Hey, why can't you just wear your old UCLA T-shirt to bed like you usually do?"

"Because I don't need to advertise our time together every time I see him," I say, even though I'm the one with the memory of an elephant that not even drinking continuously through four years of university has managed to dull.

I go back to the dressing room and add the negligee to the growing "no way, get fucked, fuck off" pile. I turn to the next option. Lacy dusty-pink shorts and a cropped white T-shirt. "I don't want him getting any ideas," I say, trying try to get these shorts to sit straight on my hips and failing.

"And what about you?" she says as I give up and step out for my grading.

This time Em throws one hand over her mouth, not even bothering to cover up her true reaction. "You know I didn't put that in your pile. It's very . . . Forever 21?" she says, letting the laugh spill out.

I turn to face the mirror. She's right. I look like I'm trying to avoid the inevitability of aging by wearing—or rather stuffing myself into—clothes that belong to a not quite legal teenager.

"Point taken," I say. "One more." I walk back to the change room, ignoring the camel toe that crept up in the five steps it took to get from the change room to the mirror. The things youths will wear to sacrifice comfort. I pick up the final item and inspect it. The summer flannel set with a red and white plaid pattern.

"Seriously, though. If I remember correctly, Xander wasn't the one who cannonballed three pints of ice cream post-ghost. He did a number on you, Ash. How will you sleep next to him for an entire month straight?"

"You do not remember correctly," I say, cutting in because the facts are always important. "I came home. We smoked. We got the munchies. We munched."

"Really?" Em says dubiously.

"Well, I munched. You couldn't stop laughing enough to put the spoon in your mouth," I say, shaking my head at the lightweight that has and always will be Em. "Come on, it was eleven years ago. We're not young anymore. Or dumb. We're old. I'm poor. He can't sleep. There's nothing more to it."

I throw on the flannel and inspect myself in the mirror. I mean, plaid is hanging off my body. This could work.

"So, you're just going to . . . *hang out* with him every night for four weeks?" she says, as I press the flannel against my chest, trying to create some sort of figure. Call it habit.

"Exactly," I say, releasing the material and letting it return to swallowing me up whole.

"You know, that sounds a lot like dating someone," Em says. "And as you never fail to remind me, you don't date. Ever."

"No, it sounds a like going to work with a coworker," I say, concluding our conversation. But I'm not sure if even I'm convinced. It does sound a lot like dating someone without any of the benefits. Fucking hell.

I step out one final time.

"I wouldn't bang you in that," Em says at the sight of me.

"Perfect."

CHAPTER SIX

I pull up to the Sleep Lab at five forty-five PM on Friday and turn off the engine. I'm really doing this. I take off my sunglasses and am instantly hit with the glare of the sun on the horizon. Being smack-bang in the middle of summer, the sun won't set for hours. It's an absolute mystery to me why we're here so early. I mean, no one is sleeping at six PM, and they know it. What am I going to do with Xander for four hours in a 330 square-foot room until I finally fall asleep at the respectable time of ten PM?

Don't answer that.

My phone pings with a missed call from my landlord. I delete the message, not needing the reminder that my rent is well past due.

Without the air conditioner on, the car immediately heats up, and that heat tries to convince me I shouldn't be here. I should be in a beer garden at happy hour with Em nursing an ice-cold cider, beads of condensation rolling down the side of the glass as the warm air hits the cold surface, reaching its dew point, really demonstrating just how ice-cold and refreshing cider can be.

My bank account reminds me to unbuckle myself and get the fuck out of the car. I can drink cider anytime between the hours of 6:00 AM and 6:00 PM.

I didn't message Xander during the week, though not from lack of trying. Every time I opened our message thread to send something, there he was. That photo of him at the Cardi B concert, hair all slicked back and sexy. Did I stare at this photo a little too long at times? Yes. For I am but a mere human woman, after all. It made me second-guess every message I could possibly send.

After opening the message thread this morning, you know, to refresh my memory as to who I'm getting back into bed with, a message popped up from him, checking to make sure I wasn't bailing.

To be honest, there had been a moment during my bimonthly waxing session when I'd considered it. I'd thought about how this batshit crazy idea would backfire and I'd end up broke, unemployed, *and* charged with fraud. If not by the police, then definitely by the dean of the university associated with the sleep study. That spiral mindfuck, as I lay with my legs spread, was almost enough to make me bail.

But then the beauty technician really ripped that wax strip and I thought, *Nothing is crazier than a grown-ass woman being convinced that it's a good idea to regularly put molten hot wax on her vulva.*

So when the message appeared on my phone from Xander making sure I was still coming tonight, I texted him saying I would rather rock up to the sleep study then be caught dead selling Wetzel's Pretzels at the mall to my former students, and when he replied, Students? we both realized that after eleven years, we know sweet fuck-all about each other.

Enter: Getting to know Xander Miller.

I learned in our quick text session that Xander is a lawyer. A lawyer in the competitive, pressure-filled legal industry. A successful lawyer who has exceptional work ethic and perseverance. An exceptional lawyer with insane levels of lawyer stress. Xander's also a *single* lawyer. So, that's why he's here, because all that pressure makes it impossible to sleep or date. So he says.

And he learned that I am, well, not a high-powered anything. I'm a chemistry teacher currently without a teaching job. Xander is *smart*. And hot. And I'd be lying if I didn't admit this combination has left me a little intimidated. Usually the guys on Bone It are, how do I say this delicately? Brainless and banging hot. But a competitive lawyer who also works out? I'm going to have to bring my A game.

I sigh. Enough procrastinating. Time to get a move on.

I grab my overnight bag from the passenger seat and yank it across my body. It's heavier than what I'd bring to a regular sleepover at a guy's house situation. We were encouraged to do whatever we would at home, and in a panic-pack, I brought my only bottle of wine. Apparently it was here as a "in case of emotional support, open" bottle.

Kicking the car door open with my foot, I hurl myself out and see Xander leaning against his trunk a few cars down. One leg is kicked back against the bumper as he scrolls through his phone.

How he has the strength in that one leg to carry the weight of his entire muscley body on zero sleep is beyond me. He's wearing what I'm going to label as Xander's capsule wardrobe from this point on. White T-shirt, faded black jeans, Chelsea boots. The exact outfit he wore last Friday.

Me? I've at least rotated through a few outfits since I saw him last. Today I'm wearing skinny jeans, my favorite Nike high tops, and a tank top. Seeing him in the flesh makes my stomach fizz. The static image on my phone does not hold a candle to the fire emoji that is Xander in real life.

As I gawk, he rubs his neck, and I'm starting to think this is a trademark move of his, although I suspect he doesn't even know he's doing it. Rubbing the tension away from what I can only assume is sleeplessness just makes me want to have those same fingers rub me.

He looks up and sees me—because when someone stares at you like you're a piece of meat, the reptilian part of your brain kicks into high gear and puts you on high alert. You know, in case of a saber-toothed tiger and imminent death. Which might not be so wrong. I *do* sorta want to nibble on his ear. Shaking my head clear, I make my way over to him.

He puts his phone in his pocket and gives me a small wave as I approach. "Hey, so thanks again for doing this," he says with so much sincerity you could cut it with a knife.

"No worries," I say, trying to match his fake nice. I will not break the nice-guy act first. I will go Method all the way if I need to. I will become the caring, loving girlfriend of the insomniac man with the one outfit every night for four weeks for four thousand dollars per week. I am committed.

"I know it doesn't exactly fit in with your *lifestyle*." The sincerity eviscerates from the air around us. "Hope you can put it on pause."

Excuse me? What the actual fuck does that mean?

"My lifestyle?" I say through gritted teeth, trying to uphold the nice-guy act I solemnly vowed to moments ago.

"The Bone It lifestyle," he says, clarifying. One-night stands. "I don't want anything jeopardizing this for me."

Like my sex life and the rules that come along with it are going to ruin his plans.

"I'm sleeping next to you every night for four weeks. When, exactly, am I going to be fucking around?" I say, putting on my best condescending teacher voice. *One plus one equals two.*

He cocks his head in response, alluding to the other twelve hours of the day that are wide open to an ex-teacher who has nowhere else to be and nothing else to do for the next twelve weeks of summer vacation. To him, the math ain't mathing.

I decide to ignore the pointed look, which says a lot more about him than me.

"We going in?" I say, refocusing on the job I came here to do.

There's a moment when he doesn't move. Like he's assessing whether he does, in fact, want to go in with me. That maybe living with insomnia forever is better than getting treated if that means he'd never have to see me again.

But then, he plasters a fake smile on his face. "Let's do it," he says. And there it is. That seemingly insignificant smile that tells me everything. If he were stuck on a desert island with me, I'm the last person in the world he'd want around. And yet he's so fucking desperate, he's going to sleep with me for four whole weeks.

Well, ditto.

We start walking toward the entrance and he grabs my hand. It seems my body doesn't give a shit about this new information about how little he thinks of me, because holding his hand feels like atoms colliding.

"Nice move, fake boyfriend," I say, just for the sake of talking.

"Well, for a couple who has sex every night, surely we can't keep our hands off each other," he replies oh-so-casually.

"Good point," I say, doubling down on the line I blurted out in our interview. He doesn't have to know I'm squirming on the inside.

Fuck. This is going to be a long night.

CHAPTER SEVEN

After we're checked in, a young man in a white lab coat, who I'm guessing is one of the lowly research assistants, is tasked with taking civilians to their sleep room and answering boring questions like "Where's the bathroom?" (down the hall to the left) and "What's the internet password?" (Sleepfine509, which is actually catchy).

He's got a messy mop of hair, thick glasses, a name tag that reads Ben, and he's wearing a buttoned-up cardigan underneath his coat that puts him firmly in the adorable geek category. Ah, to be at college again when being cash poor didn't matter because you felt like you'd won the lottery thanks to passion alone, and getting an unpaid internship was something you wanted. I remember those days well. I smile at him. *Don't give up on your dreams.*

He blushes as he opens the door to our sleep room. It's nice. Wow. I didn't expect that.

Compared to the rest of the building full of stark white walls and silence, it's cozy. The walls are a soft cream so as not to glow in the dark while we sleep. The bedspread is blue. There's a chair in the corner of the room. And we have a TV. It's like a mid-range Airbnb except the room also has a trolley filled with wires, monitors at the head of the bed, cameras in all corners, and an intercom for communicating. There's a control room right next to ours, but there's no *Criminal Minds*-style one-way mirror with people in white coats on the other side watching us sleep under a dim light—at least I hope there isn't.

Ben tells us it's standard practice to record all sleep study sessions and the analysis happens over the following days. Then he instructs us to get ready for bed the same way we get ready at home.

That's when it dawns on me. I need to get undressed. To change into my sleepwear. In front of Xander. With zero privacy. Because the damn bathroom is down the hall on the left.

Ben leaves, reminding us to be in our pajamas and ready. He'll return after settling in the other patients.

How the fuck is this going to work?

I move around to my side of the bed and throw my overnight bag at my feet. The wine bottle clangs. Xander tilts his head, eyebrows furrowed, questioning the noise.

"They said to do whatever it is we do before going to sleep," I say, shrugging. I wonder if he's going to judge me for the empty calories like any dude on the Bone It app would. I mean, he clearly works out. The jury's out on whether he owns a fedora. "Don't worry, you can't catch calories by being in proximity. Your macros are safe with me."

"Oh, great. I was worried," he says, laughing. "About the *macros*."

My eyes widen. I haven't heard that sound in eleven years and warmth spreads from the pit of despair in my stomach throughout my entire body. It's a nice laugh. Deep, genuine. A little husky.

Xander starts busying himself with his overnight bag. It's one of those nice canvas ones with a leather handle. Mine is the free bag Em got with her gym membership. Before I can answer, he looks up, holding his sleepwear in his hands. I'm still searching for mine. We're frozen.

We're each waiting for the other to make the first move, like we're in a Western movie. Instead of staring down imminent death, it's the awkward dance of trying to get changed without the other person seeing your private bits.

Xander starts to turn to face the wall and I quickly do the same, snatching the sleepwear out of my bag. I guess I'm changing now.

I rip off my tank top and bra, but my hair gets caught in the clasp and I can't untangle it. Never in my entire life of having to remove my bra has my hair gotten caught in the clasp. Am I having a stroke? I ignore that it might just be the Xander effect because in the matter of seconds since I started stripping, I'm sweating. This does not help me in releasing the clasp from my hair that shall now be referred to as "the bird's nest." Growing more desperate by the second, I bail on the bra for a moment, boobs out, and start peeling off my skinny jeans and underwear, forgetting that I haven't kicked my sneakers off. I try to use my right foot to jimmy my left foot out without having to bend over and untie the laces, but it doesn't work. Damn high tops.

So this is how I die. By humiliation.

I can hear the final piece of clothing being put on across the room. How do I know what a final piece of clothing sounds like? The silence is a dead giveaway. I frantically bend down and start undoing the shoelaces.

"You done?" I say into the silence coming from the other side of the room.

"Yep," Xander says.

I manage to get one shoe off and I'm working on the other. My jeans are down to my ankles.

"Oh shit, sorry," Xander says to my back.

I spring up and turn, the hunter becoming the hunted. We stare at each other eye to eye. My boobs are hanging out. Just swinging in the wind. My jeans and underwear are around my ankles. One hand springs up to cover as much boob as possible. The other attempts to cover my vagina area.

"What the fuck?" I say, finally releasing my second shoe.

Xander turns around, lightning quick. "I'm sorry. I thought you were done."

"I was asking if *you* were done, not saying *I* was done," I hiss, finally feeling sweet freedom as my skinny jeans come off. I pull on the flannel pajama set, but I can't get the bra free from the bird's nest.

I consider for a moment playing this off like it's a new fashion trend. I bet I could sleep with it just hanging in my hair, channeling my trashy university days. He probably wouldn't notice.

Instead, my scalp starts throbbing at the tension, so I look up to see Xander facing the wall. I've got the vantage point here because I'm facing him, so I give myself a few seconds to sweep my eyes over his body. He's wearing (surprise) a white T-shirt and gray sweatpants. His hand returns to rub his neck and his shoulders flex under his T-shirt. I move my eyes down to his butt—it's a very nice butt—and then stop. Not the time. Not the place.

I walk up to him and tap him on the shoulder.

"Is it safe for me to turn around?" he says.

Safe? Like my naked body is a threat? It wasn't a threat when he moaned my name between my legs. More like a treat, he'd said. I ignore the pulsing between my thighs this memory is solely responsible for and answer his question.

"Yes." It's one word, but it's better than none. Xander turns around. His eyes are careful not to dip below my eyeline before landing on the bra in my hair.

"I need your help," I say, as he tracks the dubious look on my face. "*Please.*"

I must do something good with my eyes when I say "please" because the hard line of his mouth tips at the end.

"Okay," he says, lifting his hands up to my head and getting to work. First, assessing. Delicately moving my hair around to see where the clasp is buried. I can't help but notice the single swallow tattoo on his right bicep. He's kept that side of his body completely clean apart from the little blue bird. He'd told me once that the swallow represents successful voyages, hope, and the warmth of home. Like even if you set someone free, their love can come back. I remember rolling my eyes at this before he quickly pinned me to the bed and made me forget. Until now.

His left arm though, is covered in a full sleeve. I tilt my head to the side in an attempt to study the intricate details, but my hair pulls. "Ouch."

"Sorry," he mutters before rubbing my scalp, and I let a groan slip without any consideration for where I am and who I'm with. Shit. He drops his hands from my head immediately before bending down so my entire vision is Xander and his curls.

"Excuse me, Ms. Hutchinson. What was that?" he says, mimicking my teacher voice I pulled on him in the parking lot.

A devilish grin creeps over his face, almost lighting him up at my involuntary admission that I like the way he touches me.

"It was an unapproved groan," I say, scoffing.

"Oh, so your subconscious is trying to tell me something?" He's still bent down, my entire vision taken up by Xander's face. And just like I have no control over my vocal cords, it appears I also have no control over my eyes because they can't help themselves and flicker to his half-moon scar on the corner of his lip. "I wonder what it is."

"You were good in bed eleven years ago. Want a medal?" I say, defending myself.

"Your muscle memory seems to think I deserve one," he says, quick with the comeback.

"Shut up," I counter, regressing to my teenage dirtbag phase. I force my eyes back on his and will myself not to break. His eyes lock on mine. My stomach does a lazy forward roll. It's official. He's staring at me. And I'm staring at him. And what we have here, is a stare off. I count my breath.

One.

Two.

Three.

There is no way I'm losing this stare off. Especially after the unconscious moaning. I'll never live it down. Don't break, Ash. Don't break.

"Come sit on the end of the bed. I need a better angle," Xander says, finally breaking eye contact.

I may have won this battle, but we've still got four weeks of each other's company, so I do as I'm told and perch on the end of the bed. I have never sat on a bed with such perfect posture as I do right now. And only when I have my back to him do I allow a victory smile.

Bed Chemistry

Of course, I am immediately humbled when I feel the mattress sinking in on either side of me as Xander kneels behind me, reminding me just how close his body is to mine. My heart beats faster as my mind conjures up another memory of Xander kneeling in a different position.

I reprimand myself by engaging my core and partaking in the longest workout I've given my abs in my entire life but, as promised, this has improved his technique.

Just when I think I'm completely in control, the coolest of the cool, an expert in being comfortable, Xander's fingers brush my scalp and my body goes haywire. I go ramrod straight from the electric shock.

I'm going to start shaking any minute from muscular fatigue when my bra lands in my lap.

Ah, freedom.

"Thank you," I say, turning around as he climbs to the top of the bed and lies down. I guess that's what we do now. We lie in bed together. So I discard my bra on top of my bag and make the climb to the top, scooching to the far side of the bed to avoid contact.

"You don't have to sleep with half your body hanging off the bed," he says.

It's true. I've created so much space between us you could fit another body in there. My right butt cheek is hanging off the bed, for crying out loud. I can't help but notice the twinkle in his eye and I know he's finding amusement in my discomfort.

"My body is on the bed just fine," I say, lying. Well, that was a short recovery time between workout sets.

Engage. The. Core.

"Okay," he says. "Suit yourself."

Awkward silence descends.

Every now and then, Xander moves his body. To rub his neck. To stretch his back. To find a more comfortable position. And it's contagious. I'm feeling more and more uncomfortable by the minute too, because every time he moves, it feels like the air has been sucked out of the space between us, so no matter how much distance I've created, it's like we're basically touching.

This is going to be way harder than I thought.

*   *   *

I creep along the hallway, returning from a quick bathroom intermission. It's so quiet you can hear the whirring of the machines behind the doors marked Observation. I can just imagine Ben and a bunch of nerds huddling over their monitors, unlocking an interesting new discovery to the human sleep cycle they'll study during the week. A loud snore cuts through the silence from behind one of the observation rooms.

Or not.

Judging by the darkness, we're miles from morning. I woke up on my side of the bed, miraculously not touching Xander (yes, I would like a medal for my effort) even though every muscle in my body is aching from the restraint that I managed to show while asleep (yes, I would still like a medal for my subconscious effort). Xander was lying in bed with his ankles crossed and arms folded on his chest, and he looked peaceful until the light from my phone lit up the tips of his eyelashes, showing he was wide-awake.

I slowly open the door back to our sleep study room, ready to creep back into bed without saying a word when I see Xander standing. Maybe I did touch him during the night and he's here to implement a pillow barrier system? But no, he's just standing. And staring.

Staring staring. At me.

Like he wants me.

Before I know what's happening, Xander closes the space between us.

Clutching my face with both hands, he lowers his lips to mine. He expertly traces kisses from my mouth to my neck, and the pace changes.

Xander slows down. He takes his time, savoring every kiss. My skin buzzes. Every touch feels like he's marking me permanently with a *Xander was here* tattoo. He lingers on my collarbone, trailing kisses along it before turning back to my lips then to my earlobe. I run my hands under his T-shirt toward his strong shoulders, feeling his muscles flex under my fingertips.

He hasn't even touched me below the neck, and I'm losing it. The guy is a sexual magician. I lift his T-shirt to signal it's time to take our clothes off, and it's the first break in Xander's mouth-to-skin contact. I'm already missing his lips when his hands graze the sides of my hips to slowly lift the flannel shirt I'm wearing and I gasp. In one smooth move he discards my shirt and gazes over my body before pressing his bare chest into mine and our lips collide again in sweet relief. His strong arms are wrapped around my back, keeping our bodies locked in place.

He presses his entire body into me, and I feel where his sweatpants frame the main event. I let out a whimper.

"I've wanted to do this since the moment I saw you," he says, whispering in my ear, sending shock waves everywhere.

Gently, he pushes me back toward the bed, and his hands start to migrate south from my stomach. I will my legs not to buckle and then mercifully I hit the bed and fall back, his body following mine onto the soft surface.

"Xander." I let out a moan. And then . . .

I'm lying on my back. The room is light. My hands are between my legs.

And Xander is not on top of me.

Oh fuck. Oh fuck.

Oh fuckity fuck.

My heart starts racing. And not the good kind of racing, like you get from heart healthy cardiovascular activities such as running. No, this is the kind you reserve for panic attacks when you realize you just had a sex dream and have literally been caught with your hand in your pants.

I look over at Xander and he's wide-awake, sitting upright and staring at me.

Just like in my dream. But not.

Oh fuck, oh fuck, oh fuck.

I throw a pillow over my face, willing myself to disappear.

If there was ever a time to make a deal with the devil, that time is now.

Dear Devil,

Is this how you do it? I don't know and I don't care. Desperate times call for desperate measures.

Dear Devil,

How are you? I hope you're well, and not too booked and busy with requests. I would like to make a deal. I am willing to trade anything to go back in time and ensure Xander does not witness me moaning myself awake from sleep masturbation. And I mean anything. I am willing to trade sleep farting, which I'm sure you'll find equally soul destroying and an absolute

58

boner killer, which will kill my confidence to hook up with hot dudes for a very long time, leaving me in sexual purgatory, which is, in essence, hell for me. This is a great deal for you. And I'll also throw in a set of steak knives.

Yours truly,
Ashleigh

I hold my breath.

Nothing happens.

"Are you okay?" Xander says, his voice a painful reminder that he's still here, and that he saw and heard everything. I cringe so hard I almost pull a fucking muscle in my face.

"No," I say, steadying myself for what I'm sure will be a full-blown mockery of my salacious sleeping habits.

But then he surprises me. "Nightmare?" he says without a hint of malice.

Wait. What? Nightmare? Oh, thank God. He thought I was moaning in fear (something I will likely overanalyze later but for now—who cares?). Yes. A nightmare! Exactly. One hundred percent a nightmare.

I remove the pillow from over my face and turn toward Xander. His hair is scruffy and messy and I want to run my hands through it. Do not flashback to the sex dream, Ash. Don't do it. I'm warning you. I'm counting to three.

One.

Two.

A flash of his hands on me.

I swallow.

"Yes. Really scary stuff," I say, clutching my heart to corroborate my story. I will take this lie with me to the grave.

There's a soft knock on the door, and Ben enters.

"Good morning," he says.

I smile. Sweet Ben. A perfect distraction. There will be no more mentioning of my one-woman show. Or of the cover-up story. Just an appreciation for fancy wires and to marvel at the relatively new science of polysomnography, which is a new word I learned, fancy speak for studying sleep.

"Ashleigh, we saw a hard spike in your vitals right before you woke up. Heart rate, breathing, eye and leg movement. I'll have to replay the tapes back when we do the analysis later, but how are you feeling?" Ben says.

And no.

No. No. No.

Do not play the tapes back.

Do not study the tapes, Ben.

Ben, please don't study the tapes.

"Bad dream," I say, with a dry throat.

Ben's eyes light up. "It's rare we get adults who are woken up from a nightmare. I'll be looking forward to studying the video with my students at my next tutorial," Ben says, confirming my worst fear that I've essentially made a porn, and it's now going to be circulated among the academic community.

My heart starts racing again.

I look over at Xander, who is staring at me with an expression that is part pity, part curiosity. Wait—does he know?

His eyes shift to the floor.

Shit. He *does* fucking know! He knows and was just trying to give me an out. A small part of me is intrigued by this gesture of kindness. The larger part is now once again horrified.

Xander turns to Ben. "I believe the contract we signed mentioned our results would be kept confidential and not shared beyond the on-site team," Xander says, putting his lawyer voice on.

"With your permission, of course," Ben says to me.

Rock. Hard place. Me. What kind of excuse can I give for saying no that won't make him even more curious to watch it on replay, slowing it down, rewinding it, zooming in like an NYPD cop trying to figure out who the Central Park Flasher is?

"We'd rather not," Xander says simply. I wait for his excuse. His reason. His rationale to explain why we'd rather not. But it never comes. It has never occurred to me until this very moment that as adults, we do not need to justify why. We can simply say no.

"No problem," Ben says without skipping a beat.

Thank you, Sweet Ben. He proceeds to de-wire us, thank us, and leave.

And that's the end of that.

A few minutes later, we're standing by Xander's car wearing the clothes we came in with.

"Thanks," I say, forcing it out before I chicken out.

"For what?" he says.

"For making sure my terrible . . ." I swallow. "Nightmare wasn't paraded around the science department."

"Sure," he says, his expression indifferent.

We stand, staring at each other. It's so awkward. He knows. And I know he knows. And he knows that I know that he knows.

I'm wondering when he's going to give me a wisecrack. Give me shit about what happened. But he doesn't.

"Okay," he says, ready to wrap this up.

"See you tonight," I say quickly, beating him to it. I turn and hightail it toward my car, hoping I can get out of there before anything else happens.

And then I hear his voice from behind me. "Shouldn't you say, see you tonight, *Xander*?" He calls out his name in a spot-on impression of my moan.

I freeze and slowly turn around just in time to see a wicked grin spread across Xander's face before he disappears into his car.

I let out a long and slow breath. Well, that's our first night done and dusted. Only twenty-nine days to go. So, if everything that could possibly go wrong went thunderously wrong the first time, am I safe to say it's smooth sailing from here? The devil on my shoulder laughs.

CHAPTER EIGHT

"You what?" Em's face does a three-way surprise expression—eyebrows shoot to the sky, eyes bug out, and mouth drops halfway to the floor.

"Unfortunately, my new one-woman show, *Sleep Wanker*, is coming to a late-night sleep study session near you," I say, straight-faced.

The fact that this legit happened to me last night registers on Em's face, and her entire body shudders as fits of laughter spill out from her.

"I will not laugh," I say in the face of Em's deadly contagious laughter. "I refuse. Because this is super serious stuff. I need advice. I need to know how to navigate tonight. Do I ignore it? Do I confront it? Do I ask Ben if he studied the tapes? No. I can't. I won't," I say as Em's laughter gets louder.

The straight face I'm holding is about to break. I clench my jaw tighter and swallow, but Em's chortling pushes me over the edge. The corners of my lips start to curl, giving me away. I avoid eye contact for a second to reset.

"I think you should, um, well . . ." Em attempts to talk her way through her laughing fit, but she can't finish the sentence. The gleam in her eye turns into a full-blown tear that rolls down her cheek—and that does it for me. I start laughing. And my laughing spurs on Em's laughing, and we're just two dickheads who went out for a café lunch on a Monday only to end up laughing uncontrollably instead of eating anything.

Em finally regains some semblance of control. The laughter subsides. And I think we're in the clear. But then she takes a sip of water and instead of swallowing it, she looks at me again and it must remind her of what I told her. She sprays it out all over our table. Our Cuban sandwiches—with the perfect crusty sourdough bread—turn soggy under the mist.

This sets me off and it's getting to the point where we're both wheezing as we recount the story to each other through a random collection of consonants and vowels that don't sound like any language on this planet. I put my hand out to cover Em's face and look away so I can't see her reacting to my reaction, which is reacting to her reaction—my last-ditch effort to break the cycle.

"I'm good. I'm good. I'm good," Em says, repeating the mantra. She starts to break on the third repetition. Yep, she's a goner. She'd be terrible at meditation. But I know without a doubt that "sleep wanker" will forever more make Em collapse with laughter.

Ten long minutes later, we have our shit under control and I can take a moment to enjoy our surroundings. We're sitting inside our second-favorite café, Roasting Warehouse. And warehouse it is. Exposed beams and bricks and pipes that do nothing to keep the heat out. It's a scorcher of a day and still, I refuse to drink my coffee cold. I take a sip of my double-shot cappuccino.

"This mess is two-fold," I say, returning to the reason I shared the story in the first place—to figure out my next move before tonight. "One. Sweet Ben. Two. Xander," I say, counting them out on my fingers.

"But you said Xander handled Ben. So where's the mess? I mean, besides the fact you're fighting deep-seated *feelings*," Em says, but I cut her off at the F word. I don't do the F word.

"Feelings?" I shake my head. "It's chemistry. Hormones. Bodily functions. I can't control it." It's the perfect defense for why my rules have held up for me personally for eleven years, why millions of women worldwide agree, and also why the execs at Netflix gave Mom a lucrative deal for her TV show.

It's flawless.

"Yes, yes, the chemistry teacher doesn't believe in love," Em says, like she's said it a million times before. Because she has. Still, I can't stop thinking about the wicked grin on Xander's face in the parking lot, and for some reason it has me wondering what he's doing right now. Or who, I guess, if he's into some afternoon delight.

"Now, I will admit," I say, smiling at her slyly, which has her leaning in for the juicy gossip. "That if I had met Xander *for the first time* last Friday, I wouldn't hesitate to . . ." I let the sentence trail off but wiggle my eyebrows.

"Okay, I need a photo," Em says, letting her speech about love go. Yes, yes, the English teacher is a romantic.

"I don't have a—wait," I say, remembering the photo he sent from the Cardi B concert. I swipe open my phone and navigate to our text message before handing my phone over to Em.

She's quiet for a moment. But her mouth drops open as she zooms in and I can't help but smile. "You need to break your one-night-only rule for him."

"*What?*" I say, which actually means "No fucking way." I ignore my stomach bottoming out at the idea that all my memories of Xander could double as future projections. Future pleasure.

"Not for love," Em says, understanding the true tone of my question. "For sex."

"No."

"Come on. Do your Bone It boys really measure up to the original?" Em says, eyebrows raised.

"Let me put it this way. If Bone It had a rating system like Uber, Morgan would get five stars. Smooth ride. Knows how to handle a stick. Arrived at my destination multiple times," I say, always ready to go to bat for my rules.

"You need to fuck Xander," she says like it's a done deal. I stare her down, but this only encourages her. "Fuck Xander," she repeats, adding on a fun little hand clap. Oh god, here we go. The theatrics of Emily.

"Fuck Xander. Fuck Xander. Fuck Xander," Em chants and claps, her voice getting louder every time she repeats it, like she's a kid in class playing the penis game.

Then, she pauses midchant. And I know she's waiting for me to join in. And I also know she won't stop until I do.

"FUCK XANDER," I chant and clap loudly.

I say it at the exact same time there's a change in songs on the "café chill vibes" playlist, so my chant echoes across the space.

And then my gaze lands on one of the patrons and I freeze in fucking terror.

"Fuck," I say in a whisper. "Xander?" Em doesn't register the question in my intonation because she doesn't stop.

"Yes, you need to fuck Xander *immediately*," she declares.

Bed Chemistry

"No, Xander is *here*," I hiss, but I'm not looking at Em anymore because my eyes are locked on Xander. Sitting right there. Staring back at me with that wicked grin.

Why are warehouses made like amphitheaters where the acoustics carry across fifty tables and reach into every corner? There's no way in hell Xander didn't hear a) his name and b) that we were just chanting about fucking him. What horrible thing did I do in a past life to deserve this kind of karmic retribution?

Just then a waitress delivers Xander's food and he breaks eye contact with me to thank her, which sends her blushing in his presence. Looks like the entire world wants to fuck Xander.

Okay, so now on top of the enormous task of figuring out how to handle the catastrophic moment of getting caught sleep masturbating by tonight, I now have to redirect my brain cells to being caught chanting about having sexual intercourse with Xander.

I am not prepared for this. Time is ticking. I have maybe three seconds to figure out how to play this out as the waitress places the food down and starts to leave.

To add sprinkles to the shit sundae I'm now eating, further neural pathways have broken off to discuss my choice of outfit, reminding me that I'm wearing yoga leggings that haven't seen a yoga pose since they were downward dog proofed during quality control before being shipped to stores, and a T-shirt that has a stain on it I only noticed when I got out of the car at the café. Also, yesterday was the absolute last day I could physically get away with using dry shampoo as a replacement for washing my hair.

Normally, I wouldn't give a flying fuck about any of this, but with the embarrassment compounding rapidly since Wankergate and subsequently getting caught red-handed chanting "Fuck Xander," forgive me for being a little sensitive.

Em follows my line of sight and studies Xander for a moment before turning back around, her face beaming. "*Holy shit*, that photo does not do him justice," she says, her voice booming with permission. "Xander's *hot*."

Yeah, I know. "Shhh!" I hiss, whacking Em in the arm for being so loud. In turn, Em yells out for being hit. That sound carries toward Xander, further pulling his attention to the sound tsunami we've created. The waitress leaves, and Xander looks at me over his coffee cup that he's slowly taking a sip from. Is he mad? Oh, no doubt he's mad. It also happens to be sexy somehow. Smoldering, one might even say. Like a predator stalking his prey.

I put my hand to my mouth, pretending to chew on my thumb.

I can't believe the way Emily's smiling at me right now. Rude.

"Put that smile away. Now is *not* the time to smile. Now is the time to strategize. What the fucking fuck do I do?" My eyes flash back and forth between Em and Xander.

"Go over and say hello?" Em suggests, like we weren't just caught chanting about objectifying him.

I give her my best "are you kidding?" look. "I can't just go over there," I say.

"Well, awkward chitchat is better than staring at him from across the room pretending you didn't just scream excitedly about screwing him," Em says, like it isn't her fault I was doing it in the first place.

Also, damn it. She's right. I can't not get up and say something.

"Okay," I say, taking a deep breath. "Okay. Okay. Okay." Maybe if I repeat it enough times, I'll believe everything's okay. "I *can* do this."

"That's the spirit," Em says, taking a swig of her coffee and sounding not at all sincere. "You can reminisce about your *Sleepless in the Saddle* incident." She waves her mug in the air and then giggles.

"Really?" I say, not giving her the satisfaction of her decent wordplay as I push back my chair. The coffee machine whirls. A dog barks in the distance. It appears I've unlocked superpowers in which I can hear all sounds, near and far.

I drag my body slowly over to Xander, every muscle willing me to turn around, but I've made it halfway across the warehouse now and there's no turning back. He hasn't taken his eyes off me. I resist the urge to run my fingers through my hair as a makeshift comb. To try and pick the unidentifiable stain off my top. And yep, that's the feeling of my leggings riding up my crotch and giving me camel toe.

I breathe out and clasp my hands together to appear put together.

When I finally reach Xander's table, a Cuban sandwich is halfway to his mouth. I stop in front of him, and he pauses mid-bite, then looks me up and down. His gaze stops on my stain. And then my hair. And finally lands on my face. Ugh.

"The Cuban sandwich is good here," I say, initiating the chit-chat Em told me was supposed to be better than staring from a safe distance. Xander takes a bite and chews. This is getting more awkward by the second. I take a deep breath, ready to apologize.

I can't believe he caught me playing the penis game with his name. In all the cafés in all the Valley, he had to eat a Cuban sandwich in mine. I am internally screaming.

"So, about what you heard—" I say just as his phone rings.

Xander looks down and studies the incoming call with brows furrowed, all serious. "I have to take this," he says, then wipes his mouth with his napkin. He stands and I step to the side, giving him space to walk past me.

"Yeah, of course. Okay. So, um, see you tonight?" I stammer.

Not answering me, he swipes his phone and walks straight past me, leaving a trail of his signature fresh scent, which short-circuits my brain. I've been dismissed.

Awesome. Now I've got five hours and forty-five minutes to think—also known as worry, stress, catastrophize, and have an ongoing anxiety attack—about how I'm going to handle Wank-gate *and* Fuckgate.

How did my drama-free life turn into a scandal worthy of a reality show?

* * *

The first thing I questioned over the following five hours and forty-five minutes was: *Will I see him tonight? Will he show up?*

That's spiral number one. It's the most important spiral because if he doesn't show, then we're not in the sleep study, and if we're not in the sleep study then I don't have a job, and if I don't have a job, then I have no money. Money that's supposed to pay the rent.

The good news here is that I was able to pull myself out of this spiral by constantly reminding myself that Xander is an insomniac and needs this study more than the money. Which is saying something.

I concluded that I would see him tonight.

This made way for my second spiral: the confrontation spi-ral. Also known as, what the actual fuck is he going to say to me? And what am I going to say to him in response? This spiral required the most spiraling. Do you know how productive the brain can get when its only job is to conjure up fifty different scenarios in which Xander could confront me, and me coming up with fifty different responses where I don't come off as some depraved sexual deviant?

So productive.

I thought about it as I watched Derek Morgan kick down doors in *Criminal Minds*. I thought about it while playing *Mario Kart* with Em. I thought about it while sticking my head in the freezer in attempts to cool down in this chronic heat wave.

In all my thinking, the biggest thing that stood out was that Xander is a lawyer. He confronts people *for a living*. And so he will, without a doubt, confront me.

And this is why, as I'm pulling up into the parking lot this evening, I am completely on edge.

A nervous wreck.

I take a deep breath. It does absolutely nothing.

I get out of the car, ready to see Xander in the parking lot— but Xander's not standing at the trunk of his car with his leg kicked back, rubbing his neck. Xander's car is not here at all.

I search the parking lot as the late afternoon sun attempts to blind me, and nope. No car. No Xander. The one scenario I stopped myself from spiraling over is what's happening right now.

After hearing himself the butt of our joke, Xander decided he didn't have the energy to spend the next four weeks with *me*.

Fuck.

I cannot twerk, swing around a pole, or drop into an aggressive squat and pop back up again like I'm some athletic stripper gymnast. I have zero core strength. I need this job.

Maybe I can go in and pretend Xander is running late from a case. Maybe when Ben asks where Xander is, I can check my phone and it says there's a voice mail from Xander. There's been an accident. Xander's at the hospital. In a coma . . .

"Hey, Ash," I hear someone say. Turning and shielding my eyes from the sun, I see Ben pop his head up from one of the parked cars.

With its rusted roof, chipped paint job, and what looks like the remnants of a fender bender that didn't get fixed, I don't have a shadow of a doubt it's Ben's pride and joy. He slams the door three times to get it to lock and walks over to me, wrangling a stack of papers.

My stomach drops. I'll have to start talking. The jig is up. I'll be jobless and homeless, all because I lost a game of penis.

Ben moves past me and walks toward the front door. I don't join him. My right foot won't lift off the ground. I stand there for a moment, my brain and body paralyzed.

"Ben, I . . ." I look around as if the parking lot will magically give me the words I need right now. He turns and smiles.

"Come on, Xander's already inside," he says, gesturing to the building.

What? I don't need to kill Xander off? I don't need to make up another story to explain his absence? Xander showed up?

"Something about his case wrapping early. He's so cool," Ben says to me, a look of approval on his face.

I nod and begin to follow him inside. Wait. Is Xander cool?

I shake it off. No way. Not in this universe.

"Look who I found waiting for you in the parking lot," Ben says as he opens the door to our tiny sleep study room for two.

Xander stops rubbing his neck and looks up at me from behind furrowed eyebrows. Holy mother of hotness.

In all the spiraling this afternoon, I forgot how ridiculously good-looking Xander is. Blood rushes from my extremities and concentrates itself in the pit of my stomach and forward flops at the sight of him. The sex dream flutters behind my eyelids when I blink. His hands. His lips. His tongue. I'm keenly aware neither of us is smiling at the other. Just staring. Xander gets the memo and breaks the stare by giving me a half smile. You know, minimum-effort style.

"I'll be back to put on the wires shortly," Ben says, and closes the door behind him as he leaves.

Xander's half smile rests on his face, almost morphing into a smirk, and I know it's coming in three, two—

"Fuck Xander? Tell me how you really feel," he says.

And there it is. The confrontation.

The smirk on his face makes me think he's slightly amused, but the tone of the delivery tells me he's hurt.

"You don't even know me," Xander goes on, before I have time to gather my defense.

"Oh, please. I know you," I say, quick to react.

Xander laughs. He actually laughs. "Just because you know what I can do with *my tongue* doesn't mean you know me," he says.

"Really?" I snap. "Is that it? You're pissed because I didn't thank you for your services eleven years ago? Okay, well, *thank you*." I curtsy on the thank-you to really drive home the sarcasm.

Xander rolls his eyes. "Wow," he says as though it's a complete sentence.

"Wow what?"

"Forgive me for not having the patience to deal with your childish behavior after a night of exactly zero sleep," he says.

I swallow because suddenly, my mouth is an ocean of salvia. Does he have a point?

"*I'm* childish?" I say, opting to fight him instead of understanding where he's coming from.

"Did I stutter?"

"You're the one who's having a tantrum about a one-night stand," I say, reducing our former friendship down to a decision we could never come back from. And the moment it comes out of my mouth, I know I'm grasping at straws.

"Oh, come on, Ash. I promise I haven't thought about you in eleven years," he says, volleying the argument right back into my court.

"You think I'm pathetic that I signed up for the sleep study even though I sleep perfectly fine," I say, projecting my worst fears onto him.

"The study *needs* solid sleepers. Why would I think you're pathetic for helping out?" he says, confused.

"Because I got fired from my job and I'm a broke joke," I say, practically screaming and simultaneously wishing I hadn't spoken.

"I don't think—"

The door swings opens, and we're both snapped out of our fight.

Ben stands there, his eyes wide. "Do I need to get security?" he says, his voice wobbling a little, but standing his ground.

Oh my god, he heard us fighting.

Xander's face morphs into a friendly smile that immediately makes Ben smile back. "Not necessary. I was just telling Ash what happened in court today," he says. "She likes to hear all the dirty stuff."

Ben raises his eyebrows, interested.

"It was some real Jerry Springer shit," Xander says.

"I bet," Ben says, mesmerized by Xander. "But, um, the thing is, everyone can hear you. Like everyone. And your acting is really good. It sounded like a full-on domestic in here. You know?" The warning hangs in the air between us.

"Roger that, Ben. No more courtroom drama at the sleep study," Xander says, motioning with his hand that he's zipping his lips shut.

"Thanks, bro," Ben says, leaving. "I'll be back soon for the wiring."

After the door is shut, I wait in silence for five seconds before I spin around to face Xander. I'm ready to go for round two, but I notice his hand has returned to the back of his neck, like he's trying to rub me out of his life.

"I'm exhausted," he says, now rubbing his temple.

"Yeah, obviously, because you're an insomniac," I say, unable to help myself.

"No. I mean, yes, I am an insomniac. But no, that's not why I'm exhausted." He doesn't explain further, but I know exactly what he means.

I exhaust him.

There's a momentarily lapse in my desire to fight to the death like we're two gladiators. I look at him. Like, really look at him. Something in his dark hazel eyes changes. It's like they're waving a little white flag.

Before I can process it, Ben knocks again and enters. He's holding—surprise, surprise—a stack of papers.

"Oh, Ash, I've got this for you. Have a read before I come in to wire you up," Ben says, handing me said papers. "I'll be back in ten." He closes the door behind him.

I look down at the papers. The title on the cover sheet says: *Cognitive Behavioral Therapy to Reduce Sleep-Interfering Arousal/ Activation.*

OH MY GOD. He studied the fucking tapes.

I can feel Xander peering over my shoulder, scanning the paper. Well, that's one way to end a fight.

"Ben studied the tapes," I say, holding up the paper and turning to face Xander.

"He probably made a spreadsheet about it." Xander is wearing a full-body smile. It seems the fight is forgotten for now because he's filled with utter delight.

"Yeah, that's much better. I'll for sure be able to look Ben in the eye the next time I see him," I say, shaking my head.

I head over to the end of the bed, dramatically turn around, and let myself fall backward. I stare up at the ceiling and finally notice how exhausted I am. Sure, I might not be able to do insane maneuvers on a pole, but I can perform mental gymnastics with the best of them.

Only twenty-eight days to go, I remind myself.

I sigh. It's going to feel like a fucking lifetime.

CHAPTER NINE

I open my eyes with a jolt, the nape of my neck slick with sweat. I'm surrounded by darkness, and it feels like the weight of the blanket is suffocating me. Kicking at the blanket does nothing to remove it, so I throw my hands at it, pawing it like I'm trapped in a nutshell. I finally manage to find sweet freedom as the blanket balls up discarded to one side of the bed.

Sitting up, I realize my neck isn't the only thing sweating. I'm drenched. I reach for my top, ready to remove it for some sweet relief until I hear a familiar voice remind me that I'm not in bed alone. Reason number take-your-pick as to why sleeping over is never a good idea.

"You okay?" Xander says. His soft voice floats across the blanket fort that I'd made in my desperate escape. My hands pause at the hem of the flannel I'm wearing. And the worst summer sleepwear award goes to . . .

The mattress moves under Xander's body and then the lamp on his bedside table is on. In the glowing light, I notice Xander's curls have gone even more rogue than normal, which I didn't think possible. Just pure mussed. There's stubble that's clearly been growing since five o'clock. He looks so relaxed it'd be easy to mistake him for someone who just woke up.

My body flushes hot again. And not because I woke up wearing flannel. I start moving the hem of the flannel back and forth, trying to create a makeshift fan. It's not working.

"The air conditioner conked out an hour ago," Xander says as his eyes land on my cheek where I feel a clump of damp hair sticking to it. He lifts his hand up, like he's about to move the hair off my face himself, like it's instinct. I bet he does it with all the girls. I freeze. Definitely instinct. He must think twice about it because he redirects his hand to his own hair. Running it through the curls. Somehow, it's even hotter than if he touched me.

We stare at each other for a moment before Xander gets up and reaches into his bag. That's when I notice he's replaced his sweatpants and hoodie for boxers and a T-shirt. He's wearing *sleepwear*. In front of me. A total stranger.

I start to feel lightheaded. This is exactly the kind of intimacy I avoid. This is exactly why I bail afterward. This is exactly why I don't stick around and snooze. Wearing your . . . Captain America—really? I blink twice just to make sure. Yep. Really— boxers breed the kind of closeness I save for Christmas with my mom. Not old friends-turned-flames. Fucking labels.

He rummages around and then pulls out a white T-shirt and boxers, which he holds out to me. "Here," he says, his eyes searching mine.

I narrow my eyes.

"They're clean," he says. He shoves them toward me and tilts his head to the side as if to say, *Come on, take them.*

I study the clothes. They are so inviting. So cooling. So comfortable. So weather appropriate. Even if they are part of the Marvel Cinematic Universe. I imagine the cotton, oh, sweet cotton, how I miss thee, soft against my skin. I want to get out of this fucking flannel so bad and wear them. More than I've wanted anything in my entire life. I want them so bad I could cry.

I reach out as he hands me his clothes.

I don't even have to ask him to turn around. He faces the wall. I can't help but notice his thighs are decorated with a smattering of tiny tattoos that weren't there the last time I saw this much of his skin. I see a wave. And scales of justice. And there's a molecular tattoo that wraps around his thigh. I can't make it out. Unless I plan on getting up close and personal. Which I do not. And so, I remove the flannel and replace it with his T-shirt. And boxers. They smell like Juicy Fruit. I breathe it in a little too deeply. The long slow steady breath grounds me. The T-shirt is soft. It might even be organic. I'm so relieved. It comes out as a sigh.

"Have you officially changed?" he says, repeating the same way I spoke to him yesterday after what I will forever refer to as The Peep Show. I look over at him and give myself a few seconds to remember just how strong I know his thighs are.

"I am officially changed," I say with the enunciation of proper British nobility and the mind of a filthy chimney sweep.

He turns around and his eyes flicker all over my body, not sure where to settle. A shiver follows behind his eyes, like he's physically touched me. "Better?"

"Yes," I say, letting the cotton do its thing and moisture wick, cooling my skin down.

He rolls his eyes at me. "You're *welcome*," he says, taking a dig, because I didn't actually thank him.

"Thank you," I concede as he settles himself, though not before turning off the lamp and plunging us back into darkness.

Now that my body temperature has lowered to within normal range, you'd think I'd be able to drift back to la la land. I can't. The chasm that was between Xander and me when I fell asleep feels like it's vanished into thin air. Without my ability to see him, my other senses are in overdrive. It's like every surface possible from my ankle to shoulder is touching him.

"Do you know what the time is?" I say to distract myself from my skin singing at the physical closeness.

"Quarter past one," he replies without having to check, which tells me he's been awake this whole time, aware of the seconds that've ticked by to get us to this moment.

"You haven't slept at all?" I ask, already knowing the answer, but if we're going to be awake for a while, I may as well attempt to make friendly conversation. Maybe we can be civil. For the sake of the sleep study, I'm willing to try.

"Nope. I'll usually get an hour or two around three, if I'm lucky," he says with a lighthearted tone that tells me he's taking it better than I would.

"How do you function?"

"Barely?" he says, his voice raised at the end in a question mark. I'm not sure if it's a confession or if he's being self-deprecating. My mind flashes back to when Xander answered his phone at the café while dealing with my shenanigans without missing a beat. I can just imagine the jury needing to break for recess due to new evidence. *Open the envelope and you'll see that it was Miss Scarlett in the photocopy room with the candlestick.* The man is functioning just fine. Definitely self-deprecating.

Bed Chemistry

"And you have no idea why you can't sleep?" The darkness makes me bold enough to ask, even if my eyes are slowly adjusting.

"That's why I'm here," he says like he's admitting defeat. I wonder how long he's had insomnia. And what his breaking point was to make him walk into this sleep study and not only ask for help but ask me to help him.

"Without sleep, I would be a pathetic mess," I say, the mattress shifting next to me as Xander rearranges himself. Into what position, I have no idea. I don't dare look.

"Er, thanks," he says, like I was calling him pathetic. I scold myself in the dark.

"That's not what I mean. You look *good*," I say, exaggerating the *good* so much that I may as well have said, "You're fucking hot" to his face.

"Thanks. You too," Xander says right back to me. Like his filter might be malfunctioning in the dark.

"Because I sleep," I say, trying to redirect the conversation away from the fact that Xander visually stimulates my senses. *And not just visually.*

"From what I remember, you look good especially when you *haven't* slept," he says, his voice lowering an octave on the last two words.

Woah.

My blood rushes from my extremities and pulses between my thighs. I can't help but wonder what memory he's in right now.

"Shut up," I say, trying to deny myself the chance to ask. Unfortunately for me, this time, it comes out like I'm begging him.

"Make me," he says.

I finally dare myself to look over at Xander. The streetlights outside slice through the blinds, illuminating his mouth.

That fucking mouth.

My eyes crawl up his face to find his locked on mine for a moment before they flicker to my mouth.

And something in me snaps.

I lean forward and kiss him.

On contact, I lose all self-control.

Xander slides his tongue over mine and my entire body leans into his, making full frontal contact. I tilt my head back, giving him access. I feel the hard lines of his chest, the detail of his waistband on my lower stomach, his thighs. He is all over me, and I still can't get enough.

My hands are in his hair, twirling first, then tugging him closer.

His hands roam from my jaw down my back, and he squeezes my ass. I groan into his mouth before he slides them underneath my T-shirt—*his* T-shirt—and makes his way up my stomach, his fingers putting on a show as they dance over my ribcage.

Then he abandons my ribs and slides his hands around my back, pulling me flush to him. Our bodies meld together. His warm hands splay across my back, like they're trying to cover as much surface area as possible. My skin heats up to the flame that is his touch.

Kissing Xander is like muscle memory. I don't have to think. I just *feel*, my body remembering exactly where to burn for him.

And when our kiss deepens, I know it's reciprocal.

My spine bends in a perfect arc as we create seamless contact and I feel him growing hard against me, the pressure intoxicating.

He scrapes one hand down my side to hold my hip, his thumb circling there. A request. But then his thumb digs into me. Frantic. Begging me. I open my legs ever so slightly and he fills the space with this thigh.

The friction.

I sweep my hands down his back and trail them gently along the edge of his boxers. Xander shudders at the light touch of my fingertips that dip below the waistband, teasing him.

"Ash . . ." Xander moans my name in my mouth, but he can't finish the sentence as his warm tongue finds its way back to mine.

The hand he had on my back has moved to my side. He's applying enough pressure to my ribcage to keep me from moving. His thumb starts tracing along the soft curve of my breast.

I ache everywhere for him.

BEEP. BEEP. BEEP.

I pull back from Xander. What the fuck was that?

The horny haze lifts at the sound of one of the monitors going off next to me. And I remember where I am. And who I'm with.

BEEP. BEEP. BEEP.

I snatch my hands away. Xander follows.

There's a knock on the door before Ben enters. He rounds the bed quickly and pokes a few buttons on the machine next to me.

The beeping finally stops.

And then we descend into awkward silence.

I refuse to look at Xander, so I watch Ben as he studies the machine, watching my heart rate.

I feel so exposed.

I will my heart rate to slow down. But as it turns out, embarrassment is a hell of a stimulant.

I don't dare look at Ben. I don't dare look at Xander. So I keep my eyes forward.

"Another nightmare?" Ben says, finally cutting the excruciating silence.

"Yep." That's all I say.

"Have a read of those papers I shared in the morning," Ben says before turning back toward the door. "Goodnight."

When the door clicks behind Ben, I count to three before turning to face Xander.

He's wearing the most self-satisfied smile I've ever seen.

"Not a word out of you," I say, warning him. It looks like the lawyer learns quick because this time he doesn't ask me to make him.

CHAPTER TEN

"That was a mistake," I say, shoving my flannel into my bag with a little too much force. Like I'm trying to shove that idea into my brain. Forcing it until I submit.

It can never happen again. Can it? Nope.

It's morning. We're fully clothed. And I haven't said a word to him since Ben interrupted us last night.

From the hours of one thirty until ten minutes ago, I thought I was never going to sleep ever again. I thought I was going to have to march into Dr. Waitley's office and tell her she's got two insomniacs now. *Congratulations! You've just discovered insomnia is contagious. Now please submit my body for further study in solitary confinement.* But as my eyes fluttered open this morning, I realized that I did manage to get some shitty sleep among the squirming. And squirm I did. Every time I closed my eyes, there he was.

His hands. His lips. His moans.

It shouldn't have been that good.

Chapter nine of Mom's book: *The Illusion of Rekindling Desire & Why It Usually Fails.*

I glance up at Xander, who's studying me from his side of the bed. "Are you telling me or you?" he says, one eyebrow raised.

"Both," I say. This makes Xander bust out in full-body laughter. I look past him toward the door. Longingly.

"Will I see you tonight?" he says, a strain in his voice as he catches me fantasizing about walking out of here and never coming back. Never seeing Xander again. Never having to deal with the aftermath of my lapse in judgment.

His eyes widen when I don't answer immediately. Those red-rimmed eyes. I ignore how it tugs on a piece of me that I usually reserve for Em and instead focus on my empty bank account.

"I'll be here," I say, reassuring him with a tight nod. "But I think we might need to set some—"

"Rules?"

"Exactly."

"No dating. No sex. No falling in love," Xander says, reciting the rules we made the day we met eleven years ago. When we decided to become friends. That we inevitably broke, because you can't deny chemistry. I can't believe he remembers. "Looks like we didn't break any rules last night."

Technically, he's right.

But my brain is still trying to make it make sense. How was it so fucking good? Why is my body still vibrating six hours later? And how is it possible to feel like I'm one flashback away from coming undone? I squeeze my eyes shut. Ignore it.

"Ash?"

"What we had was nothing more than chemistry," I say, trying to find an explanation.

"Right, Miss Ashleigh," Xander says, anchoring into the frame of reference for this conversation. I am a chemistry teacher. I will use chemistry to explain this.

"A chemical reaction," I say, looking down at my hands.

"Is that why it felt so good?" he says, his voice thick like smoke. My eyes snap to him.

"Yes." I breathe out. His voice pulling me in. And for the second time in my entire life, I wonder if breaking my rules might be worth it. And then I remember the reason I don't break my rules. "Wait."

"Can't a chemical reaction ever be repeated?" he asks. Normally, the teacher within me would perk up that someone has expressed genuine interest. But when it comes to Xander, I have to tread carefully.

"A chemical reaction is irreversible," I say. "Like when a log burned in a fire turns to ashes, but the ashes can't be changed back into a log." I omit the new evidence thanks to last night that our chemical reaction *can* be repeated.

"Okay," he says, accepting his fate. "So just to clarify then, what we just did was so incredible, it changed *your* life *irreversibly* forever?" He says it like he's delivering his closing argument to the jury.

"No," I scoff. "It's not my fault you're too dense to understand."

"You're an excellent chemistry teacher. Don't sell yourself short," he says, smirking.

Fuck. And just like that, I've managed to walk myself into another battle of the comeback. Every time I think I've got him, I realize too little too late he's got me. It seems our dynamic is that I set him up, and he knocks me down.

I literally have nothing to say to this. It's true. The awards hanging in the dark room of Principal Holland's office, in the empty hallways of a school that's shut for the summer, are proof. And yes, I am smart. Regardless of how good Xander is at making me squirm.

I look at him and he's carefully placing his folded T-shirt and boxers into his bag. Like his methods—compared to my haphazard stuffing—give him the high ground in this. Not for long.

"You're projecting," I say, launching my counter.

"What?"

"You're the one whose life changed *irreversibly* forever," I say, unleashing a smile right before changing to a mock shock expression. "What? You think you walked away unscathed? Please, it takes two elements to tango."

He frowns but doesn't speak. I revel in reducing Xander to silence, a much welcome change from his carefully crafted comebacks. "You were the wood. I was the fire. Now, you're ash."

"Your name is literally Ash," he says, bumbling the delivery. Fuck, it feels good to take him down a few pegs.

"You're grasping at straws. It's pathetic," I say, feeling like I'm circling a victory here. "So in that case, I want to apologize, for cataclysmically changing your life." Now it's my time to smirk at him.

"You didn't," he says, scoffing.

"So we were both equally unaffected?" I say, trying my best to remain innocent on the outside. But if he's going to talk shit then I owe him nothing.

"Yes," he says through gritted teeth. Like lying isn't his day job. Please.

"Good boy," I say, my stomach dropping at the innuendo. *Oh Ash, you didn't just say that.* It's out in the open now—if I want to win the battle of the wit, then I must commit.

I force myself to look at him, willing myself not to break. His eyes lock on mine. My stomach does a lazy forward roll. It's official. He's staring at me. And I'm staring at him. And what we have here, is a stare off. I count my breath.

One.

Two.

Three.

There is no way I'm losing this stare off. Especially after the "good boy" comment. I'll never live it down. *Don't break, Ash. Don't break.*

The only difference is that his eyes have grown dark and I have no idea how to recover from this. So I break.

"Here," I say, throwing his T-shirt and boxers across the bed, doing my best to wrap this up.

Of course, trying to throw the lightest, softest, most comfortable cotton across the bed doesn't work. They both flutter to the mattress, landing in the middle. "Shit." I get up on the bed to reach for my pathetic attempt, when I feel them being shoved into my hands. No. I push against the resistance, trying to return them to their owner, but then they're immediately back in my hands.

I finally look up and see Xander. Leaning on the bed. Meeting me in the middle.

"Keep them," he says, and the clothes are back in my hands.

"I don't want them," I say, shoving them back into his hands. It lasts all of two seconds because they're back in my hands.

"You might not want them. But you're going to need them."

"I don't *need* them," I say, making another attempt to return them. This time, though, I put my back into it as I shove the clothes in his hands and hold his wrists. *I will not be walking out of this sleep study with your fucking sleepwear.*

Physics, though, is not on my side. Because Newton's Third Law of Motion states that whenever one object exerts a force on another object, the second object exerts equal and opposite force on the first. It appears we're at a stalemate. Fucking Newton.

What happens next happens so quickly I'm going to need Ms. Chatterjee, the physics teacher, to explain it to me, because Xander stops pushing against me and I end up facedown on the mattress, his clothes still in my hands.

I see Xander looking down at me, pressing his lips together, holding in a laugh. His whole unfazed demeanor sends white hot anger through me.

I am so fucking sick of Xander Miller.

My rage unlocks access to the self-defense class Em and I took a couple of summers back and I reach up and get a fistful of Xander's T-shirt, yanking him hard toward me. This coupled with the edge of the mattress sends him off balance and falling toward me. I grab hold of his other sleeve and use it as leverage to roll on top of him.

Holy shit. I can't believe that worked.

I am officially on top of Xander Miller.

"Fine, I'll take the clothes back," Xander says, waving the white flag. It comes out low and a little harsh. I stuff the boxer shorts into one hand and the T-shirt into the other. He mercifully takes them.

And just when I think it's over, his eyes skate down my body and rest where our hips are pressed together. Fuck. I am officially *straddling* Xander Miller.

"Ash," he says, strained. "You're going to need to get off me *right now*."

I scramble off him as quick as humanly possible, ignoring the hard lines of his belt buckle. At least, I *think* it's his belt buckle.

I turn to grab my bag before walking out the door, not looking back.

I hit the speed dial on Emily's number. She picks up after one ring.

"Xander Miller is going to be the death of me," I say at the exact moment I almost bump into Dr. Waitley.

Oh, shit.

"Morning, Ashleigh," she says, unreadable as always. I hang up on Em while she's in the middle of rallying me.

"Morning, Dr. Waitley," I say, trying not to freak out.

Did she hear?

Are we fucked?

She studies me for a moment.

Oh, we're so fucked.

But instead of calling me into her office, she offers me a curt nod. "Have a great day," she says before continuing on her way.

Crisis averted. For now.

CHAPTER ELEVEN

I round the corner from my bedroom with my freshly showered wet hair, acting like I know how to fly-kick the air like a certified ninja.

"Okay, Rocky," Em says, stirring the hollandaise sauce. I throw a few air punches while running in place. A poor impression, but it makes her laugh.

Once the air conditioner of my car cooled me down, I called Em to let her know that our summer of self-defense did not go to waste. When she asked if I saw the eye of *his* tiger, I promptly replied, "Ewww," followed by, "No, but I might have touched it."

No, I have not told my best friend, who has explicitly told me to fuck Xander, that we had a little late-night make out session. No good can come from her knowing I practically mauled him in the middle of the night. And yet, I can't get the strained sound of my name in his throat out of my head. Like he had to muster up every ounce of restraint including past, present, and future just to function. I refuse to let myself smile at this, even though I am in the safety of my own home. I am not safe around Em, the enabler.

I bite my bottom lip as I walk behind her and pour us two giant mugs of coffee. "One day, you're going to teach me how to make your hollandaise sauce," I say as Em plates up. The thing I love about Em's eggs benny is that she replaces the muffin with hash browns. She's a genius.

"You know, today could be that day, it's really not hard," she starts to say, but is cut off by my phone vibrating on the bench next to her. Not gonna lie, one day is more of a state of mind than an actual moment in time. She peers at the screen and says, "It's your mom. Am I answering it, or are we ignoring her?"

"Answer it. She'll just call back," I say, taking a sip of my coffee. She hits the answer button.

"You haven't RSVPed to your father's wedding," Mom blasts through the loudspeaker. Never with the hello, how are you . . . Wait, *what*? "It's next month!"

Before I have the chance to process, Mom says, "When we signed the contract, we were promised full creative control, and we all know sex sells," which I have learned is not part of our conversation, but the second conversation she's having at the same time. I called her out on it once, to which she replied, "If you don't take the reins, no one else will."

Today, though, I am thankful for her multitasking. I look over at Em as if she might be able to shed some light on this situation. In response she takes a sip of her coffee. Equally clueless.

"I'm sorry," I say, walking up to the phone like distance has distorted the news. "But what did you just say?"

"Why haven't you RSVPed to your father's wedding?"

I'm clearly hallucinating. I pick up my coffee cup and look inside at the dark brown matter. Is coffee a hallucinogenic now? Did the DEA reclassify it in the last month? I take a sip anyway.

"Dad's getting *married*?" I ask finally. Dubiously.

My dad isn't the kind of guy that goes and marries someone. I mean, that's why he and Mom got divorced. It's why they're both perpetually single. Love is family. Sex is fleeting. Marriage is a sham.

It's the Hutchinson way. We don't find The One. We find family. And we find lovers. They aren't ever the same person—and we're better off for it. We're *happy*.

"Are you sure?" I ask, trying to muffle my laugh. I mean, last time I checked, hell had not frozen over.

"Yes, Ash. Next month," she says, almost annoyed at my incompetence. And then, just like this is regular old news on par with the world getting warmer and corrupt politics, she adds, "You should have gotten the invitation."

I look to Em. She can read my expression like the blurb of a book. She's gotten the entire rundown of my brain in a simple eye-bugging stare. She grabs my hand on the counter and squeezes it. Reassuring me that *Yes, I'll be your date*. Of course. And we can debrief this batshit crazy idea later. As the warmth from Em's hand spreads from my fingers to my brain, warming me up, hell is alive and kicking. And I'm living in it.

"Right. Of course. The wedding invitation. To Dad's wedding. Which I knew about, obviously." I make a strange sound I hope comes off as a carefree laugh as I move my coffee mug off the pile of envelopes that I've been using as a coaster, the multiple dark-stained rings reminding me I've been avoiding this pile for a long time. I sift through envelopes I will never open until I find a cream-colored one addressed to me in hand-painted calligraphy. The one Mom gave me when I saw her last. It's all becoming clear now.

"I thought I sent my RSVP weeks ago," I say, continuing to play the game. There's a long pause and I'm not sure she's buying it. I don't ask, and instead wait her out.

"I'll just text your dad to let him know you're coming," she says and goes quiet for a moment. For someone so hip for her age, she's the world's slowest texter. Usually, this annoys me. Today, I'm grateful for the silence it provides.

I look up to see Emily busying herself in the kitchen, turning our breakfast into brunch with Bloody Marys. She is a good friend.

"Who are you bringing?" she says, still typing, I assume.

"Emily," I say, without thinking twice. Mom laughs through the phone. That's her way of confirming that of course she's RSVPing for us both. Em gives me a thumbs-up.

"I'm flying solo," she says, offering up this information like I asked for it. I didn't. Because I know she's going to say, "No need to involve anyone I'm involved with. I don't need to be giving them any ideas about a future. Can you imagine?" I can hear her shudder on the other end.

Now that is the kind of reaction I expect from my parents. Not collecting RSVPs for table placements for weddings.

"Done," she says, exasperated.

My phone pings seconds later. It's from my dad. The time stamp on the prior message is from months ago.

Glad you're coming to the wedding. Want money for a dress? Love, Dad and Keeley.

It hits me again.

My dad.

Is getting married.

Elizabeth McKenzie

To a random woman named *Keeley*.

Marriage. Until mere minutes ago, I didn't think my family bought into that institution anymore. I think back to fifteen years ago, when I was in high school and I caught Dad cheating on Mom, and how devastatingly heartbroken I was for those few days before Mom finally confronted me and I had to be the one to tell her. For a moment, she was eerily calm when she told me it was okay that Dad was "being intimate" with Alice, the receptionist (he's so cliché, I know). She said she loved my dad with her whole heart. And that we're family—we'll always be family. Love is family.

Sex, she said, is about chemistry. And it's fleeting.

She spoke so highly of my dad and their love—a love so unconditional, not even extramarital sex could ruin it. And when a love is as great as theirs, it's beyond sex, she said.

I admit, I was skeptical as fuck. And with good reason because as it turns out, Mom's compassion was also fleeting.

That's when all hell broke loose in the Hutchinson household. And subsequently when Mom started writing her bestselling book. And the motto women across the world have adopted as their own. Myself included.

"Okay, I've got to run. Love you," Mom says and hangs up.

"What the actual fuck?" I say, just as a Bloody Mary appears in front of me. I discard the half-drunken coffee and take a sip of the spiked tomato juice. Not strong enough. I reach my hand out expectantly and Em slides over the Tito's bottle. I top mine up with more vodka.

"I did not have this on my bingo card for our summer," Em says, sliding in the seat next to me and holding out her Bloody Mary. I top hers up as well. We each take a long sip in silence. Then another.

I reach for the cream envelope with the coffee stains and open it with a pop. I am covered in pink glitter. Great. I attempt to pluck the glitter shrapnel off my clean wet hair. It's useless. Motherfucker. I dust the invite off and skim-read it.

"Saturday the twenty-fourth?" I say, handing the invite to Em to read. That's in four weeks.

What sort of wedding gift does one buy their dad who explained that the reason he constantly cheated on their mom was because love is unrealistic and who is now throwing what appears to be, based on the thickness of the paper stock for the invite, a very expensive wedding to proclaim that, in fact, love isn't a sham anymore, anyway? A SodaStream?

"Want to talk about it?"

What's there to talk about? My chemistry is glitching with Xander. Dad is getting married. The system's breaking down. The only thing holding my rules together right now is the image of the billboard on the 101 of Mom's show going number one across fourteen countries.

And so, I settle for saying, "It's a bit rich expecting us to celebrate when he's setting *Keeley* up to be ex-wife number two." I practically shrug as I take another long sip. The subtext: *There's nothing to talk about.* "I am, however, declaring today a total write-off." We were planning on venturing to the beach to cool down. My air conditioner coupled with the giant bottle of Tito's that lives in the freezer permanently is a perfect substitute.

"Happy hour on the hour?" Em says, not missing a beat.

"Exactly," I say.

And before we know it, we've quit the tomato juice, which to be honest was just slowing us down and sitting heavy in our stomachs, in favor of straight vodka shots.

* * *

"SWIPE RIGHT!" Em shrieks from on top of the coffee table. I've swapped fulfilling my fifteen-year-old Coyote Ugly dreams for the sofa, leaving Em to solo on the karaoke machine she got me for Christmas when we first got our teaching jobs and knew we'd landed the jackpot of getting paid to party all summer long. Is it old? Yes. Do we only have one CD remaining that isn't scratched? Also yes.

I'm holding my phone out for her approval. On screen is Morgan 2.0. "He's wearing a fedora! A V-neck T-shirt! It's a gym selfie! He's perfect!" A smile spreads across my face while Em attempts to fight the moonlight. And can't.

My thumb hovers over the image, ready to swipe right when I remember Xander.

Xander, who I promised I would not spend my days "boning it." Xander, who I'll be seeing in two hours. Fucking Xander.

I take a screenshot of Morgan 2.0 and open my messages to Xander.

I attach the photo and type out a message: This is who I'm declining for you.

Send.

I throw my phone across the sofa. And right when I think LeAnn Rimes is done, the song starts up again. I look up at Em, who casts out a fishing rod and reels me in. With this much vodka running through my veins—I can't help but oblige. I take Em's hand and she helps me up on the table.

She hands me the only working mic, like she's handing over the reins to the show. Considering she's the self-proclaimed thespian in this duo, I am honored, and so I prowl around on the coffee table like I've just arrived in New York to pursue our dreams of becoming songwriters while working for tips. And I too, cannot fight the moonlight, no matter how hard I try.

Out of the corner of my eye, I see my phone lighting up and I immediately know it's Xander. He replied. I know it's going to be a master class in dry humor. Instead of dreading it, I feel every inch of skin prickle with anticipation.

Em must track my smile back to my phone because after she hands me one of the two shots of vodka, she walks over to the discarded phone to see what's distracted me mid-performance. "You know who you should swipe right on?" I know the answer before she says it. "XANDER!"

She raises her shot glass up at me from across the living room, beaming. I hold mine up, saluting her. And damn it, I find myself smiling back.

* * *

"You!" I say/shout/slur in Xander's general direction, pointing/ waving/swaying. Oh, she's drunk, all right. I'm momentarily distracted by the Uber driver who floors the engine in reverse, grinds the clutch, and kicks up dust as he leaves the parking lot. Was he not happy with me serenading him at the top of my lungs? Blame Em, passing her panache onto me via vodka shots. I blink a few times before my eyes land back on Xander, standing by his car. He's got that dumbass smirk plastered across his face.

He holds up his phone, arm outstretched, the screen displayed for me to see. Yeah, like I can read that from nine yards away. I begin dragging my feet toward him, slinging my bag over my shoulder and forgetting that there's a rogue bottle of wine in there (oh yay, wine . . . tonight is already looking up). That's how I end up stumbling the last few steps. That's how I end up officially entering Xander's personal space. The unexpected close contact makes me breathe in sharply and definitely not gasp in his presence.

"Hutchinson?" he says, smirk ever present.

"Miller?" I say, mimicking his tone, although I'm currently not a good judge of whether I pulled it off. The ever-growing smirk on his face tells me I did not.

"You good?" His smile unable to smile anymore, for he is wearing his biggest smile. And so he raises his eyebrows at me.

"Good?" I say, scoffing. "I'm fuckin' gre—" I smoosh my words a little too close together to get away with it. "Great. With a T," I say. Smooth. Nice recovery.

He studies me, so I hold his gaze, which is infinitely easier when your reflexes have slowed significantly over the last few hours.

Then, he tilts his head at his phone, waiting for an explanation. I reach out and grab his phone. He lets me take it, so I bring it right to my face to read whatever is sooooo important to him.

The messages from me.

I scroll to the top of the thread and land on the photo of Xander with Cardi B.

"I still don't understand how you were at a Cardi B gig," I say, more to the photo than to the man standing in front of me. He laughs at this. That full-body, deep and husky one. "You go to gigs?"

"Keep scrolling," he says. I start scrolling, but the tiny words blur on the screen. Why does he want me to read the messages I sent him when I was in the Uber? After I sent him a screenshot of Morgan 2.0, who I would (sigh) not be sleeping with, he texted back and said, "You're so welcome," to which I texted back and said, "Why am I thanking you?" to which he texted back and said, "That guy doesn't know how to satisfy you," to which I barked a laugh in the back of the Uber before texting back, complete with eyeroll emoji, "What? And you volunteer yourself as tribute?" I threw in a laughing emoji and proceeded to put my phone in my bag, extremely satisfied with my response.

Instead of rereading this, I shove Xander's phone back into his hands. He takes it.

"Your point?" I say.

He studies me. Again with the staring. I widen my eyes and lean in, imitating him.

"Holy shit, you're drunk," he says, and if I didn't know any better, I'd say he's delighting in the discovery.

Cat's out the bag. Alcohol's out the bag too.

"If finding out my dad is getting married in a few weeks and then proceeding to drink a bottle of Tito's with Emily while she forces me to do living room karaoke all afternoon," I say, like I'm a mumble rapper, words just blending in together, "then yeah, I'm drunk." This time I over pronounce everything to within an inch of being equally unrecognizable.

His eyes roam my face at this admission. Shit. I hold my breath, hoping that if I don't move, he won't ask about why my dad getting remarried drove me to day drink. While our chemistry might be repeating itself like the dodgy half-eaten burrito you can't help but take a bite of the next morning after a particularly ambitious night at the bar, there's absolutely no need to *connect* with him.

Then he makes the right decision by cocking his eyebrows and saying, "What song?"

"'Can't Fight the Moonlight,'" I say, straight-faced. Daring him to make fun of me. "Want to know a secret?" I lean forward, not realizing how close we've actually been this whole time, because now, I can practically taste his neck. Sweet and salty.

"Sure." He tilts his head ever so slightly to me, and I feel his breath hit the shell of my ear. It sends shockwaves through me.

With Tito's running through my veins, my filter is nonexistent, and I let out a squeal as my body squirms and I jump back, the movement causing my bag to pull me off balance. Again. This time, instead of watching and waiting to see if my body will recenter itself, Xander decides intervention is necessary and puts his hands on my shoulders, steadying me.

"What was that?" he says, still holding me. It has the centering effect my balance is incapable of giving me right now. Rock solid.

"What are you talking about?" I say, playing dumb, which seems to pair perfectly with vodka on the rocks.

"The squeal?" He must decide that I'm capable (just) of holding myself up because he lets go of me.

"A bug. Landed. On me," I say, impressed with my improv.

He bends down so his head fills my vision, curls curling, and says, "And the secret?"

"Wine," I breathe out in a terrible whisper. This time unable to hide my amusement. "I'm getting you drunk."

I start to stomp toward the building, and this time, I am nimble like a dancer because I do not stumble, sway, or struggle to put one foot in front of the other. I'm basically sober at this point. All the more reason to open that bottle of wine. I don't plan on nursing a hangover before falling asleep.

"I'm getting you water," he says, and I turn around in dramatic fashion and find him assessing me. I stomp back a few steps so I'm standing in front of him.

"Whatever," I say, pulling on his T-shirt sleeve to bring him in line with me. He reaches over and hooks his fingers under the strap of my bag, slipping it down my arm and slinging it over his. This catches me by surprise in the sense that no man has ever carried my bag for me. "What. Are you doing?" I say aloud, unable to process my shock internally.

"Carrying your bag," he says, shrugging like he does it all the time. "I fear your *magnum* of wine is trying to take you out."

"Chivalry's not dead," I say, like I know what the latest reports are on chivalry. Because I sure as shit don't know from firsthand experience.

"No, it's in the kitchen where you ghosted it," he says, fucking flawless with his comeback as ever.

"You know there's too smart. And I *fear* you just crossed that line," I say looking over at him, one eyebrow cocked. He tips up one side of his mouth in a half smile. Almost apologetic. Like he's acknowledging he can't help being this clever.

"I'm not just going to get you legless, Miller. I'm going to ply you with so much wine it'll render you speechless," I say, vowing to get Xander so drunk, I have the final say.

"Red or white?" he says, accepting my challenge.

Bring it on.

CHAPTER TWELVE

"Can I tell you a secret?" Xander says, slurring his words.

I look over at him, dubious. He sees my expression and it sets off a chain reaction of delight. It starts at his eyes, which are already hooded thanks to the Malbec, but still manage to crinkle in the corners. Then, the delight spreads to his nose as he scrunches it up. And finally, landing on his lips, which spread wide, splitting his face in two. It's contagious.

Turns out, Xander is a fucking lightweight. And no amount of alcohol could ever shut him up. If anything, it's removed the last of his restraint, which I didn't realize he'd been exercising.

We're both sitting on the bed, our backs against the headboard, passing the *standard*-sized bottle of wine between us. And in a turn of events I didn't see coming, not that my vision has been 20/20 since I subbed my tomato juice for straight vodka this morning, but Xander is drunker than me.

"This better be good," I say, knocking his elbow with mine. "The last five secrets you've told me were lame."

"As if," he says, and there's lightness to him I haven't seen before. It makes me think of what he would have been like as a kid growing up. And from his last couple of secrets, I'm getting snapshots of what it was like. Getting picked up by two loving parents from a particularly rowdy house party. Piling as many teenagers as possible into the back of his parents' car to avoid getting busted by the cops. In-N-Out burgers to soak up the alcohol before dropping everyone off at home.

Xander Miller is fucking wholesome.

He leans in so our entire sides are touching each other, like we've formed an alliance. I ignore how every single cell has rallied to the touch. "Did I tell you about my role in the Enron collapse?"

I whip my head to look at him. Is he for real?

He watches me for a moment before laughing. "Got you. I was still in high school when that happened."

"Oh my god," I say, laughing, and Xander takes this as a cue that I'm forgoing my turn because he takes the bottle out of my hands and sips. I watch as his Adam's apple bobs.

After his sip, he puts the bottle between his thighs and leans his head on the headboard. "Thanks." He lolls his head toward me.

"For what?"

"For getting me drunk," he says, sighing with content. I study him a moment, with his eyes nearly closed, but his mind still wide-awake. Could this be the closest thing Xander's had to a solid sleep in who knows how long?

"Please, I do not need any more encouragement when it comes to that domain," I say, brushing off the genuine gratitude. I know he's not literally thanking me for getting him drunk, but more so what being inebriated brings. A dullness that gives your brain a break. Which might be worth its weight in gold when you're suffering insomnia.

"Which domain do you need encouragement in?" he says, all relaxed. "Oh, I know. Breakfast."

"I eat breakfast just fine," I say, giving him side eye. "And that was a weak-ass attempt to bring the conversation back to me sneaking out," I concede. Looks like we're having the conversation about what happened eleven years ago.

"How'd you do it?" The way he asks, there isn't an accusatory tone to be found. Morbid curiosity, maybe?

I hesitate. I'm starting to learn Xander's way of getting his point across, and it involves asking questions I can't seem to connect the dots with until he delivers the punchline. Usually knocking me on my ass. And yet, I can't ignore the question, so I proceed with caution. "What do you mean, 'How'?"

"In order to get to the front door in that apartment, you had to walk through the kitchen," he says, and my mind immediately flashes to the commando crawl I expertly performed the morning I accidently fell asleep and found myself awake in Xander's bed. "But I was in the kitchen."

"I don't remember," I say, lying. I will not admit to armyapproved techniques I've deployed to get out of hostile situations.

"Why not just say goodbye?"

I'm about to shoot back, "Why does it matter?" when Xander lets out a soft sigh. "You missed out." I hesitate because I'm concerned he's going to get all emotional drunk on me. "I make the best eggs Benedict."

"No you don't. Em does," I say.

"Your best friend, from the café, who was shouting, 'Fuck Xander'?" he asks.

"That's the one," I say, giving him a finger gun and shooting it in his direction like Xander's dad probably does followed by the word *champ*.

"How can you be so sure Emily's eggs are better than mine? You left," he says.

"I'm well aware I left commando-crawl style. I was there," I say, conceding.

A soft laugh comes from his throat. "I knew it," he says, matter of fact. Then he scrubs his face with his hand. "Okay, so you want to know what's so embarrassing about that?" Embarrassing? That's new. My silence invites him to continue.

"My housemate walked past you in the hallway on the way back from the croissant run I asked him to do." He was going to make eggs and include croissants? Okay. Not bad. A bit considerate.

"And?"

"I told him we had a connection," he says, before sipping from the bottle. "I told him that you were *into* me." He coughs out a laugh. "And I went on and on about it until he told me that you were gone. And I still didn't believe him until I walked back into my room." He offers a shrug at the end and it's so earnest I know it's not about his ego, and yet I can't help but say it out loud. Call it a defense mechanism.

"So fragile masculinity," I say, like a smartass.

"Just a fragile human heart," he says, correcting me. And I know he's right. Because in my drunken slushy mind, I know exactly what he's talking about. There was a connection. I just had to sever it before we could both really get hurt. Because I don't do feelings. Feelings are bad. And he made me feel way too much.

"I'm sorry I snuck out."

This apology lends itself to intense staring on both our accounts.

"We've established how you did it. I want to know why," Xander says, still staring. "Did I get the wrong impression that you liked me?" There's so much honesty in his eyes, I decide not to deflect and instead answer the damn question.

I shake my head. "No, you didn't get the wrong impression." Xander's eyes go wide at this confession. "Everything you felt, I felt it too. I just know that relationships don't work—and statistically speaking, we're no different. It was easier to bail before things got complicated. And hard. And messy. And sad."

He nods slowly, accepting it. "Okay."

"Okay."

"How'd you get fired, anyway?" he says, moving us along.

The change in conversation throws me. "You really want to know?" I say, thankful he decided that talking about my termination is better than continuing down the path of apology, which we all know is the gateway conversation to deep and meaningful. And I don't think I'll ever be drunk enough for that.

"I mean, you are talking to a lawyer," he says, raising his eyebrows. "Do you think you have a case for wrongful termination?"

"The idea of taking a case like this to court and not winning, it'd be over for me," I say.

"Case like this?"

"Putting a woman's sexual activity on display like she should be condemned," I say, looking straight ahead, avoiding eye contact. And that's truly why I could never hate my mom. In a world that still slut shames women, my mom doesn't just celebrate it. She writes a *New York Times* bestselling book about it. She produces a show about it. She leads a revolution about it.

I will my eyes to stay straight, because it seems that while we've avoided any deep and meaningful between us, we've stumbled on vulnerability, and it's making my skin itch. I feel my heart pound a little faster at this confession.

"Can you walk me through what happened, start to finish?"

"You're going to judge me," I say, still avoiding eye contact.

"I'm not here to judge you."

"One of my Bone It hook ups," I start, but stop and look over at him. His eyes are steady and soft, so I continue. "Picked me up from the school and was a little handsy at the school gates. So apparently I'm a pervert now."

"I could win it for you," he says, like it's a done deal, and he must read the shock on my face because he says, "Hello, I'm Xander Miller. A lawyer. Nice to meet you."

I shake my head. "Aren't you in corporate law? White-collar crime shit?" He laughs at this.

"Correct, but part of that white-collar crime comes under employment law. Let me look into it for you," he says, and this time I can tell he's asking for approval. It dawns on me that even in this drunken haze, I'm getting pretty good at reading Xander Miller and his intentions.

"You'll have to get me way more drunk to even consider that," I say, reaching for the bottle between his strong thighs that I am not hyper-fixating on. I take a Xander-sized gulp. It turns out that Xander-sized gulp was the last one. "Shit," I say, inspecting the empty bottle. "Do you think we can DoorDash another?"

Xander springs into action and gets his phone out. He smashes the screen a little too hard but declares with a grin: "Done."

CHAPTER THIRTEEN

"Boo!" I jump up from Xander's side of the bed, trying to spike his heart rate. I look over at Xander's monitor, hopeful. But no such luck. It's steady as she goes. Not even a blip.

Xander slowly turns his head to look at me. He shakes it, pitying me.

"You know, I'm actually so embarrassed that I wasn't able to see you commando crawl out of my apartment because I just watched your ass in the air as you made you way around the bed," he says, smirking.

I shove him.

"I didn't say it was a bad view," he says, slow and deliberate.

Is he flirting with me?

If so, pathetic. And yet, my mouth reacts involuntarily, acknowledging this flirty exchange between us. "Thank you, I *don't* work out." I then proceed to crawl back to the safety of my side of the bed.

Bed Chemistry

I have tried and failed three times now to spike Xander's heart rate. With a second bottle of wine discarded, we've found one way to entertain ourselves until I pass out.

It's a victimless crime. Harmless fun. Innocent trouble.

There's no deep and meaningful. No chance we can stumble into vulnerable territory. And absolutely no way we're connecting over these stupid games.

The first attempt was challenging him to a push-up contest. I went for pure physical exertion, but that motherfucker smashed out twenty push-ups while practically yawning. The second was rapid-fire math, hoping I could get his heart racing at arithmetic. He bombed out, but didn't care. In fact, he laughed it off with a steady calmness. The true mark of someone who doesn't just know himself but is comfortable with himself.

My third attempt was a classic. Scare him into a heart rate spike. I just botched the execution. Less Casper, more Ass Clapper the Friendly Ghost.

Once I'm settled, Xander perks up. "My turn."

"Go for it. I've drunk enough to put down a small horse," I say, hiking my thumb over my shoulder to my own heart rate monitor. It's low and slow like a brisket. "There's no way."

"A challenge." Xander rubs his hands together. Then he stops and looks me in the eye. How they shimmer, I have no idea. "And just to be clear about the rules?"

"The rules are, there are no rules," I say, palming him off. "You spike my heart rate, you win."

I watch him as his teeth scrape his bottom lip, deep in thought. "Which you won't," I say, a little too distracted by what I'm witnessing. I find his eyes. There's mischief written all over his face.

"But I have. *Twice* now," he says, his register lowering an octave, and the drop in his voice sends a shiver down my spine. And I realize that he's playing for keeps.

I snap my eyes forward, looking straight ahead. I will not lose. I will not lose. I will not lose.

"Is this within the rules?" Xander says, his breath hitting the shell of my ear. Oh God. How did he close the distance between us so quickly? How was I not prepared that he would use chemistry against me? How is it I'm letting out a "Mmmm" in response that's a mixture between a yes and a moan?

Jesus fuck. Rein it in.

"I'm going to need verbal confirmation." His warm breath hits my ear again, sobering up every single nerve ending, making them come alive. I feel his words all over my body. I squeeze my thighs together.

Shut it down.

"Yes. It's within the rules, because it means *nothing*," I say, my voice grating on the words. I'm trying so hard to convince myself I feel nothing. The hardest. And just when I think I've got control, he pulls me into his lap.

And time slows.

My hands fall to his strong shoulders. My knees press into the mattress on either side of his hips. My eyes finally lock on his.

I listen for the heart rate monitor.

Nothing.

That's probably because every single cell is diverted to the seam of my boxer shorts that are digging into me right *there*. The pressure, perfect.

"Nice try," I breathe out but before I can claim any sort of victory in this game, his warm hands make their way to my waist, and he shifts me.

Bed Chemistry

Slowly, deliberately, achingly, he grinds me into him. And I have no choice but to go with it because I feel everything.

I let out a slow, soft sigh as I settle into him.

I find my fingers running through the curls at the nape of his neck. So soft it feels like water. I grab a fistful of hair and tilt his chin up.

Our lips are so close. The anticipation sets every nerve cell alight with pleasure.

He pulls back, wearing a shit-eating grin. Absolutely just beaming. "I win." His voice comes out husky.

I pull back, brows furrowed. *Huh?*

And that's when I hear it. The heart rate monitor going off.

Fuck.

Before I can form a comeback, he plants a strong, solid kiss on my lips, rendering me speechless. And all I do is go along for the ride as Xander returns me to my side of the bed in one smooth motion.

I sit, arms crossed over my chest, and stare at the wall ahead.

That's when I notice—there are *two* sets of alarms going off.

I want to laugh. I want to smirk. I want to poke fun at him for losing.

But before I can, there's a knock and the door opens.

My eyes snap to Ben, who's got his arms crossed over his chest, not impressed. "Guys."

CHAPTER FOURTEEN

Fingertips trace lazy circles around my stomach, slowly coaxing me out of my sleep. The solid wall of warmth behind me pulls me right back under.

I need to wake up. I need to leave.

As if reading my mind, and deciding against it, my Bone It buddy pulls me in closer. There's a soft sigh from behind me, that's apparently music to my ears, because it lulls me right back to sleep.

I'll get up soon, I bargain with myself. Ten more minutes.

Newsflash: it was not ten more minutes.

I fling my eyes open, only for my head to start throbbing immediately. It takes me all of a nanosecond to remember I'm at the sleep study clinic. It's morning. And the messy mop of brown curls that are so close I can feel a few strays on my cheek belong to Xander.

I'm big spooning Xander.

The entire back of his body is making direct contact with my entire front. My arm is also draped over his solid torso, fingers resting on his chest.

I lift my fingers off his chest and freeze so I can assess the situation, all while willing my sensory receptors not to register what his back feels like pressed against my chest. Too late. My heart starts thundering. I can't remember what happened last.

Did we sleep together? With wires on? And a camera crew?

Did I make the sequel to *Sleep Wanker*, turning it into an actual porn that Emily would love to name?

Besides the blood pumping through my veins at an alarming rate, I am completely still. And I stay that way, not willing to risk waking him. I feel the clothes I'm wearing create a flimsy barrier between us, so at least I'm not naked. Silver linings. I catch a glimpse of the white T-shirt on my shoulder. I'm wearing Xander's clothes. Fuck. Surely, I would know if we had sex. Like, *down there*, I would know. Yet, all evidence points to not having a fucking idea in this moment. Fuck.

And as if by some cruel joke, Xander shifts and his firm ass presses against my lady bits. Ignore it.

I need to create as much distance as possible. Maybe I can roll over subtly, go back to "sleep," and we both naturally wake up on our own sides of the bed. It'll be my little secret. Yes. Great plan.

I hold my breath and as slowly as possible, I slide my arm back to my side of the bed. This action elicits a soft groan from Xander. Oh, shit. Before I can get my arm off him, he reaches for it and pulls me closer, tucking my arm under his arm and anchoring me in place. There's a series of soft sleep sounds and I wonder if he's falling back asleep, but then his entire body stiffens.

He's awake.

A moment of utter stillness.

I can practically hear his mind processing.

And then he almost throws my arm at me as he scrambles to get up first.

I follow suit, kicking off the sheet and jumping out of bed.

We stand facing each other in some sort of spoon standoff.

And that's when I see it.

His erection.

He must notice my eyes bug at his crotch because he does something with his boxers in a failed attempt to hide it.

I snap my eyes back to his face. "Did we sleep together?" My voice is raised and I'm on the edge of losing it. I cannot have slept with Xander for the second time. That's against the rules. Rules that are in place for a reason.

"What? No," Xander says, and the seriousness of his tone combined with him reaching for his pillow to hold it in front of him is almost comical.

I keep my eyes on his face, waiting for the punchline. *Psych! We did! Hahaha!* I raise my eyebrows and cock my head at his pillow without averting my eyes from his face. My eye contact will burn a hole in his face before I dare to look down there again. "Your penis seems to suggest otherwise." My voice is loud and shaky.

"That, is mechanical," he says, one hand rubbing the back of his neck as the other holds the pillow in place. "We didn't sleep together. We fell asleep together." He looks up at me from under his curls that are so relaxed on his forehead they're probably still sleeping.

My immediate reaction is to excitedly shout at him, "OMG, you *slept*!" But the logical part of my brain, which is currently wincing at the units of alcohol it's been forced to deal with, wants to get to the bottom of what happened last night.

The truth is, I know there's nothing to fess up. I know Xander would never sleep with me drunk. And I hate that I know him this well after seven fucking nights together.

I focus my mind on last night, trying to pull on any thread that'll give me something, anything to hint at what happened. An unwelcome thought filters through my mind. Okay, we didn't sleep together, but did I try and kiss him?

An image flutters behind my eyes. Me sitting in Xander's lap. Lips so close . . .

The wince on my face must translate into me further questioning his integrity because Xander raises his eyebrows at this. "I'm not one of the assholes from your dating app."

I scrub my hands down my face and groan at Xander bringing that up.

"Again with that?" I say, almost pleading. I am too hungover to take another trip down memory lane. I mean, I can't even remember last night.

Another hazy memory surfaces: *We're laughing. At what? No idea. We're laughing so hard that Xander falls off the bed. A second later he raises his hand, red wine bottle unspilled. I am appalled at the cuteness level of this memory.*

"Let's not forget you were the one spooning me," he says, snapping me back to the situation at hand. I notice the pillow is no longer required. And he's put on his jeans. Meanwhile, I'm standing in *his* sleepwear. I'm losing this battle.

"You were spooning me first," I say, throwing it back at him, trying to recover some ground.

"What? When?" Xander frowns, no recollection of this.

Another memory of last night makes itself known. Xander, crawling back onto the bed. Me, patting my lap. Him, lying there. Me, stroking his hair. Gross. I am utterly horrified at this. I feel my stomach roil.

"I don't know, in the middle of the night?" I say, refocusing on Xander and trying my hardest not to projectile vomit at that memory.

"And what'd you do about it?" he says, giving me the full cross-examination. He removes his sleep T-shirt without warning, revealing the hard lines of his stomach and sculpted chest before replacing it with a clean black replica. Turns out there are no tattoos on his torso.

"What?" I say, shaking my head at him in frustration.

"When you realized I was spooning you? What did you do?" he says, articulate as ever, functioning at level 100. *I fell back asleep.* Still, I don't say it. I can see a "gotcha" smirk creeping across his face at my silent admission that I did nothing.

"That's not fair. I was lulled back to sleep," I say, already realizing I've lost.

"You liked it?" he says, embarrassed for the both of us. He shakes his head. "Oh, Ash."

"I did not," I say, flailing now.

"I think you like me," he says, cocky.

"Like you? I don't even *know* you," I say at the exact time I'm interrupted by a female voice.

"Good morning."

It's the record scratch that sends both Xander and me snapping our heads to the door because that voice sounds a lot like . . .

Dr. Waitley.

Bed Chemistry

"Can I have a word with you two in my office, once you're dressed?" she says. That was a dig at me, since Xander managed to get fully clothed in the span of our fight.

The question is rhetorical. Of course we're going to her office once we're dressed. Which is why she doesn't wait for a reply and disappears.

I stare at the door.

We're fucked.

CHAPTER FIFTEEN

We're back sitting in Dr. Waitley's office, opposite her. I can't believe we only made it a week before we got caught. Still, that hasn't stopped us from launching a full-blown PR campaign. We! Are! Together!

We haven't stopped touching each other, both of us with a mutual understanding that we need to fix this poor performance from daytime Emmy to Oscar worthy.

Xander put his hand on my back as he guided me through the bedroom. I reached out and we held hands as we marched to the gallows. Xander pulled his chair close to mine when we arrived at her office so we could continue to present the picture of a perfect couple.

Will the simple act of Xander's hands on me create a tectonic event that's going to set alarm bells off at the Cal Tech Seismological Laboratory?

Hands that have gripped my waist. Dug into my pelvis. Rocked my hips.

Ignore it.

I look over at Xander, who unleashes his now infamous sickly sweet smile he used the last time we were in this room that won us a coveted spot in this sleep study, before he reaches over to brush a strand of hair from my cheek. The act shouldn't have any effect on me. Because I am part of this performance. I see how the sausage is made. I've seen him switch it on and more importantly, switch it off. And yet, I can't stop myself from swooning.

Stop that right now, Ash.

You're in the equivalent of detention.

Xander's ability to go from freaking the fuck out back in our sleep study room to doting, caring boyfriend is remarkable. I guess that's why they pay him the big bucks. Although, I'd like to thank myself for the rousing half-time speech worthy of winning the Superbowl.

We can do this.

We've convinced Dr. Waitley before.

We can do it again.

We've just got to keep it as close to the truth as possible.

Now, my bravado starts to waver under Dr. Waitley's piercing eyes as she studies us, her gaze methodically moving from one of us to the other. Like one of us is going to snitch. My fingers curl tighter around Xander's, and he reciprocates. We're in this together.

"Our sleep study is affiliated with UC Berkeley," she says, her voice sharp like she's lecturing a hall full of unruly students. "We are able to pay our participants because this sleep study enhances the educational programs."

The guilt starts curdling my stomach juices. I feel physically ill.

"What is going on with you two?" Dr. Waitley comes on heavy, turning this detention into an interrogation.

"Can you explain what you mean?" Xander replies, his timing perfect. He didn't jump to answer. He didn't wait too long to question it. In this moment, I realize that Xander is a professional and he will get us through this.

"Setting off the heart rate monitors. Fighting like cats and dogs. Your actions are compromising the integrity of this sleep study." She stares me down, like I'm the weak one. It's hard to believe this is the same Dr. Waitley who was rattled by my confession about our active sex life. She is scary. A fierce protector of knowledge.

"We're sorry," I blurt out.

"This study will be submitted into the *Journal of Sleep Research*, with our students' names on the article," she says, stern.

Ben's name will be on a sleep study with fake results that will stay with him forever, if we're ever found out. Shit. Fuck. Shit. I didn't think any of this through. Of course I didn't. Because I am an awful, terrible person.

I look over at Xander, wondering if he's thinking the same thing. And he looks so tired. The reason why he's here in the first place. He qualifies. He deserves to be here. He needs to stay in this sleep study.

"I'm not going to lie, it's been hard. With the insomnia," Xander says, coming to bat for us.

She stares at us a little longer. And then her face softens.

"I'm sorry," she says, shaking her head. "I know what it's like." It's the perfect segue to Dr. Waitley's origin story which, not going to lie, I would be interested in hearing. But wrong time.

Her eyes move between the two of us. Less interrogation. More sympathy.

Shit, this is actually working.

"Have you felt Xander pull away?" Dr. Waitley says, looking to me now.

No. He's never pulled away from me in my life. Not during the friendship we had together. Not during our one night together. Not when he noticed me in the waiting room in the sleep study. Not when he got into my car to thank me for doing this for him.

If anything, he aways leans in. The only truth I have access to are my own actions.

"It feels like we're not on the same page anymore," I say, opting for vague.

"It was like, we were so good. And then she, I mean, I, just shut down," Xander says, and I can't help but feel he's referring to my actions eleven years ago when I snuck out, effectively ending things.

"We just disconnected," I say, nodding. "And we stayed disconnected."

"Mmmmm," Dr. Waitley says, an obligatory pause that has me wondering if she double majored in psychology. "When was the last time you did something fun together?"

We look at each other. But we don't answer, worried we'll say the wrong thing at the same time. She reads this silence as the answer: a long time ago.

"I want you to go on a date this weekend," she says, and a nervous laugh escapes me before I can control myself. I glance at Xander, and he's looking at me like he knows exactly what I'm thinking right now.

Objection: I don't date.

"I need you to reconnect," she says, breaking our silent conversation. We both snap our heads back to her "And you're not going to reconnect at a sleep study filled with wires. Or in your day-to-day routine."

Fuck. This isn't a suggestion. This is a prerequisite of the sleep study.

I need to date Xander. I need to make an exception to my rule for the sake of the sleep study. For the sake of Xander's insomnia and my paycheck.

I puff my cheeks and blow out a steady stream of air.

"Okay," I say, agreeing with the minimal amount of enthusiasm possible that I will go on a date with Xander. "Let's go on a date."

*　*　*

"We're not going on a date," I say, Xander finally letting go of me.

He led me all the way down the hallway, past reception, through the doors, and dropped me off at the passenger side of his car. Because of course my car isn't here. I got rip-roaring drunk yesterday, and I've got the shitty Uber star rating to prove it.

"Oh, we're definitely not dating," Xander says, practically laughing. His hand has returned to the back of his neck, again like he's trying to rub me out of his life.

"Rude." I cross my arms over my chest.

"You said it first," Xander says, now actually laughing at me. "You can't seriously be offended?"

I can. And I will. Of course, I don't say that out loud.

Instead, I say, "We need a truce."

"Can you be civil?" Xander says, without thinking. I shoot him a look. He holds his hands up, like they're two giant man hand-sized white flags. A truce. "We can be civil."

Then, he leans toward me. For a moment I think he's going to kiss me and I hate that anticipation zips through my body, practically begging for Xander to be anything but civil toward me.

Thankfully, he reaches for the passenger door but it's too late, I'm already flustered. And if you think the hint of his slept-in-so-fresh-and-so-clean-scent that's been marinating in his skin for the last twelve hours would lose its effect, well, you'd be wrong. It acts like a narcotic, a shot straight to my nervous system. I am intoxicated. In broad fucking daylight.

He opens the passenger door to his slick black BMW-something-series, then turns to face me. Waiting. I hesitate.

"I can Uber home," I say, offering him an out. Instead of taking it, he rolls his eyes. "It's fine," I insist. Not that I want to get hung up on what constitutes as civil, but where does the humble eye roll fall?

"Get in the car, Hutchinson," he says, tilting his head toward the open door. The act makes his curls flop, and if Xander and the curls want me to get in the car, then I will get in the car. "Our truce starts now."

I get in.

Xander shuts the door and I'm free to sigh in peace, without scrutiny under our new civil act. I rest my head on the leather headrest and close my eyes, trying to process what the fuck just happened.

One moment, we're getting freaky. The next, we're snuggling. Then we're being ordered to date. And now I'm his passenger princess. The destination? Somewhere civil, I guess.

I hear a click and turn around to see Xander putting his bag, and mine, in the trunk, and I try to ignore that this basic act of courtesy feels warm and fuzzy.

Once Xander gets in the car, I make a concerted effort to thank him. He puts on a pair of Wayfarers that make him look like a heartbreaker before looking over at me and throwing me an equally concerted, "You're welcome."

"Ten points for basic manners, *Captain America*," I say, the memory of his thick thighs wearing the hell out of those boxer shorts a few nights ago.

"Ten points for recognizing them," he volleys right back.

"Thank you," I say, acting like it was a compliment of the highest order and not some half-baked diplomacy wrapped around something pointed. Well, joke's on Xander because I barely recognized it.

Of course, I don't say any of this out loud. We're mere minutes into this truce, and I will not take the bait. But I do watch as Xander's lips curl at the ends. Like he's getting off on working me up. So I decide the safest place to look for the sake of our truce is out my window. The sun is full throttle in the sky.

"Another day, another heatwave," I say, evoking the social code of surface-level conversation. The weather.

"There's supposed to be a cool change tonight," Xander says, equally mundane. "Thunderstorms and all."

"In Los Angeles?" I question as my retinas slowly begin to melt without my sunglasses. "Doubtful."

"That's what the weather app says."

"Like they ever get it right," I say, before remembering that there's a treaty that's relying on me filtering myself.

I look at Xander, who's concentrating on navigating a lane change. The blinker like a countdown, reminding me that this conversation, like every other one, it seems, is a ticking time bomb. Once we're safely in Xander's lane of choice, he looks at me for a moment before returning his eyes to the road.

"That's an interesting perspective, and I can see how it could be interpreted that way," Xander says, his tone measured. Every consonant precise. I feel like I'm getting the full lawyer treatment right now. And I look at the clock on the dash. Yep, that was a whole minute into our truce before Xander managed to get under my skin.

"If by 'interesting' you mean because we practically live in a desert," I say, unable to stop myself from testing how far Xander will go with this lawyer word salad.

"That's an important point," Xander says, noncommittal. And the filtered version of Xander somehow pushes my buttons more than the fighting. Or the fucking around. "It definitely adds depth to the conversation."

And just when I think he's done, he says, "Let's revisit this conversation this evening and see how it all ties in."

Well, it's official. Xander's gone full lawyer bot on me.

I sigh. That's fine. That's just fine.

In fact, it's more than fine. This is exactly what we need to get through the rest of this car ride, and sleep study, without any more drama.

I close my eyes and lean my head on the headrest. Disengaged.

Xander takes the hint and doesn't talk. The robot lawyer is learning.

The inviting smell of coffee has me flinging my eyes open like my life depends on it. Because it does. I must have fallen asleep. And this hangover headache is throbbing.

I look at Xander, who's holding out a takeaway cup of coffee. And it's warm. Not iced.

"Cappuccino," Xander says, handing it to me. How'd he know? I finally look up to see we're in front of Roasting Warehouse. The café that's half a mile from my house.

You can't fault lawyer logic.

CHAPTER SIXTEEN

Thunder booms, rattling the windows as lighting streaks attempt to stand out in broad daylight. This storm wants to be dramatic, but even dark clouds can't create an ominous atmosphere in sunny Los Angeles.

I roll my eyes knowing Xander is home, getting off on being right. And then I scold myself for thinking about Xander. Who cares about whether or not he's getting off.

Not me.

I am not now thinking about his own hand wrapped around his—

Another thought-shattering boom. *Thank you, thunder.*

I haven't moved from the couch since I arrived home with a double-shot cappuccino in hand. Actually, I lie. I got up for the DoorDash delivery. Because I didn't think it was appropriate to give a complete stranger explicit directions on how to access my apartment without a key. Even though the hangover warrants it.

I glance at the clock. It's five thirty. Fuck. How did that happen?

I look down at Mom's book on the coffee table. Did I really sit here and read through the book again, looking for an explanation as to why I can't get Xander and his hands, Xander and his curls, Xander and his fucking mouth out of my mind?

When I got to the part in chapter three about the Madonna Whore Complex & Why Your Brain Categorizes People Into "Love" or "Lust," I felt better. Because the horny little whore in me recognizes the horny little whore in Xander.

It's pure lust, baby. And that, I can live with for now.

I sigh.

I should already be on Ventura Boulevard. I'm going to be late. I wince as I haul ass into my room to pack my sleepover bag. Which will absolutely not include wine. My head throbs even though I feel like I'm walking in slow motion. The hangover still hasn't passed.

I mentally make a list of what I need for tonight, like this is my first rodeo, and not at all like a seasoned veteran who's been doing the same thing every single night for the past week.

Pajamas. Toothbrush. I sniff my armpit. And clean clothes.

I catch a glimpse of my open wardrobe from the door and notice it's bare. Where the fuck are all my clothes? The answer is underneath me as I trip over the laundry pile—once a dormant volcano now exploding dirty clothes everywhere.

Turns out spending every evening at the sleep study has set me back on domestic duties.

Shit. What am I going to wear to bed tonight? I refuse to wear Xander's sleepwear for another night in a row. Not after I practically rode him in them. Not after that heart rate monitor advertised exactly how he gets me going. And especially not after waking up with my limbs snaked around him, snuggling. Now *that* was embarrassing.

And yet, it's slim pickings. I stare at my empty wardrobe hoping something will materialize when a pastel pink set of folded sweats catches my eye. I haven't seen those in forever.

I stretch on my tippy toes to pull them down.

Printed on them is: *To mate, date, or masturbate. That is the question.*

I completely forgot about the free merch Mom sent me after she recorded her exclusive interview with Oprah. I suppress a gag at the cringe creeping up, threatening to reject the bacon eggroll I DoorDashed earlier.

Oh, Mom, who signed off on this merch slogan? And then I recall an earlier conversation where my mom demanded full creative control for the Netflix series and there is no doubt in my mind that she didn't just sign off on this. She created it.

And while I fully support her, I refuse to wear that shit in public. I'm about to fold it right back up and find a bikini that could double as a tank top when right on cue, thunder booms followed by the pelting of rain on the window, reminding me that Los Angeles just dropped thirty degrees in the span of three minutes and a bikini top won't cut it.

Looks like I'm changing into Barbie-pink sweats that advertise wanking as a valid alternative to dating and mating.

As I slide into the sweats, I'm thankful for the truce. Surely, Xander will bite his tongue, no matter how hard he wants to tease me for it. I think back to the lawyer bot from the car ride home and surmise that he'll bite it until he bleeds, if that's what it takes. I throw my hair up into a high ponytail and make my way back into the living room, searching for my phone.

It pings, reminding me it's on the charger.

Thinking it's Em, I swipe it unlocked, and that's when I see it. A message from Xander.

I'd like to revisit the weather we discussed earlier.

That motherfucker.

My eyes slide to the clock.

5:37 PM.

Time of death on our truce.

And just when I'm about to throw my phone into my bag, a photo loads.

It's Xander. Wet.

White T-shirt see-through. Black running shorts gripping his sculpted thighs. Curls stuck to his forehead.

Fuck. Off.

I pull my hoodie up over my head and close my apartment door behind me.

* * *

Angelenos don't know shit about driving in wet weather.

I'm not just late. I am *fucking* late. And honestly, I'm lucky to be alive.

I race to the sleep study, skidding to a halt outside our room before flinging the door open and announcing, "I'm so sorry I'm late."

I pull my hoodie down and see Ben standing with Xander.

Xander's wearing dry clothes, but his thick curls are still damp and clinging to his forehead. I ignore how badly I want to witness him run his hands through his hair and tousle them.

Ben offers me a kind smile. "It's totally fine. Everyone is late today." I project a smile toward Ben that tells him thank you before my eyes slide to Xander, who's mouth is set in a straight line. "I'll be back to wire you up later." And then, Ben is gone.

I stare at the closed door. Every second I don't turn around, the tension ratchets.

I don't know why but with the gag order in place, the energy is charged.

"You're late," Xander says. A statement. Not a question. And I don't know if he's upset. Or if he's making friendly conversation in Switzerland. Neutral territory.

"Yep," I say, even-toned. I still haven't turned around.

"Why were you late?" Xander says, and this time there's no doubt there's a touch of accusation around the edges of his voice.

"Because I left on time," I say, a white lie for the sake of civility. That's when I turn around to see a furrowed brow. Xander's concerned. If he's going to blame me for ruining this sleep study because it's wet outside, I'm going to—

"There was a three car pileup on Ventura," he says, giving me a totally different response. He was worried. About me. My heart unclenches for a whole entire second. For all he knew, his sleep study buddy was crushed under a pile of metal. In this moment, I know my tardiness warrants an apology, but right before the words come out of my mouth, he cuts me off. "I told you it was going to thunderstorm this evening."

"You did," I say, slow, trying to regroup after this U-turn right out of our truce and into hostile territory, where the temperature is hot. The satisfaction that Xander caved first has me biting my lip to suppress a smile. The truth is, unfiltered Xander does things to me.

"And you ignored me why?" he says, pressing me for more. "Because meteorology is a scam?" His sarcasm zips through my body, and I feel like I'm coming alive after lounging around at death's door all afternoon.

I opt to remain quiet and watch as his jaw clenches. The last restraint leaving his body. And suddenly, I want nothing to do with this bullshit truce.

I want unfiltered Xander.

And almost like he can read my thoughts, his eyes slide over my sweats. "What are you wearing?" The judgment is coming through thick.

"Merch," I shoot right back.

"You paid for that?" Xander scoffs.

"Fuck no."

Xander's eyes skirt over the slogan.

Date, mate, or masturbate. That is the question.

It's printed directly over my chest. I don't want him to look away.

"Well, what is it, Ash?"

"What is what?"

"Date, mate, or masturbate," he says. Fuck, why is it such a turn-on when he says it out loud? Is that what my mom intended?

An involuntary smile creeps across my face, which Xander takes as an invitation to hook his finger along the waistband of my sweatpants and pull me closer. I stumble the distance between us, landing right in front of him.

"Definitely not date," I breathe out loud. Our lips are so close.

"And we're definitely not mating," Xander says, his hands steadying my hips. "Which leaves us with . . ." He doesn't finish the sentence. His fingertips dip below my sweatpants, playing with the lacy edge of my underwear.

Fuck.

I grab onto his forearm and pull him closer to me. Encouraging him.

Suddenly, the cure to my hangover is obvious.

"Chemistry."

He pulls his body back and I'm about to protest when he says, "That's not an option, Ash." I'm not sure if he's referring to the sweatshirt I'm wearing, or the conversation we had earlier about our chemistry being irreversible. What I do know is that when I look into his eyes, there's smug amusement. He's fucking with me.

And I am thoroughly enjoying it.

"Is our chemistry a scam too?" Xander says, low.

I swallow. I don't speak. I don't know.

Without another word, his hand falls away from my panties and I have to do everything in my willpower not to pout at him. His hand travels up my waist, skimming over my ribcage, up to my shoulder, and down the length of my arm until he's holding my hand.

Then, he drags it under my sweatpants with him.

Mate. Date. Or masturbate.

And the third option is . . . oh.

Oh.

This is so fucking hot.

Together, our fingers glide over my underwear. The lace creates friction that I feel everywhere, but it's not enough. I am so wound up that I slip my fingers under the lace, giving myself access to my wet, hot bare skin.

"How do you feel?" When I look at him, his usual sunburst hazel eyes now resemble aged whiskey. He's drunk. On me.

"So good," I say, voice raspy with want. Something flickers in his eyes and then he's kissing me, drugging and addictive, like he can't get enough.

It's never enough.

I bail on myself in favor of fumbling with Xander's belt when there's a knock on the door.

I freeze.

Xander breaks contact but instead of pulling away from me immediately, he rests his forehead on mine, lingering for a split second. I can see that I've managed to get the top button of his jeans undone and I'm *thisclose* to ripping his belt through the loops and discarding it on the floor.

"Give us a minute," Xander calls out to Ben. I take a step back, adjusting my sweats while Xander fixes his jeans.

When Ben finally enters, it only takes him one look between the two of us before he shakes his head and turns to leave again. "I'll be back in ten minutes, *please* be ready." A pang of guilt sets in, and I look over at Xander.

He runs his hand through his curls. Stressed. Then, he opens his mouth and says, "Date me."

"Date you?" I say, my mouth echoing my thoughts. *Objection: I don't date.*

"Come on. I don't think we'll last in this study past tomorrow at this rate. Date me for the sake of staying in it?"

I puff my cheeks and blow out a steady stream of air.

Xander's eyes slide to my mouth, unintentionally suggestive, before his eyes shoot back to mine. This time, his eyes do all the talking. Or pleading.

Fuck, he's right. Because if there's one thing I know to be true, it's chapter four. *The dating scene: where love and lust go to die.*

"For the sake of the sleep study." I nod, reluctantly agreeing.

"For the sake of the sleep study," Xander agrees.

As I head over to my side of the bed, my arm brushes past Xander's chest. How the arm nerve is connected to the thigh nerve I'll never understand, but they're talking to each other. I tell them to calm down.

Because I may have agreed to this, but there's one thing we need to get clear right now—dating is not mating.

CHAPTER SEVENTEEN

I didn't realize that entering this establishment with Xander would turn my desperate attempt at getting as much caffeine into my body as humanly possible into date material, but let the record show, Xander and I are officially on a date. Dr. Waitley, are you seeing this?

After Ben finally wired us up after our shenanigans, Xander clocked the stressed-out expression on my face. He asked, "What's up?" to which I said, "So . . . dating?" to which he said, "Ash, you do know *how* to date, right?" to which I lied and said, "I do," to which Xander called out my bluff and said, "Dating isn't fucking."

That's when I challenged him and said, "Oh yeah, what do you know about dating?" And that's when I got the full rundown about what dating actually entails.

Apparently, to quote Xander, dating is about "spending time together."

Groan.

"Getting to know each other."

Sigh.

"Having fun together."

Ew.

And "learning about each other's goals and dreams."

Thank you, Patron Saint of Dates. It sounds fucking horrible.

And yet, I'm on a date. And not just any date. One where I didn't have to spend hours sweating under the intense lights of my bathroom only to fuck up my winged eyeliner using the kohl jet black waterproof one before sobbing in a heap on the floor, my confidence shattered thanks to a pencil.

I did go to the bathroom to splash my face with ice-cold water and stuff my long, unbrushed hair into a messy ponytail that looks more intentional and less slept in. I also texted Em to raincheck our hang, citing overtime at work, which she took as innuendo.

"She'll never believe I'm on a date," I say, shaking my head as I hold my phone out to show Xander the wall of one-sided text messages from Em. I look up at him, but he's not looking at the phone. He's staring at me.

"What?"

"You never date? Like, actually?" he says, not asking. Affirming. Like he's rearranging how he sees me. He runs his hands through his curls and laughs. "I just thought it was a line."

"It's a *lifestyle*," I say, quoting his choice of word back to me when he was condescending about my preferred dating app. I instantly regret it. Since we've arrived at the coffee shop, we haven't bickered, fought, or been absolute dicks to each other. And it's been, I don't want to say nice, but bearable.

We hold eye contact for a moment, and I hope he doesn't say anything. I don't know how long this date is going to last, but I don't have the energy for fighting fire with fire.

"What's your longest relationship?" I say, right as he opens his mouth to speak. He raises his eyebrows at this. "We're *getting to know each other*." I use air quotes to really add to the sarcasm of it all. But alas, it's time to fulfill the duties of this date.

"She listens," he says, shaking his head, a half smile on his face, completely bemused by my actions. I don't know how he does it, turning a half-assed smile into something so sexy, but he does.

"I am a *very* responsive to instructions," I say, and I don't know why it comes out suggestive, but there's no denying it. I have introduced innuendo to this conversation. I bite down on my lip to shut myself up.

Xander scrunches his face but can't stop smiling at what he's seeing.

"Your talents are unparalleled." He leans into the sexual overtone I've unleashed, and there's an immediate shift in the energy around us. I feel my cheeks heat up.

Then, Xander holds up his coffee cup. "Cheers."

We clink cups carefully but our fingertips brush and before I take my sip, a flash of a memory flutters behind my eyes. *Xander's fingers pressing into my hips.* I watch as Xander lifts the cup to his mouth. *His lips are roaming up my sternum.* I track the moment Xander swallows, watching his Adam's apple. *I'm kissing the column of his neck as he swallows a groan.*

I finally make my way back to the present moment and look Xander in his eyes.

"Five years," he says, and I almost blurt out, *What are you talking about?* until I remember the question I asked. Xander's longest relationship was five years. That's basically forever.

"Half a decade?" I say, shocked at this discovery. That's not just a long time. That's the longest time. The caffeine I've been mainlining since we got here starts to slosh in my stomach. There was someone else. Who Xander promised himself to. For five long years. For some reason, this new information doesn't sit right with me.

"What happened? Why'd you break up?" I don't care how nosy I sound. Suddenly, I really need to know. And if she left him with a broken heart.

"She was supposed to help me . . ." He pauses, thinking of his next line carefully. "Get over someone else and we got too comfortable." This is the first time he looks past me. It's not his usual MO. Usually he holds eye contact long enough to make me squirm.

"A five-year rebound?" I say, eyebrows raised. His eyes slide back to mine.

"I'm a sucker," he says, back to his somewhat intimidating eye contact.

"Are you over her?" I'm pressing now. I don't know why it's so important, but suddenly it is.

"God, yes," he says, coughing out a laugh before looking over at me. "What about you?"

"You know I have no relationship war stories," I say, shrugging in relief that my past doesn't come under scrutiny.

"What about your relationship with your dad?" he says, and the mention of my father catches me by surprise.

"What about it?" I say, defenses going up. I don't think familial relationships count as "getting to know each other" on the first date.

"You seemed pretty upset when you found out he's getting remarried," he says, persisting.

"Upset? Come on, that was your standard day-drinking karaoke session," I say, trying for neutral and coming off like a dick. It dawns on me that this could go one of two ways. We end up fighting. Again. And consequently, end up annoyed, frustrated, and filled with pent-up energy at the sleep study tonight. Or I meet him halfway. Let him get to know me. Even if it means talking about my relationship with my father.

I really want to keep it classy tonight. So I'm going to talk about my dad.

"I just feel sorry for the new wife. The man has proven time and time again he can't keep it in his pants."

"He'll cheat again?" Xander says, even-handed. "That's your conclusion?"

"Absolutely," I say, this time with the kind of cocky confidence that you'd expect from Xander in his closing arguments to the jury.

"What if he doesn't, though?" Xander presses. "What if he's *in love* with her? Like, truly, madly, deeply head-over-heels *in love* with her?"

I take Xander in for a moment. His slept-in stubble. The tattoos that snake around his arms and seem to pop against his white T-shirt. His curls. He's wearing an intense look on his face.

"What are you talking about?"

"You need a crash course in love, too?" he asks, but the blank expression on my face is all he needs to go on. "Being *in* love with someone means you feel a strong, almost inexplicable desire for that person. It's a yearning," Xander says, eyes darting all over my face. "You think about them constantly. You crave spending time together whenever you're apart. It's such an intense feeling of joy that you can also feel a bit unsure because it feels so strong."

I study him for a moment. And his big hazel eyes. Then I burst out laughing. "What the fuck was that, Romeo? Holy shit. Do you want to write the vows for this wedding?"

His face lights up before he snaps his fingers. "Actually, that's a good idea."

"What? I was joking." I shake my head.

"Not that. But me, coming to your dad's wedding, as your *date*," he says, finally explaining his brain wave.

"No fucking way," I say, choking on how ridiculous this sounds.

"Did you really think we'd be able to get through the sleep study on one date alone?" he says. This stops me in my tracks because obviously the answer is yes.

But every touch, tease, and taste we've had in said sleep study rushes to the surface.

Ugh. Xander's right.

I repeat my new mantra: *Dating is where lust and love to go die*. And that's when I find myself whispering, "Okay."

"Okay," Xander says, slowly, like he's realizing that we have both agreed to date each other.

"For the sake of the sleep study," I say, more to remind myself than to remind him.

"For the sake of the sleep study," Xander repeats, raising his coffee up for a toast.

I clink his coffee cup with mine.

And he can barely hold back his smile. "This will be fun," he says, a full-blown smile blooming across his face.

CHAPTER EIGHTEEN

"I didn't say it was nice. I said it was bearable," I correct Em, who's been teasing me since I got home from the impromptu date with Xander.

"Bearable," Em says, from her basically horizontal position on my couch. Then she smiles as she continues, "Allowable. Acceptable. Sustainable."

"You and your thesaurus need to relax. This is not voluntary. It's contractual," I say in between scenes of *Cocktail*. The movie just happened to be on, and neither of us have bothered to make the effort to find something else.

"The biggest injustice of this film isn't that Tom Cruise can't pour a cocktail to save his life, or the misogynist speech he gives at the end. It's the fact that 'Kokomo' plays for only three seconds in the entire movie," I say, waving my hand at the TV. *Aruba, Jamaica, ooh, I wanna take ya . . .*

"No," Em says, shaking her head.

"What?"

"You're not changing the topic, even if your commentary is warranted. You just went on the first date you've ever been on in your entire life. You are giving me details," Em says, while Tom gives Elisabeth (with an s—yes, I had to IMDB her) a tropical contact high.

I peel my eyes off the screen and steal a glance at Em. She's trying to keep a casual face, but there's a hint of a smile. Em—the ever romantic—is happy I went on a date. I guess that tracks after I promised her all the juicy details if she stopped texting me.

"Xander drinks lattes," I say, starting with something easy, but Em cuts in.

"Boring."

She's right. "You can tell a lot by a person's coffee order," I say, grasping at straws.

"Is that what Buzzfeed told you?" she says, smartass coming through thick. "Give me something real."

"He was in a relationship for five years," I say, offering the piece of information that's been stuck in my head since he dropped me off. Xander doesn't just date. He settles down. For the long haul.

"Xander's a relationship guy," she says, echoing my thoughts. "How long ago was this?"

"Ages," I say, keeping it vague. I've already done the math. His rebound to five-year relationship has nothing to do with me. And I don't need Em trying to manipulate information for shits and giggles. But this vague answer doesn't stop her from asking more questions. If anything, it spurs her on.

"Why'd they break up?"

"Dunno."

"Did *she* break up with him?"

"Dunno."

"Did *he* break up with her?"

"Dunno."

"What do you know?"

"He was in a five-year relationship with someone. He is not anymore." I shrug.

"Sounds like a fun date."

"It was bearable." I realize I have not fulfilled my promise of juicy gossip. And so I decide to offer her the one morsel of gossip I know she'll have no problem dining out on for a week.

"There is one other thing," I say, slyly keeping my eyes forward.

"What?" she says, interest piqued.

"We kissed," I say, sliding my eyes over to her. I decide to go for the PG-13 version. She doesn't need to know Xander had me *thisclose* to fondling myself last night. And I would have, if it wasn't for being interrupted by Ben.

"What?" Em says, whipping her head to me. "When?"

"The other night. In bed . . ."

"I don't care. I don't care. I don't care," she says, cutting me off after realizing she's asking the wrong question. Here it comes.

"How was it?" she says, almost singing out the words in excitement. I don't respond immediately. Last night's indiscretion is all consuming in my memory.

The flicker in his eyes the moment he made the decision to kiss me. The way he cupped my face. How it started off slow. My inability to restrain myself as I pressed my entire body into his. How he pressed back. The electrical current that ran along every single nerve in my body.

"You're rendered speechless," she says, mouth open.

"I have speech," I say, a little too shrill to come across like I wasn't just daydreaming about said kiss. Em laughs at this. "This is me talking."

"Always in denial," Em says, pushing my buttons.

"I mean, of course it was fucking great. We know this," I say, coming at it from a practical standpoint. "The reason I decided to spend the night with him eleven years ago was not because he's terrible with his mouth, is it?"

This shuts Em up for all of a second. "We also know he's helpful, open, and generous," Em says, like she's piecing together a profile of Xander. Not to hunt him down for heinous crimes like they would a serial killer. Something much more serious. A dating profile.

"How do we know this?"

"He drinks lattes," she says, and this sends me over the edge.

"Buzzfeed." We both shout at the same time, collapsing in laughter.

When the laughter subsides, Em gets up and heads to the kitchen. She returns a moment later with a bottle of beer and more slightly salted potato chips. This woman can drink beer like it's freaking water. Me? The yeast factor makes it like eating a loaf of alcoholic bread, which would be a great afternoon snack if I wasn't heading to a sleep study later this evening.

"I can't," I say, exercising restraint. I can't be inebriated around Xander anymore. I don't need less inhibitions around him. If anything, I need more. Way more.

"Coughlin's Law: Drink or be gone," she says, quoting *Cocktail* while producing a bottle of water.

"That is very kind of you," I say, taking the bottle gratefully and drowning myself in the cool H20. How does water taste so good when it has no taste?

Seconds later, the bottle is officially empty and I already feel better.

Em settles on the couch next to me.

"So, what'd you get up to last night?" I ask.

"I went drunk shopping online and found you the perfect dress for the wedding," she replies. "Want to see?"

She whips out her phone and shows me a photo of a blood-orange, puffed-sleeve, deep V neck, exposed back, cut above the knees wedding dress.

"It's perfect." I've been feeling guilty about ditching Em as my wedding date but apparently she doesn't care to take my feelings into consideration because she says, "Xander is going to lose his mind when he sees you wearing this."

"Do I really have to bring Xander as my date?" I raise my eyebrows, but it's no use. Me dating is like crack to her. I can see the unhinged written all over her face. She's on a mission now.

"Emphatically yes."

"*Pffft*. Is there a rulebook on dating?" I say, almost sarcastic.

"Many. Why?" she replies, serious. Because of course there's a self-help section at Barnes & Noble filled with dating advice, with my mom's book smack bang in the middle. See what I mean by incompetent?

"You have so much to learn," she says, patting my arm. "Since this is what you do now. You date."

"Do I?"

"Don't you?"

I study her. No, I don't date. I have one-night stands. And then I sneak out before the morning. Although I notice my heart beats a little quicker as I picture Xander all dressed up, hair styled, opening car doors, kissing on sidewalks.

And then I think about the reason why I'm even thinking about dating Xander to begin with. For the sake of the sleep study.

"I am dating Xander Miller." Officially. On the record.

"Holy shit," Em says at the confession. That's all she says. It appears that dating Xander Miller has rendered us both speechless.

We turn back to the movie as Tom Cruise cheats on Elisabeth with the older rich woman. And *this* is exactly why I don't date.

I reach over and swipe Em's bottle of beer. I take a sip.

Coughlin's Law: Drink or be gone.

* * *

Xander and I stand at the entrance to a rando carnival I've never seen before in my life. It's complete with a circus tent, grown-ass men wearing clown costumes, and a Ferris wheel. Here I am. Wednesday afternoon. On a second date.

We have been the height of respectability during the last few nights of the sleep study. I would like to publicly thank me. I want to thank me for keeping my hands to myself. I want to thank me for keeping my hands out of my own pants. And I want to thank me for keeping Xander out of my dreams.

"When you said 'carnival,' you really meant carnival," I say, turning to Xander, who looks like he's a celebrity in disguise trying to do "normal people things" with a red plaid shirt and dark blue baseball cap. Turns out, the man with the capsule wardrobe has range.

"What does 'carnival' mean to you?" Xander says, raising his eyebrows.

"A murder scene waiting to happen," I say. "There isn't a single crime procedural show that doesn't have a circus serial killer episode."

"You're dark," he says, laughing. "And have questionable taste in television."

"Fine, if you get murdered in the haunted house, I will not go out of my way to find the killer to avenge your death. I will wait for the F.B.I.," I say.

He's laughing even more now. Until he stops.

"Wait. Why am I getting murdered in the haunted house and not you? You're the pretty one. And the type to get seduced by Ted Bundy."

"Not a brunette. Not his type," I say, correcting him. He reaches over and holds a piece of my blonde hair, studying it. There's a faint smile on his face and I don't know what exactly he's thinking—or remembering—but just as quickly as he picked up the strand, he lets it go.

"Can we go have fun now and debate who gets killed later?" he says and hands over our tickets to the operator who clicks them, old-school style. I follow him through the gates.

There's a spring in Xander's step. I'd say the guy's a morning person, but I don't think that applies when you don't sleep—ever. Maybe he's a carnival person. There's an adorable light-hearted wonder to him as his eyes scan from left to right. Between Xander calling me pretty and me even thinking Xander is adorable, the evidence is undeniable. Dating is the death of love and lust.

I follow Xander's line of sight and spot a clown. *Gross.*

Em wouldn't come within a ten-mile radius of a carnival. The phobia of clowns is strong in that one. Although to be fair, there's nothing creepier than a grown-ass man hiding behind a fake smile, basically plotting your death. One Halloween at university, one of the fraternities all dressed up as clowns. They roamed the campus scaring the shit out of everyone. We were on our way back from a party, Em in her Buffy costume and me in my Giles costume, you know, from *Buffy the Vampire Slayer.*

One of the clowns ran out from behind a tree. There was a cackle behind us and so I turned and kicked that clown right in the nut sack. He bitched as he went down.

And that's how I learned that it's simply a matter of realizing that a clown is just a sad man in a costume. And they all have a crotch you can kick them in, should you need to.

"First stop," he says cryptically, interrupting my thoughts. He takes my hand and gently pulls me farther and farther into the carnival, turning back to wink at me, which I want to say is grosser than the clowns but I can't. Because it gives me a little dopamine hit and I find myself smiling.

We weave our way through the legs of the guy on stilts breathing fire and an elephant wearing an ugly hat, which I'm pretty sure constitutes animal cruelty, my feet continually tripping up as I start to process my surroundings. The soundtrack is basically an electronic keyboard whose battery is about to run out and die. The shrieks of children remind me I should not be here. The only other adults are those chaperoning the children. Whichever Buzzfeed correspondent wrote *carnival* into their list of Top 10 Date Ideas should be fired.

And then I smell it. The scent of deep fried everything. And sugar. And it smells so good, my mouth starts watering.

Okay, maybe the carnival isn't so bad.

Xander stops us directly in front of the cotton candy booth and turns to face me. "This is the only way one should consume sugar," he says, before ordering the puffiest cloud of sugar on a stick.

Then, he holds the stick with a cloud of candy bigger than my head between us and proceeds to rip off a massive chunk and shove it in his mouth. There's a bit of cotton candy sticking out that his tongue sweeps up in a matter of seconds. He's the one eating cotton candy, and I'm the one who's drooling.

"Is this the 'fun' you were talking about?" I say.

Xander takes another chunk and holds it inches from my lips. "You tell me," he says, waiting.

The longer I wait to swipe the cotton candy, the more suggestive this gesture gets. So I open my mouth and lean ever so slightly forward to take the chunk while trying to avoid his fingertips, but I misjudge and only get the tiniest whisp of spun sugar between my lips.

Before I know it, Xander's palm is over my mouth, essentially shoving the entire chunk in. Something I'd expect from Em, not my "date."

The cotton candy melts in my mouth on contact, but I'm too distracted to care that I've just mainlined sugar in the tastiest format. "Hey!" I say, reaching for a hunk of cotton candy myself. I shove it in his mouth.

He ducks my first attempt, a twinkle of mischief in his eye, but I get him on my second one. The difference between us is that I keep my hand over his mouth.

"Oh, this is the only way one should consume sugar, is it?" I say, mocking him. He tries to say something, but it's all just muffled noises. "Are you enjoying it?"

He's eyes widen and before I know it, he bares his teeth and takes a nibble of my palm.

I pull my hand back really quick. A smug expression is on his face.

"Do you know where these hands have been?" I say, cocking my head. "From the sleep study to the carnival. I haven't washed them, once."

"Ew, gross," he says, trying to channel the sass of a preteen who found out girls have cooties.

We both descend into fits of laughter before he grabs my hand and we're off, past the food vendors and into rows and rows of rides.

"This way," Xander says, as he does a double take before veering us off the path. He pushes me up against the back entrance to the haunted house, keeping us out of sight.

I look down and his chest is so close to mine that if I take a breath, we'll be touching. So I don't. Then, he leans forward and looks past me. The problem? His neck is inches away from my lips. And that signature smell dares me to nibble on his skin.

Okay, so turns out carnivals aren't just a great place to murder someone. It also seems like a great place to hook up with someone. So many places to make out off the path, hidden between rides, and moaning so loud no one can hear you.

I do not take the dare to nibble Xander's neck, though.

"What are we doing?" I say instead, and he turns to look at me, a lingering smile on face.

Then, he leans in. I want to say that I remain completely frozen. I want to say that I will not kiss Xander. I want to say that dating is the death of lust. But I can't. Because I feel myself leaning in.

Instead of meeting my lips, though, he pushes on the door behind me I didn't realize I was leaning on, and we fall *into* the haunted house.

Nope, I am not going to make out with Xander against the haunted house.

"I call this the private tour," Xander says, as he spins me around. Now I'm the one leading the way in this total darkness.

"Xander?" I say, wondering where he is.

"Here," he says. His voice is next to me.

I feel his fingers interlace with mine, and then he starts leading me farther into the Haunted House. With our vision now lacking, my body focuses all its attention on the other senses available. Xander's signature scent mixes in with the smoke machine used for spooky effects. I'm sure the soundtrack is a Spotify playlist called "Murder House."

Every single nerve ending in my body has migrated to my fingers that are intertwined with Xander's. Sure, we've held hands when pretending to be a couple at the sleep study, but there's something more intimate when you wind your fingers around each other's. There's more surface area to touch.

A spine-chilling scream echoes through the house. An evil cackle erupts. Xander wraps his fingers around mine even tighter as he steers me to the right, past a skeleton that plunges from the ceiling, without flinching.

"Should I be worried that you seem to know your way around a haunted house in complete darkness?" I ask.

"My best friend worked in one during our summer break when we were sixteen. He snuck us in all summer."

I did not expect that answer.

"So not because you take all your dates here to be scared horny?" I tease.

"Busted," he says, deadpan. "Is it working?"

"*Totally*," I say, sarcastic to hide that I am finding this groping around in the dark kinda hot.

"Tell me, what do you do for fun in your summer breaks?" he says, steering the conversation back to the theme of this date, it seems. Fun.

"What *don't* I do?" I say, reminiscing about all the summers Em and I have spent together. I feel the faintest squeeze of my hand, reminding me that sharing is caring.

"Last year, Em and I took a self-defense class."

"Is that how you flipped me the other day?" he says, amusement in his tone.

"Ummhmm," I say, willing my mind not to remember how it felt to have our groins completely smashed into each other.

"What else?"

"Another summer, Em and I entered a salsa dance competition and won a month's supply of margaritas," I say. I leave out the part that every time I took a sip of the bloody thing, I thought about the first time I had one. The night I met him.

"A perfect victory," he mutters, his playfulness toned down. Is he thinking about the night we met? Don't know. Don't care.

"And a very rowdy summer," I say, trying to bring the F! U! N!

"Ummhmm," he says, lost in his own thoughts. My turn to give him the faintest squeeze.

"What about you now? Your inability to lead us through this Haunted House clearly shows you do not attend carnivals like you used to. Are lawyers allowed to have fun?" I say, elbowing him gently.

"Lawyers are. Insomniacs not so much," he says, and the image of Xander front and center at a Cardi B concert flashes in my mind.

"But you like music?"

Before he can answer, someone grabs my other arm and a blood-curdling scream filters through the air. Without thinking, I yank myself free from Xander's hand, turn around and kick the perpetrator responsible as hard as possible in the general crotch region.

A pubescent voice lets out a howl, echoing through the darkness, and just like that the lights are on. Standing in front of me is a pimple-faced teenager, doubled over with his hands covering his crotch.

"I'm so sorry," I say, walking toward the kid in an attempt to placate the situation.

"You assaulted me!" the kid squeaks, his voice shaking, backing away from me while still clutching himself.

That stops me in my tracks. In the stark light of day, the only thing scary about this haunted house is getting arrested for assault, even if it was self-defense.

"There's a clear sign at the entrance saying our staff won't take abuse from customers," he says, lifting a shaky hand in the direction I assume is the front.

I turn to Xander, expecting him to step forward and spout some fancy legalize. But instead, he grabs my hand and drags me as we break out into a run.

"Hey! Come back! I need your details to sue you!" I hear the kid squeak, but his threats are lost over the sound of Xander laughing his ass off. I can't help it, I join in.

We run past the food vendors and the Gravitron, through a maze of baby animals, finally stopping at the Ferris wheel. Without skipping a beat, Xander slips us into the next carriage before the attendant can even register what's happening. The carriage lurches forward, and the carnival disappears below us.

"What that the hell just happened?" I say when I've caught my breath. I can't tell if this is the best date. Or the worst. And I realize I don't care.

I'm having a blast.

CHAPTER NINETEEN

I fly through the front door and throw my keys on the counter, skidding to a halt.

"Want a drink?" I say, remembering my manners as Xander walks in behind me, hands in his pockets, like we're not going to be late for the sleep study. I blame the bumper cars. I couldn't resist ramming into Xander three times in a row.

"I'm good," he says, his eyes roaming my entire apartment. I'm impressed there are only two empty beer bottles next to the sink. I thank past me for putting the dishwasher on before I left for the sleep study last night. I also note that Em tidied up. My quick stock take means I have nothing to be embarrassed about, and so I make a mad dash into my bedroom and stuff my pajamas into my overnight bag, which has taken up residence at the foot of my bed.

"Nice place," I hear Xander call out from the kitchen. I know he's not using the word *nice* in a neutral way because yeah, my apartment is nice. I mean, it's small. And the rent is on the higher end. Hence why I'm in this sleep study. But my landlord lets me do whatever I want. Which is why the place has personality. There's a sage-green feature wall and a shit ton of colorful framed photos of mostly Em and me.

I bolt into the bathroom for my toothbrush and toothpaste only to run directly into Em.

I scream, more out of shock, before grabbing onto her arms and doubling over. "You scared the shit out of me."

"Sorry," Em says.

"Shouldn't you be flirting with our tennis coach to get us discounted lessons?" I say, but she's looking behind me now, her eyes bugging. And I know I'll have to do introductions.

I turn and see Xander running his hand through his hair, his T-shirt riding up, a sliver of taut abdominal skin on show like it should be illegal. He looks disheveled, as if he's recovering from the heart attack my scream triggered.

"Not a serial killer. Just Emily," I say, straightening back up. Since Em and Xander never met in college, I proceed to introduce them. "Em, meet Xander." I look from Em to Xander and notice he's already recovered with a winning smile. "Xander, meet Em."

"Nice to meet you," Xander says first, extending his hand for a shake, which Em promptly ignores and goes in for a massive hug.

"It's so nice to meet you," Em says into his shoulder. I look at Xander, who's looking at me. And that winning smile has turned into a face-splitting grin. "I've heard so much about you."

Xander cocks an eyebrow at me. A question. *You've been talking about me?*

I shake my head at this in response. *No, I haven't.*

He scrunches his nose by way of smiling. *Bullshit.*

I bite my lip. *You'll never know.*

His eyes light up at the lip bite. *Oh, I see. Say less.*

I glare at him right as Em pulls back. Her eyes dart between us, like she caught us fondling each other in public.

Then, a Cheshire cat grin spreads across her face. She thinks we fucked. And in some ways, it'd be so much easier to handle *that* conversation. Instead, we're looking at each other like two idiots who spent way too long at a carnival having so much fun that it appears we have some sort of secret language that includes communicating in stares.

"We have to go," I say, interrupting her thought pattern, while vigorously shaking my head, hoping my best friend of eleven years can also read my face. "We're late."

I walk right past her and give her a kiss on the cheek before grabbing Xander by the sleeve and dragging him behind me.

"It was nice to officially meet you," Xander says, over his shoulder.

"Don't encourage her," I say, chastising him. I won't let go of his T-shirt until we're in the hallway and in the clear.

"Wait!" Em calls. Xander's physically bigger and stronger than me, so when he turns around and takes five steps back into the living room to meet Em, who's followed us out, I go with him.

"Do you know how groundbreaking this is?" Em says to Xander, her generally happy predisposition gone. "Or should I say rule breaking."

Oh god, I was not prepared for this. Mostly because Em has never had to do this. But it seems she's decided that since I've been on two dates, now is the time to go all confrontational father figure from a teen movie on Xander's ass.

"Em," I say, shaking my head. "We're good."

She breaks eye contact with Xander and looks at me, the sunshine returning. She's really going Method for this. "Let me do this, please," she whispers before turning back to Xander, intimidation rolling off her. Fuck, she's a good actress. I remind myself to push her to sign up for the community production of *Grease*.

Xander, to his credit, doesn't falter under the look. He takes it.

"If you hurt her, it will not end well for you," she says, all business.

"Yes, ma'am," he says, playing his part. My grip loosens on his T-shirt and my hand falls to my side. I feel exposed having my best friend talk about me like I'm precious, and the guy I'm in an arranged relationship with agree with her like I'm not here.

"She might act all tough, but she's all gooey inside, like a self-saucing pudding," she says, always a flair for the dramatics.

"I promise the only person getting hurt is me." Xander tilts his head slightly as he delivers the perfect line. Before I can roll my eyes at him, I watch as Em almost melts on the spot.

"Nawwwww." Em unleashes a swoon.

"You were this close to playing it cool," I say to her, holding up my thumb and pointer finger, almost touching.

"I felt the fear," Xander says to Em, smiling.

"All right, enough of this. We gotta go," I say, nudging Xander. Then, he slides his hand down my arm and interlaces his fingers with mine. I don't know why this act has me in a chokehold, but his fingers heat up my entire body.

"It was lovely meeting you, Em," Xander says before turning toward the door and taking me with him. When we're clear in the hallway, Xander turns to me and says, "I like her."

"She's single," I say, joking as I stab the button for the elevator.

"Jesus," Xander says, letting go of my hand. He shakes his head. "When will you realize that I'm not one of your douchebag Bone It boys?"

The elevator doors ping open and we both step in.

What I think he meant to ask was, *When will you realize that I'll never hurt you?*

My heart rate starts thundering at the realization that I'm fluent in Xander. When did that happen?

"I know you're not," I say quietly, keeping my eyes on the elevator buttons. "I'm just fucking with you."

"If you want to fuck with me, there are other ways," he says, his voice low. I turn to look at him. His eyes have grown dark. The energy shifts around us. I raise an eyebrow at him, daring him to go on.

He reaches out and hits the emergency stop button, the elevator jerking to a standstill. He turns to face me. My heart rate picks up, pumping blood everywhere. My whole body vibrates. There's a sudden urge to look at his lips.

"That little moan of yours, especially when I have my hands in your hair. That fucks with me," he says, stalking closer. And holy shit, it is the hottest thing I've ever seen him do. The end of his lip curls up. Oh, he's not done.

"When your eyes glaze over, thinking about that night. That fucks with me," he says, prowling even closer. Excuse me, what is happening and why am I so fucking turned on? He reaches out and grabs my hand, turning the palm facing up.

"When you hold my hand and your thumb absentmindedly traces my palm," he says, his finger dragging circles around my palm so lightly it sends a shiver straight to the pit of my stomach. "That fucks with me."

I didn't realize I did that.

I look past my palm, which he's holding with two hands, up toward his eyes, which are curtained by his curls. I can see they're burning. For me. And it's enough for my entire body to ignite. Want scorches through me.

"Fuck with me."

One moment his lips curl up at the ends, the next his mouth is on mine. There is no control. It's hot and hard, like every ounce of restraint we exercised over the last few days was merely kindling, fueling the fire.

He releases my hand and grips my waist, pulling me closer. The lingering taste of cotton candy on his tongue as he expertly strokes mine has me languishing. My hands fist his shirt, pulling him closer. I don't care if it's obvious. I just can't get enough.

I am so worked up with want that when he releases the grip he has on my hips, I can't help but protest.

"Xander," I whimper. Without much more than a plea, Xander's mouth is back on mine as he slides his hands to my ass and lifts me up and onto the railing. I open my legs for him to fill the space, pleasure pulsing in my thighs when I feel him there.

My back arcs off the elevator wall as one of Xander's hands roams down my legs and wraps my ankle around his waist. Once my ankles are hooked around him, his hands tunnel through my hair, angling my mouth to kiss me harder, devouring every inch of my lips, my mouth, my tongue.

I feel like I'm one delicious pressure point away from coming undone. I can't keep my hands from roaming his entire body as they slip under his shirt, making contact with soft skin over hard muscle. I scrape my fingernails over his shoulder, which elicits a groan from the back of his throat. Then, he hums over my neck, and I lose my goddamn mind. I dig my fingers into his shoulder, letting him know we're not stopping anytime soon.

Then, he pulls back. Eyes fully blown out.

"Tell me you don't want this," he says, voice on the edge of self-control and completely losing it. Like he's holding onto his last shred of restraint.

"I want this."

He groans at my consent, crashing his lips back onto me hard and heavy, before his fingers drop to the hem of my sundress as he skims his thumb over my inner thigh. The throbbing pulse between my legs turns from insistent to desperate.

His hand slips between my thighs and I am achingly aware of every single nerve cell he touches. "You want me," he murmurs into my mouth as he glides the fabric of my underwear over me, the friction creating a seismic event of pleasure cracking through every cell of my body.

Fuccckk.

I capture his mouth with mine, muffling the moans he expertly draws out of me with his talented fingers as he strokes me through the lace, using the fabric to make my body sing with want. *I want you.*

He's barely got his hands on me and I'm losing my mind. I'm stuck in between begging for more and riding this wave of anticipation as he teases me with the thin piece of fabric that's now drenched.

I pull back from our kiss and stare at him.

His fingers freeze.

"Stop fucking with me and fuck me," I say. And then there's a flash of a grin before his fingers slide underneath the lace and he drags his fingers over my hot, wet bare skin. It's slow and drawn out and it feels like he's touching me *everywhere*.

He kisses me desperately now, his tongue sliding against mine, like holding back was painful for him. His fingers trace over me as pleasure builds deep inside. My body responds to his every move.

I need more. And he knows it. He slides two fingertips inside me, no more than half an inch. And he starts dipping his fingertips down and up.

Edging me.

Down and up.

Teasing me.

Swirling.

Taunting me in the best (breathe) possible (breathe) way. *Breathe.*

"Xander," I say, turning feral. That's all the confirmation he needs as he slides his hooked fingers deep inside me, finding in *seconds* the exact spot that has baffled scientists for centuries.

He works me right there while his strong palm rubs me down.

I let out a moan, and I have nothing else to do but ride his fingers. And right when I'm on the edge, he whispers in my mouth, "Give me everything."

His demand sends an orgasm rippling through me—sparks flying along every nerve ending. I bury my face into my arm as I come back down.

The intercom squeals and a staticky voice says, "Security operations center."

Holy shit.

We both glance up toward the little camera in the corner near the ceiling.

My eyes bug out. *Busted.*

Xander scrunches his nose. *You think he enjoyed the show?*

I bite my bottom lip. *Not as much as I did.*

This earns me a beam that can be seen from fucking space.

"Remain calm," the voice says.

We both burst out laughing.

"We can't restart the elevator remotely so we have emergency services arriving at the scene."

Shit. I try to push Xander off me so I can get my underwear back on but he doesn't move. Instead, he slowly drags my panties up over my hips. Then pulls my sundress down, all delicate and precise. Deliberately savoring every second that he gets to touch me.

Like he doesn't want this moment to end. Like we have all the time in the world. Like it's just the two of us and I did not just ride his fingers in public.

Then, he slides his hands around my back, holding me in place, as he offers me a long and drawn-out kiss.

He rests his forehead on mine, lingering for a split second, before he steps back, grabs my hands, and pushes the elevator button. I let out a slow, steady breath as we resume our descent in silence.

When my phone vibrates, I thank the universe for a distraction. Em's text flashes across my screen. I like him. You should too.

I read the text five times over.

The elevator doors open and we're greeted by five hunky firemen in uniform. My eyes drink them in one by one, each hotter than the last.

And I feel nothing.

Xander has most definitely fucked with me.

CHAPTER TWENTY

Using the posted speed limit as a suggestion, Xander screeched into the parking lot on time. I was about to congratulate him until I found out that on time is late in Xander world. I hope for his sake that flash I saw while he fanged it through a yellow was the sun catching a mirror and not a red-light camera.

I'm not complaining about why we're late. Not one bit. The legend of the sexual magician lives on. After two dates and getting to third base, I'm proud to say that of all the sleep study nights, this has been the best so far.

We arrived. We headed straight to our room. Then Ben came in to wire us up. And he was smiling. No annoyed "guys." No grimacing. No scraping his hands over his face in frustration at the two of us.

Today, everything went off without a hitch. There was even a fist bump between Ben and Xander.

What a difference an orgasm makes.

Once Ben disappears, it's nothing but Xander and me, our every bodily function being monitored via wires and a camera. You know, very relaxing.

And yet, I *am* relaxed.

I repeat: What a difference an orgasm makes.

"Are we finally clocking this sleep study?" I say into the darkness. I mean there is only one answer and it's yes.

We're lying next to each other and while I'm still aware that the hard lines of Xander's body are in proximity, my body doesn't malfunction like it used to. I almost find comfort in it. Call it exposure therapy.

"Xander?" I say, turning to face him when he doesn't respond. Even though we're in the dark, a sliver of moonlight through the curtain casts shadows on the tips of his eyelashes, and they're downcast.

I scooch a little closer.

Those eyes are closed shut.

Holy shit. Xander's asleep.

Xander Miller is *sleeping*.

What do I do? Do I call Ben in here? Does he need to be made aware of this development? It's a fucking miracle. Give Dr. Waitley and her team all the awards.

I can't look away. His curls fan across his forehead and the pillow. His half-moon scar on his lip looks a little less sharp. The frown lines that are usually etched into his forehead are softer.

He really is fucking beautiful.

I reach out to him, my fingertips gently smoothing the frown lines. His face relaxes instantly.

There's a soft, sweet sound that comes on his next breath. It sounds like what I imagine peace sounds like. And I wonder how long it has been since Xander experienced peace. I like that I'm the person that gets to do that for him.

My hands freeze at this confession—this *revelation*.

Oh, fuck.

Alarm bells sound in my body, signaling a whole bunch of adrenaline to be dumped in my bloodstream. The pages of Mom's book flick behind my eyes.

Chapter 1: *Bonding Versus Boning & Why Oxytocin Is Cockblocking Your Sex Drive*

Chapter 4: *The Dating Delusion & Where Love and Lust Go To Die*

Chapter 7: *Monogamy, the Libido Killer & the Truth About Sexless Relationships*

This can't be happening.

Dating Xander is transactional. It's as fake as my spray tan. Surely none of this applies to our situation. And yet, I can't gaslight myself. Feelings have entered the chat. Sure, it was a brief moment. A single feel was given.

I blame Post-Orgasm Ash.

What an idiot. She got all up in her *feelings*.

My kingdom for a one-night stand instead of this mess.

I slip out of bed all stealth-like and grab my phone off the table. I look over and see that Xander hasn't been disturbed. I can't help but smile.

There I go again. Feeling. What, exactly? I don't know. Happy? Content? Gross. I wipe that smile off my face immediately. Although, I can appreciate and marvel at the results of the sleep study. Science and all. And so the enforced frown on my face turns upside down because it really is a miracle Xander is asleep and it's only—I look at my phone—11PM.

Perfect. Em will most definitely still be up.

In the safety of the bathroom, I hit dial. She answers immediately, which tells me she's been scrolling her phone on the sofa with something on in the background she's seen a million times before that requires exactly three brain cells to follow.

"Chapter three," I say. In the stark light of the bathroom, I don't feel as sure of myself as I did in the darkness. I need reinforcements. I need my best friend to tell me that everything is going to be okay.

"Refresh my memory," Em says. That's the beauty of having a best friend like Em. It's like our conversations are never-ending and so there's never a need to interrupt with a basic salutation like, "Hi, how are you?"

"The paradox of sexual chemistry and why it evaporates once you care too much," I say.

"Hold up. What happened?"

"Xander . . ." I start but stop myself. Where do I even begin? Xander finger banged me in the elevator, I rode his fingers like a cowgirl, he made me come so hard that the firefighters they sent didn't do it for me—

"What?" Em reminds me I'm having this conversation in my head and not with her.

"Xander fell asleep," I say, deciding that Xander's manual labor is an entirely different conversation that we need to have over drinks.

"That's amazing!"

"Nope," I say, cutting her off before I chicken out on this conversation and truly gaslight myself. "I watched him in the dark."

I suck in a breath, waiting for Em to jump in with a comment. Instead, the line remains silent, so I brace myself for what I'm going to say next. "I reached out and stroked his fucking face."

"Okay," Em says, slowly so as not to spook me.

Here goes nothing.

"And it felt good being there for him," I say, punctuating every single word with disgust.

"Did you just say the F word?" Em says, almost choking on her own spit.

"Yes."

"You have feelings?" Em asks, and this time I can tell she's using her first-day-of-school-don't-scare-the-freshmen voice. Don't scare the emotionally unavailable woman.

"Xander is making me feel," I say mincing the words. Not taking responsibility. Because why would I? "Chapter five: 'The Trap of Passion: Why the People Who Make Your Heart Race Also Make Your Life Hell.'" I don't have to read that chapter. I lived it with my parents when The Cheating happened and my home became a war zone. "I need an exit strategy from this sleep study, like now."

"You're not bailing on Xander because of feelings," Em says, calling me out.

"Chapter seven—," I start, but she cuts me off.

"Fuck your mom's book," Em says, her voice morphing from caring to cutting.

"That book has sold millions of copies worldwide," I say, defending the book and, by extension, my lifestyle.

"So has *The Lord of the Rings*. Do you believe hobbits exist?"

"I don't understand the reference." Of course I understand. I'm being a smartass. And Em knows this.

"It's fiction," Em says. This catches me off guard. "Catching feelings isn't a death sentence."

"Isn't it?" I say, seeing red. I'm unable to keep my cool about the topic I've so carefully managed with my rules. "Because why would any parent put their kid through what I went through if it wasn't absolutely fucking necessary?"

The line goes silent for a moment. No quick comeback.

I'm thankful for the respite.

"I'm sorry your parents are a bag of dicks," she says, and a bubble of laughter escapes my lips. I'm so grateful for the comment. I wish she was here to hug. "But you're wrong."

"What?"

I hear her taking a deep breath. "Your negativity bias is showing."

"You're going to try and use science to change my mind? Really?" I say, unconvinced.

"What? I can read research papers too," she says. Before I can argue, she continues. "You know studies show that it takes five positive interactions to outweigh just one negative interaction in a relationship. And if you count how many interactions you've had with Xander . . ." She doesn't finish the sentence, letting me fill in the blanks.

I make a *pfft* sound, trying to show how unbothered I am that she's using science against me. The truth is, I love/hate that she's using science right now. She's right, though. Negative bias in scientific theory is real.

"Catching feelings doesn't mean you immediately have to get Xander's name tattooed in an arrow heart across your forehead. It just means you acknowledge something is there, and you get to decide what to do with it."

"It can mean nothing?"

"If that's what you decide, yes," she says.

What comes next from me is a mammoth sigh. Relief spreads through my shoulders and I drop them down an inch.

It can mean absolutely nothing. And while I might have to physically be in Xander's presence for the rest of the sleep study, there's my exit strategy.

"You make me feel warm and fuzzy inside," I say to her. My way of thanking her.

"Hugs," she says.

"Hugs," I say back.

When I slowly close the door to our room, I turn around to see Xander awake.

"Come here," he says, opening the duvet. It's an invitation. But before my flight, fight, freeze response kicks in, I remind myself it's not an invitation till death do us part, and I can do this. It doesn't mean anything.

So I get into bed and snuggle Xander to sleep.

* * *

"Twizzlers for life," I say, using my mouth to tear open the family-sized packet while clinging onto my third cup of coffee like my life depends on it. I hear Xander scoff next to me, and I turn to him and his heartbreaker Wayfarers. "Let me guess, you're a Red Vines guy?"

"They're both terrible options," he says, shaking his head as he reaches for a packet of candy corn. I didn't even know you could buy that shit outside of Halloween.

"That's your idea of a good time?" I say, my turn to scoff.

"Party in my mouth," he says, before he throws a single piece into the air and catches it between his lips. He looks over at me, chewing vigorously on the hardened piece of trash candy before driving us out of the parking lot.

Bed Chemistry

Welcome to the third date, in which we went from leaving the sleep study to the gas station for snacks, to driving along the 101 in peak rush hour. Because Xander is fucking insane. This might end up going down as the worst date in history, if we ever finish it. Or we might just die here. Bumper to bumper.

Also, I have no idea where we're going. And I don't know if Xander thinks it's cute to keep it a secret, but the traffic we're crawling in has me muttering under my breath.

This morning at the sleep study, Ben woke us up like a kid on Christmas morning, informing Xander that he'd slept for a total of four hours. "That's your new record," Ben said, like he was announcing an entry into the Guinness World Records for sleeping. And after my debrief with Em in the bathroom a few nights ago, I've been sleeping like a goldendoodle that just got adopted by a rich white woman. You know, warm, tucked in, and taking up most of the bed.

Basically, we have continued to attend the sleep study without any more *incidents*.

"Care to share where we're going?" I say through a mouthful of red flavored plastic. Yum. I glance over at him, and with the windows down, his curls are whipping around, having the time of their lives.

His lips tip into a smile and the text from Em flashes in my mind. *I like him. You should too.*

"To learn all about our hopes and dreams . . .," Xander starts but deliberately stops, giving me time to react.

"Gag."

"We need to go back to the very beginning," he finishes, like he's perfected when to talk, when to let me cut in, and when to continue. Okay. Not bad. A bit considerate.

"What cryptic shit is that?" I say, while simultaneously trying to crack the code like I'm Bruce Willis in *Die Hard with a Vengeance*.

The hopes and dreams bit is from his/society's definition of what constitutes a date. But what's the "very beginning" of Xander's hopes and dreams?

"Are you taking me *home*?" I say, lifting my eyebrow.

Two hours later, we pull up into a parking lot on the side of the road, just outside of Santa Barbara.

"Rincon Beach," Xander says, which, judging by how full the parking lot is, and how many fit surfers there are running to and from the beach, is the one decent surf spot in Southern California.

"You grew up *here*?" I say, trying to consolidate the sharp-tongued corporate lawyer with the laid-back beach boy vibes of the three surfer dudes hanging around the trunk of their car. Their naked torsos ripple with every movement.

I tear my eyes away to scan the parking lot. We're surrounded by greenery. Shrubs, trees, and general coastal vegetation. I can't see the beach, but I'm assuming it's down the narrow pathway that seems busier than the 101 we were driving on—at ten AM on a Thursday.

I focus on Xander through a new lens, taking him in. Those wide, strong shoulders, solid hips, strong thigh muscles.

His body is carved by fucking Poseidon himself.

The aircon is still blasting as the engine idles, but it's getting hot in here.

"Santa Barbara, yes," he says as my eyes fly back up to his face. "But this is where you'd find me and—"

"Xander!" A woman that looks around my mom's age comes jogging up to the car, the saltwater drying on her skin in white blotches, sand up to her ankles, and her dark brown curls fighting their hardest against being slicked-back wet. She's holding a surfboard. Dread fills me at the realization. Surely this can't be. He wouldn't . . .

"Mom," he says, startled. He does a double take to me before getting out of the car to greet his . . . MOTHER.

I am meeting his mother. This cannot be happening. This has to be against dating protocol. I watch as he goes in for a big bear hug, not caring that it'll get his white T-shirt wet. I hear his mom say something about the waves pumping.

I've got about three seconds to figure out how to play this.

I don't date. *And yet, I am dating Xander.* I don't have relationships. *And yet, I'm in a fake relationship with Xander.* I don't meet the parents. *And yet, I'm about to meet his fucking mom right now.*

Stoked, dude.

I unbuckle myself reluctantly and haul my ass out of the car. The sun immediately beats down on me, reminding me that Ventura County in the dead middle of summer might just be in the hottest place on planet earth.

I look over to Xander's mom and offer her a smile. She beams right back. "You must be Ash," she says, her voice warm and sparkling. I wait for the coronary I expect to have, knowing that Xander has spoken about me enough that his mother can recognize me by sight, but it never comes. In fact, she is so inviting, it makes me instantly want to hug her. As if on cue, she goes in for a hug but pulls back at the last moment, thinking maybe I don't want my T-shirt wet. With one hand extended, she says, "I'm Eva. It's so nice to meet you."

I look to Xander. "I swear I didn't know she was going to be here," he says. Apparently, my face is an open book, and he just speed-read the whole thing in one glance.

"It's true. This isn't an ambush. I couldn't resist the swell," she says, running one of her hands through her long, loose curls, shaking out the water. Like mother, like son. "But while I'm here, can I be of assistance?"

I cock my head at Xander. *Assistance?*

He puts his hands in his pockets. *I've got nothing to hide.*

"I have embarrassing stories. I have the first love letter he ever wrote to his high school girlfriend," she says, offering up the first anecdote I've heard from Xander's childhood. "It was so bad, she broke up with him."

I steal a glance at Xander. *Naw. Poor baby*, I convey to him wordlessly.

His shrug is so casual he could be lying down. *What can I say, I'm a romantic.*

"Not nearly embarrassing enough," I say, turning back to his mom, rubbing my hands together. "What else you got?"

"Oh, he once had the stomach flu at the same time as a junior surf competition," she says, shaking her head. "I told him not to surf, but he was determined."

"Oh no," I say, enjoying this way too much.

"They had to stop the competition. The water was deemed unsanitary," she says, shaking her head in shame.

"I was winning my heat," Xander says, defending his decision. "So that makes me the winner."

"He's not even embarrassed. He's bragging," I say, protesting to his mom at this piece of information. I can't help but be impressed she raised Xander with the kind of self-esteem that borders on a fully functioning, healthy grown adult. If only he could get seven hours of shut-eye a night. I guess we can't all be perfect.

"Right," she says, pondering. Then she clicks her fingers. "I walked in on Xander in the bathroom surrounded by candles and my very expensive lotion slathered all over his hands," she says. *Oh, shit.* "I've never seen someone slam a laptop shut so fast."

I burst out laughing. "I cannot picture Xander watching porn."

"Oh no, he wasn't. He was watching *Romeo + Juliet.*"

I look to Xander, clutching my heart. *So romantic.*

He winks at me. *Gotta love yourself first.*

My cheeks heat at the implication.

"Thank you, for sharing so generously," I say, in my most professional yet approachable parent-teacher voice. "I will use these stories against him should I need to bring him down a notch," I say, and this sends her reeling.

"Exactly as I'd hoped," she says back, beaming at me like a proud parent. And I can't control it. My heart swells.

This is the pure goodness I've seen in Xander. Directly from the source. Before I can analyze my own reaction, the moment is interrupted by a cacophony of cheering and I turn around to watch a fit as fuck younger woman emerge in a bikini that shows off her lean, long, and strong frame. She's carrying a surfboard under her arm, her golden-brown hair dripping with water.

"Scar! Wicked cutback!" one of the dudes shouts from the car next to us, grinning ear to ear.

"Thanks, Bodhi," Scar—short for what? Scarlett?—says as she jogs to what I assume is her car when she does a double take at Xander standing there. She stops.

"Xander?" she says, at first confused. Then, her eyes light up, not even bothering to rearrange her face into something chill. She is genuinely excited to see him. And she's not afraid to show it. "What are you doing here on a Thursday at ten AM?"

"I could ask you the same question," Xander says, offering her his winning smile. The casual nature of his greeting tells me they have history.

I ignore that my heart starts to pound as I get to watch the meeting of the exes unfold in front of my eyes.

And then it clicks.

Is this the ex? The half a decade together ex?

"Didn't Eva tell you I went part time?" she says before stretching on her tippy toes to kiss his cheek. He leans down and obliges.

"He's a very busy man," Eva says, in her defense. "I see you more than I see him."

Definitely the ex.

Definitely not my heart rate picking up the pace.

"Enough about Xander," Scar says, ignoring him in favor of his mom. "The carve you did on the last wave. Incredible." Scar goes in for a fist bump that Eva obliges.

"Thanks. Your cutbacks are coming along," Eva says, her mother-loving-warmth radiating off her. I take them in. They are as comfortable as two peas in a pod as they fall into easy conversation.

I imagine the five Christmases they've shared together. The five summers. The five New Years. Just the sheer amount of time they've had to spend together to feel this comfortable. Then. And now. Post breakup.

Like breaking up didn't break their bond.

Unlike my relationship with my dad.

Who forgot that I existed the moment Keeley came into his life.

And that does it for me.

Jealously flares throughout my body. Followed by anger.

What the actual fuck am I doing here? Why would he bring me to a fucking family reunion? How this pertains to Xander's "hopes and dreams" is beyond me.

Xander catches my eyes for a moment, and I hate that he can read how uncomfortable I feel crashing this impromptu family gathering.

That is, until I feel Xander's hand wrap around mine. The immediate comfort that I feel has my heart rate picking up all over again.

I snap my gaze to Scar and Eva. They're in their own world, using their hands to gesture wildly at each other, so I dare to look up at Xander.

Instead of communicating via a stare, though, he leans into the shell of my ear and says, "I swear I'll make this up to you." The heat of his breath. The promise of his words. His fingertip that's circling the inside of my palm. I hear his thoughts echo in my head. *I want you.* It's like he's letting me know that I'm the only one he's thinking about. "Anything you want."

I pull back. Our faces inches from each other.

"Anything?"

CHAPTER TWENTY-ONE

I dunk my head into the sixty-three-degree water. Fuck, that's cold as shit. We're out the back—a term I learned as Xander was helping me paddle out past the crashing waves—with Old Yello', his ten-foot bright-yellow log of a surfboard he promises anyone can stand up on.

It just so happens that surfers never rock up for a surf with a single board. His mom had Old Yello' strapped to the roof of her car *just in case*. Scarlett had a spare swimsuit in the truck of her car *for emergencies*. And one of dudes had some board shorts for Xander *because you never know*. Everyone's so helpful around here. Like one big happy family. Not going to lie, do I feel uncomfortable wearing Scarlett's swimsuit? Yes. Is it the most comfortable thing I've ever worn in the ocean? Also yes. I don't need to worry about a wardrobe malfunction wearing this. Unlike the flimsy two-piece I have at home.

I rest my elbows on the board that floats between us, trying to get as much of my body out of the water as possible.

I look over at Xander, whose entire body is submerged in the ocean. He's just a floating head at this point. His curls are sticking up every which way, on the account of the hair whip he did after dunking his own head that had no business being sexy. Fat water beads drip down his face, making me look at his lips.

He's so open and relaxed. There's a softness about him that makes him so inviting, like being in the ocean is a big exhale for him. I'm the complete opposite right now. On edge. Tightly wound. Closed off.

"I can't believe you grew up in the Valley and you've never been surfing," he says, taking some salt water into his mouth and spitting it out.

"It's fucking freezing," I say as Xander's eyes skim over my bare arms that are now flushed with goose pimples. From the water or Xander? No one will ever know.

"Get up on the board," he says, swimming around, clearly unaffected by the cold. "I'll hold it in position."

I do as I'm told, climbing onto the surfboard that barely budges as I straddle it, my legs now the only body part in the water. The sun immediately starts to warm up my skin. I look up and see the shore ahead of me, with its sandy dunes and lush green vegetation. Regardless of how many people are coming and going, out here, we don't hear any of it.

It's—dare I say it?—peaceful.

Another piece of the Xander puzzle attempts to fit in with what I think I know about him.

I look down at him, but he's not looking at me. He's got his eyes cast out to sea. Looking for a wave, no doubt. The way he's holding the board, my left leg is caged in. I can't help but notice how close he is to me as he holds the board steady like he promised. Holds *me* steady.

No time like the present to ruin it.

"So, your mom and your ex are close," I say, trying to keep it casual. "Was that your hopes and dreams?" Smartass oozes from my voice.

He turns to look up at me. "Scarlett?" For a moment I think I've stumped him. But his eyes sparkle with amusement. "I was *hoping* for a civil breakup, so yeah, I suppose so."

My brain glitches at this.

Civil breakup? That's a thing?

When my mom found out my dad was cheating on her, she tore the fucking house down, declaring, "Sex ruins everything." Then she did a 180 kick-flip declaring that they—my parents— were still "madly in love." Then she cried so much I thought she was going to drown in her own tears. And then Dad told me love was unrealistic and left.

So my mom became a sex therapist. And my dad stayed true to his word. Until now.

"The divorce wasn't civil, was it?" Xander says, reading my mind. I hate this new development between us.

I smile through gritted teeth. *No.*

He lifts his hand off the board and squeezes my knee. *I'm sorry.*

"Why did you want to become a lawyer?" I say, changing the subject. *Hopes and dreams.*

"I feel sexy and powerful in a good suit," he says, deadpan. I can't help but laugh at this, and I'm grateful that he cut the somber mood with a joke.

"Come on," I say, splashing him. "Be for real." The water drips down his face, catching on his long eyelashes. He locks eyes with me and the fucking look on his face tells me everything that's about to happen.

"No, I'm sorry," I say, raising my hands up, but it's too late. Xander pulls me in. I squeal as my body hits the water, a shock-wave reverberating through every cell.

When I surface, I'm inches from Xander. Suddenly, I'm not so cold.

"Was that necessary?" I say, wiping the hair from my face. No fancy hair whip for this kook.

"You have to get used to falling if you want to stand," he says, oh-so-wise. I feel the water whirl around my waist as his arms methodically move back and forth. "But I got you."

That last line makes me squirm, so I ignore it. "The question, Miller." I raise my eyebrows.

Xander kicks out on his back and creates a little distance between us.

"I love being my clients' trusted adviser. I love becoming a part of their lives. I love helping smooth the path forward," he says. It's so simple yet so profound, my mind boggles. Not because of the fat paycheck? Wait—are lawyers *nice*? Do they not go around laughing that they got some murdering bitch off on a technicality, only to release her back on the streets for her to kill again?

"People tell me their deepest, darkest secrets. I not only keep them, I use them for good," he says, turning onto his stomach and swimming back to me.

It's so sincere I have no choice but to believe him, and it gets me wondering. If Xander is busy being everyone's confidant, offering his shoulder for everyone to unload on, who does *he* have?

"That sounds like a blessing and also a burden," I say, unable to keep my observations to myself. He pulls up right in front of me.

"How so?" he says, eyes roaming my face. This time, we stay exactly where we are. Close.

"Who do you spill your deepest, darkest secrets to?" I ask, a little quieter this time. The idea that Scarlett was once that person hits me. The idea that he'll find someone else hits me harder. And the idea that I might want to be that person hits me so hard I feel sick. Sucker punched.

He breaks contact first, looking back out to the ocean like it has the answers, when he says sharply, "Get up."

"What?" I say, confused by the change in tone and delivery.

"The board. Get on the board now," he says, tearing his eyes off the horizon. They're lit up. "There's a wave coming."

In a flurry of activity, I lay flat on the board and am instructed to paddle. And not stop paddling. Xander is out of view, in the water behind me, pushing me. I do as I'm told and paddle.

And paddle. And paddle. And paddle.

And just when I think surfing is actually paddling, I feel it. The pull. The surfboard catches the wave and I don't have to paddle anymore.

"Stand up!" I hear Xander shout from behind me.

Here goes nothing. I press my arms into a push-up position, like Xander showed me on the beach, and I'm on my feet. Somehow, I'm on my feet and I'm fucking surfing.

Holy shit.

I can hear Xander cheering from behind me. And I look ahead and see Eva and Scar on the beach cheering too.

My mind clears. All the overthinking, gone. My past quietens down. My rules don't matter.

In this moment, it's just me and the wave.

Supporting me. Lifting me up. Carrying me.

Bed Chemistry

It's so liberating. And it's all because of one man.

I turn around and throw my hands up at Xander to celebrate and immediately fall off.

A moment later, Xander pops up next to me. Did he just surf without a board? I don't care.

"I did it!" I say, reaching both my hands up for a double high five.

"Yeah, you fucking did," he says, high fiving me. "I knew you could."

"That was the fucking best," I say, jumping up and down on the spot until I jump directly onto Xander in a celebratory hug.

His hands slide under my thighs and I wrap my legs around his waist.

And then we just grin at each other until he cocks his head and says, "Want to go again?"

"Fuck yes," I say. And somehow it feels like we're talking about more than just riding another wave.

My heartbeat picks up at the implication until the moment is lost when he throws us directly into an oncoming wave.

CHAPTER TWENTY-TWO

"Can I tell you something?" I say, the words muffled between ginormous bites of my double-double burger. We're sitting in the parking lot of the In-N-Out on the way back from the beach.

I am fucking starving.

After I caught a couple more waves, I opted to sit on the beach and warm myself up in the sun like a cold-blooded lizard, which felt a little too accurate when describing my own heart after spending time with Xander, his mom, and Scarlett.

As the sun thawed me out, it dawned on me that Xander has more than enough love to go around and he doesn't need to safeguard it. It's just ever-expanding, free-flowing love.

This idea is so foreign to me that I focused on spending the rest of the time on the beach perving on Xander as I sent him back out to surf himself.

I saw him ditch Old Yello' for a surfboard that looked impossibly small to stand on to which I said, "Are you for real?"

to which he said, "For real" to which I said, "But how?" to which he said, "It's physics," to which I said, "I only teach chemistry." And so off Xander ran, straight into the surf, slicing through those waves like a hot knife through butter.

By the time he caught his first wave, I vowed that physics was cool.

So fucking graceful. And powerful. And soulful.

Just beautiful, really.

I realize I've been staring at Xander a little too long. I swallow. "I don't care for animal style." I look pointedly at Xander and his animal style fries.

"You're lying," he says as he scoops up a couple of fries that are dripping with saucy, melted cheese and hauls them into his mouth without getting any on his T-shirt. "Everyone loves animal style."

"I didn't say I didn't like it. It's just so messy, I'd rather not," I say, taking another bite of my burger, the lack of animal style sauce keeping it easy to eat.

"Story of your life," he says, shaking his head at me through a smile.

"What do you mean?"

"You deny yourself what you really want just to avoid the mess that comes with it," he says, and now I know he's not talking about animal style anymore. "But the mess is the best part."

This hits me right in the feels. "What do I want?" I whisper. The words are absolutely as loaded as the fries Xander is eating.

"You tell me," he says gently. I watch as his lips curl around his straw and he sucks on his soda. When I don't answer, he doesn't ask—he demands. "Tell me what you want."

It comes out low and suggestive. I tear my eyes away from his lips.

"I want animal style fries," I say so quickly the words almost blend together.

And before I can reach over and steal a single fry, he hands the entire tray over to me. "You got it," he says, taking my plain fries from me.

"It's that simple, is it?" I say, taking a fry and dipping it into the sauce so it's completely drenched before shoving it into my mouth. I look at Xander, who's looking at my mouth. Before I can reach up to see if I've got animal style smeared all over my face, he reaches over and thumbs some sauce off the corner of my lip.

Then I watch as he brings his thumb to his lips and sucks on it, effectively turning animal style fries into amateur porn. "Yes."

I take a sip of my soda, too stunned to say anything else, when a memory of Xander sucking on his fingers flashes in front of my mind.

I choke.

"You okay?" he says, leaning in to pat my back. The gentle, rhythmic patting has a soothing effect.

"I'm fine," I say, daring to take another sip of the soda that attempted to assassinate me moments ago. This time I swallow like a champ. "Just went down the wrong pipe."

Xander removes his hand from my back, and I look out the window. I just need a moment of not looking at him. A moment of not wanting him.

"I actually worked here during the summers to save up for university," he says, offering me more of him. I turn to see him munching on his newly exchanged plain fries like he ordered them. "I know the secret to animal style."

"They don't erase your memory when you leave, *Men in Black* style?" I say, trying to distract myself with banter instead

186

of acknowledging that as Xander continues to offer up information about his life, I continue to find myself gravitating toward him.

"I had to sign an NDA," he says, giving me side eye. "That's more ironclad than a neuralyzer."

I do a double take at him. *Really?*

He cocks his head. *What do you think?*

I flick my wrist as I backhand his arm. *Smartass.*

Still, I can imagine teenager Xander. With his curls popping out of the comically tall white chef's hat they make everyone at In-N-Out wear. Getting comments from the elderly about how polite he is. Every teen girl who came in secretly hoping he was on the register that day. So adorable.

So unnecessary to be thinking that.

"I wanted to be a chemistry teacher because it's the study of literally everything around us," I say, clearing my throat. Maybe if I start *talking* about myself, I can stop *thinking* about Xander.

Xander and his curls. Xander and his fingers. Xander and his lips.

Xander and his heart.

"Everything?" he says, chewing on the word. "Including the chemistry between two people?"

"Yep," I say, continuing to nod, nonchalant. "That too."

I take another French fry dripping in sauce and eat it, making sure this time I lick my entire lip. I don't dare look at him while I do this, but I feel his eyes burning into the side of my face.

"Can you explain it to me, Miss Ashleigh?" he says, and I immediately feel itchy everywhere. Because even though I've learned that Xander is a surfer boy, he's also the smartest person I've met.

I clear my throat. "Certain chemicals in your brain create feelings of desire, pleasure, and connection," I say, the same spiel I do in class except this time, my student doesn't fall into a giggling heap at the word *pleasure*, so I continue. "We have dopamine, serotonin, and norepinephrine, which help determine if you are initially attracted to someone." I look at him.

"So you were my shot of dopamine that night?" he asks.

I suck on my lip and offer a tight nod. "Yep."

"And me? Was I a shot of dopamine for you?"

I continue nodding. "Yep."

We hold eye contact and the way his eyes darken, I know exactly what he's going to ask next. I brace for impact. The L word.

"What about love? Is that a chemical reaction?"

"When we find a connection, there's an increase in oxytocin. This rewires our brain so that now we have an emotional attachment to that person," I say, taking a sip of soda. The only problem is, it's finished, so all we hear is my poor attempt at sucking the last few drops through ice.

Xander automatically hands his soda to me. I take it. But I decide that if he wants to talk about how oxytocin creates love, he can also learn about what erodes love too.

"And just as chemicals can rewire your brain when you're in love, stressors can break down those bonds and reshape your brain, too."

"Stress like infidelity?"

"Turns out, cheating's a real buzzkiller," I say, deadpan.

"Avoid the connection, dodge the oxytocin, and never get hurt," he says, perfectly summing up my rules. "One commando crawl at a time."

I look at him with an eye roll. *Touché.*

Bed Chemistry

He throws me a self-deprecating smile that reverberates in every cell of my body. Including my heart.

Ignore it.

Then he clears his throat and says, "I've got one more place to show you."

"Oh?" I say, more so to help move this *chemistry* along.

He dusts the salt off his hands and turns the engine on.

I don't know how much more Xander I can take.

After driving for a while, he turns off Sunset Boulevard and onto Hilgard Avenue, the stretch of road that houses twenty-three fraternities and sororities of UCLA.

And I can't control it. I'm back in the memory of the night we met.

*   *   *

I can't see you again. Sorry.

I stare at the text message I'm about to send to last night's hookup for what feels like the hundredth time in the middle of a frat house living room turned dance floor. My phone says it's 10:59 PM, which is college o'clock for party time. I should know; I'm in my junior year. But I'm no longer in a partying mood. My phone lights up again. For the third time in as many minutes.

Words of warning from my mom, printed on reams of paper, displayed across every bookstore in the nation, splashed across every magazine, flash through my mind: *Love and chemistry can't coexist.* She's right.

I decline the incoming call and hit send.

Note to self: Never fall asleep in someone else's bed. Never accept breakfast. And never *ever* get sucked into morning sex. It always gives the wrong impression that there could be more. But there's never more. Sure, he'll be hurt for a hot minute. But this too shall pass. At least that's what I tell myself.

I take a deep breath and slip my phone into my jean shorts pocket, then use my thumb to gently press my blackened eyelashes for a spot dry. Time to pull a Houdini.

Before I can make a beeline for the exit, a roar goes up in the corner, snapping me out of my shell-shock. I look over to see a pair of jeans and white high tops floating upside down in the air. Correction: 10:59 PM is college o'clock for keg stand time.

"Ash!" a voice calls from across the living room. It's Leo, one of the hot frat guys from Sigma Chi. "You're up!"

I try to wave him off, but it's no use. The peer pressure is strong in this one.

I lift up a single finger as Leo comes barreling up to me like an overexcited golden retriever. You do one hell of a keg stand and you're treated like frat royalty forever.

"I mean it," I say to Leo. "One." Then I'm bailing. Because no matter how many times I have to end it, it doesn't get easier.

I shut down my heart, which starts racing as my phone vibrates in my pocket. He's responded to my message. And I'm too scared to read it. Not that he'll say anything new that hasn't been said before. Whether they're begging for another chance or calling me a cold-hearted bitch, it's nothing new.

Rules be rules.

Post keg stand, I am ready to get out of here. Find a place to read this message alone, in peace. Maybe throw my phone without hitting a drunk frat guy.

Bed Chemistry

As I flee, I notice the makeshift bar out of the corner of my eye and swerve for a quick detour because that beer didn't even touch the sides. But there's something somber in the air.

The bartender is a generic frat boy with short blond hair, sunglasses on his head even though we haven't seen the sun since seven, and a salmon polo shirt that screams nepo-frat-baby. I wouldn't be surprised if he was conceived here. He's shaking a cocktail like he's pleasuring it, distracted by his deep conversation with another frat guy who's leaning on the bar in a way I can't see his face. Just a mop of curly hair.

It takes me less than a second to register they don't notice me. And there's a barely touched bottle of peach schnapps within arm's reach. I snatch it and pivot toward the door. Beggers can't be choosers.

In the warm, late-summer night air, I make my way to the quad and take a seat on a bench, creating enough distance from the scene of the crime so it's safe to remove the sticky cap of the schnapps, and take a large gulp. I choke. It's sickly sweet and so thick, it should come with a warning. Not to be drunk fast from a bottle in moments of self-preservation.

Not that I'd heed the warning. I take another large gulp. The quicker I get this down, the faster I'll stop feeling. At least that's what I hope.

The burning in my stomach is not from the sugar syrup they call schnapps—it's a knowing. An understanding.

Love is family. Sex is fleeting. Marriage is a sham.

I repeat it like a mantra until the screaming in my head stops.

"Hey," a male voice says, interrupting my trip down memory lane. Me, fifteen years old, upstairs in my bedroom listening to the yelling match between Mom and Dad I wasn't supposed to hear that went down the night she finally left his cheating ass. Annoyed, I look up and see the unmistakable thick mop of curly dark hair of the frat boy from the bar. *Busted.*

"Here," I say, stretching out the bottle, though I'm still not facing him, assuming the reason he followed me was to get the schnapps back. For what? Other than a toothache, I don't know.

There's a soft chuckle, and I turn back around to see him taking a seat next to me. I return the bottle to my lap. His black ripped jeans show off his bare hairless knees. I glance up at his face and finally get a good look at him.

Behind his soft hazel eyes, is concern. *Calm the fuck down, bro. It's one bottle of schnapps from your $20 cover charge frat party.*

"Are you okay?" he says, ignoring the contraband.

I take a deep breath. Okay, so he's not here to reprimand me for stealing from the stash. And his concern is not for the schnapps. Interesting.

"I'm Xander, by the way," he says. "I saw you leave in a rush . . ." He holds eye contact with me. "With a bottle of schnapps." His lips tip up at the ends, making his eyes sparkle. "And I know no one in their right mind would actually drink that stuff out of pure enjoyment." His tone is so gentle, it almost gives me goosebumps.

For a split second, I consider being embarrassed. An objectively hot male, named Xander, with very nice forearms and hairless knees, has locked his eyes on me. But being embarrassed only matters if you want someone to think about you in a certain way, and it turns out, I don't care what this guy thinks of me. I'm never going to love him. Or sleep with him. *Love is family. Sex is fleeting. Marriage is a sham.*

I decide honesty is the way to go.

"I'm Ash and I'm a 'cold-hearted bitch.'" I let go of the schnapps to air quote "cold hearted bitch" without thinking through the physics of it all.

Xander catches the schnapps before it lands and places it gently on the ground, without skipping an intriguing eyebrow raise.

I continue, ignoring how his actions have closed the distance between us on the bench.

"I just cut someone loose via text message," I say, shrugging. "I'm an asshole."

Before I can launch into the worst bit about all this, Xander interjects. "I highly doubt that."

I press my lips together to stop myself from smiling.

"You don't know me. I could most definitely be an asshole." I cock my head and look at him. Say what you will about the schnapps, it's pumping confidence through my veins.

"What'd you say in your text?" he says, and there's a glint in his eyes, like he's testing out whether he can get away with teasing me. "I'll be the judge." And for the first time since 10:59 PM, which is approximately forever in breakup years, my heart feels lighter.

"Like you aren't already judging me," I say. At least he's pretending to be captivated. Which is all I need to continue. "See: peach schnapps." It's a segue I can't resist. I pick up the bottle and take another long gulp, grimacing at the end.

"You're right," he says, standing. "If you're going to drown your sorrows, don't do it with that."

I glance up at him and his ripped jeans and white T-shirt. He runs his hand through his hair, but his curls can't be tamed. They flop back in place. It's adorable. I notice a small tattoo on his bicep. A blue swallow. Cute. And hot. Plus, he's got a personality. All things that any sane human woman would want in a guy. And then, he flashes me his dimpled grin that, when combined with those curls, makes my stomach bottom out.

"Let me buy you a real drink," he says, taking the schnapps out of my hands and discarding it in a conveniently located garbage can. "Then you can tell me all about exactly what makes you an asshole. I'm curious."

And for some reason, I find myself nodding.

Five minutes later, we're sitting at a hole-in-the-wall Mexican bar off campus. One that's imperceptible to university students who favor ramen and stealing food from the dining hall, which is a total rookie mistake because the drinks are cheap and they don't card here. I'll never tell. Xander found it the first night of O week when he was craving tacos.

"Two margaritas," Xander says, giving me a gentle bump in anticipation, as if to say, you're about to drown those sorrows real good. Funny thing, on the walk over, I hadn't thought about the breakup. Or my mom. Or The Cheating.

I learned about Xander.

For instance, I learned that he isn't a frat boy. He's a junior, like me. He's just got that raw charisma that sucks even upper classmen into his orbit. And he's majoring in criminal justice. I want to make a joke about that, but somehow the words escape me. Instead, I can't stop thinking about how my cells are vibrating at the direct contact.

The bartender slides two salt-rimmed margaritas across the bar. Xander and I clink our glasses, and each take a sip at the same time.

"Holy wow," I say, my mouth still watering, wanting more. The most interesting alcohol I've had so far has been White Claw Citrus Squeeze. This is something else.

"Right? Sweet, sour, salty, bitter—sounds like a Taylor Swift breakup song," he says.

"Sounds like chemistry," I say, turning the glass in my hand, like it's the subject of a thesis. Title: "Margaritas and the Effects on Happiness." As I take another sip, a voice in my head corrects the title. *Xander and the Effects on Happiness.* Shuuddduppppppp, brain. His lip twitches into a half smile, his hazel eyes amused by my response. I can feel myself slipping into his orbit. And one thing I know for sure: I can't.

"If we're going to hang out, I need to set some ground rules," I say, deciding to get ahead of whatever this is. I want to taste the margarita in his mouth. I also do not want to be sending a text message to Xander in the near future: *I can't see you again. Sorry.* I just don't think I'd recover. Something tells me I must protect whatever this is at any cost.

"Ground rules?" Xander says. I pick up the coaster stained with my glass outline.

"Do you have a pen?" I ask the bartender. He hands me one.

"Ashleigh & Xander's Rules for Hanging Out," I say, dictating the words I'm writing in my terrible chicken scratch.

Xander leans in closer to me. I can smell the freshness of the lime on his breath. It sends a shiver down my spine. A preview to what his mouth would taste like. I ignore it.

"Rule number one. No dating," I say. After I finish printing it on the coaster, I steal a glance at Xander. I wonder if he knows he might be the reason for this list. For me to get some self-preservation going before it's too late.

"Like for a month?" he says, and it comes out low.

"Forever," I say, matching his tone of voice. I bite my lip as I look over at him. He steals a glance at my lip, and I subconsciously release it from my teeth. He returns to looking me in the eyes.

"Fair enough," he says. This time, his voice comes out harsh, like he's exercising every ounce of restraint not to convince me I'm making the wrong decision. My pulse races. The chemistry crackling between us is undeniable. That is until I remember seeing a flash of bare legs on top of Dad's office desk that belong to Alice, his receptionist, and not my mom. His pants around his ankles. A fucking cliché. And a memory that has the effect of a wet blanket.

I remind myself that this isn't an emotional decision. This is strategic survival. And so I solider on.

"Rule number two. No sex," I say, the word *sex* lingering in the air between us suggestively. This time I don't dare look at him even though I feel his eyes roam my face.

Let's not linger here a moment longer.

"Rule number three. Never fall in love," I say, finishing it off with a very pointed period. Nothing like uttering the L word to a guy you just met to pump the brakes.

I hold up the coaster and examine it.

Ashleigh & Xander's Rules for Hanging Out
Rule #1: No dating.
Rule #2: No sex.
Rule #3: Never fall in love.

I smile at my handiwork.

Xander takes it out my hand, our fingertips brushing, setting off a chain reaction of wanting.

He places the coaster down and leans into me like he's going to tell me a secret.

"So, friends?" he says, and he looks up at me through his mop of curls. His lips are wet from his most recent sip. My body gravitates to his, already willing to discard the coaster along with the rules.

Before I have a chance to respond, the bartender slides two shots of tequila across the bar.

* * *

Xander cuts the engine.

Just like that, eleven years have passed and I'm brought back to the UCLA parking lot.

CHAPTER TWENTY-THREE

We flick through the racks of T-shirts at the UCLA gift shop. The repetitive nature of sliding a hanger to reveal the next piece of branded apparel has given me way too much time to continue my trip that memory lane.

We hung out for a month before the chemistry sent us straight to Xander's sheets, effectively ending any chance of a connection beyond what we did to each other and with each other in the bedroom. And I've never regretted it. Not once. Especially when half the graduating class who hooked up and ended up getting married are posting their divorces all over their Instagram accounts. *On the grid.* How psychotic is that?

I pull out a white UCLA Bruins graphic tee complete with the beloved anthropomorphic brown bear, our team mascot. "This one?" I say, offering it to Xander.

He looks up and studies it a moment before shaking his head. "Nope."'

I put it back. "Can you tell me exactly what you're looking for?" I catch the clock on the wall and know this triple-header of a date will be coming to an end soon and it couldn't come soon enough. The nostalgia has got me straight in the feels.

Xander ignores my question in favor of pulling out another T-shirt, this one with the stoner turtle from *Nemo* on it. It's got the words "Crushing It! UCLA Bruins" written on it. He makes a funny face. "UCLA did a collab with Disney?"

"UCLA *is* the leading arts and cultural center in the western United States," I say, like when I was back in my childhood bedroom reading the brochure that came with the acceptance letter word for word.

"Come for the degree. Stay for the performing arts," Xander says, quirking an eyebrow.

He holds the T-shirt up to me and studies it. I shake my head, letting him know that a Disney collab eleven years post-graduation is not the T-shirt he's looking for, even if he hasn't told me exactly what he's looking for.

Xander takes my cue and puts it back. "Does it matter whether I like it or not?" I ask.

"Sure it does," he says, like it's the most normal thing in the world. To me, it's another stirring of the feels.

"Surely it doesn't," I counter.

He shakes his head with a single laugh like I told the world's wittiest joke and continues to search the racks for who the fuck knows. And so I continue to flick through the racks of T-shirts.

UCLA Proud Parent. UCLA Mom. UCLA Dad.

As if anyone's parents would be caught dead wearing this.

Xander looks over my shoulder. "My mom wouldn't stop wearing hers for my entire first year." Okay, so I guess there *are* parents who would rather die showing their support.

"Found it!" Xander says, and just when I feel hope that we can wrap this up, I see him holding out a light blue UCLA T-shirt with the word *LAW* stamped on it.

I freeze.

That's the exact T-shirt I stole from Xander the night we . . .

The exact T-shirt that's sitting in a cardboard box in my storage unit, along with my graduation certificate and other random university mementos. Untouched for years. Leaving me completely unbothered. Until now.

Standing here, staring at the exact replica has me remembering the details of the night and the next morning that I've forced myself to forget . . .

* * *

We're sitting at the bar of the Mexican hole-in-the-wall like we're part of the furniture, which we basically are after a month. Xander and I are still relatively fresh when it comes to our friendship.

Every moment we spend together is a lesson in each other. As it nears midnight, our final drinks are made. Miguel, the bartender, teases us that this'll be the most lethal one yet. We laugh. He's right. We stumble off the bar stools and wander back to campus. We talk about our favorite songs. I confess my love for One Direction. He starts singing "What Makes You Beautiful." I give him one of those side hugs that's perfectly designed to continue walking. He asks me what my favorite power ballad is. I tell him it's "I Don't Want to Miss a Thing" by Aerosmith. He spins me around and we dance while we sing the lyrics slowly and softly until we break apart and air drum and karate kick our way through the dramatic final bridge and scream the rest of the lyrics until our voices are raw.

Bed Chemistry

After our rendition of "I Don't Wanna Miss a Thing," Xander stops, breathless. He grabs my hand and turns me to face him. "You're incredible," he says. The tone of his voice changes. It's low. It's slow. It's gentle. Even with all of Miguel's margaritas, I know this is an important moment. A defining moment. A moment where Xander is going to push this to a new level. And I'm scared shitless. Because I want the same thing. Because Xander is the most incredible person I've ever met. No denying it.

But I also know that even though from the moment Xander walked up to me in the quad it was like signing our names in blood that we'd be inseparable, it doesn't matter. It would never work.

Love and sex can't coexist.

And still, in the middle of the quad with Xander smiling at me, I start to think maybe I've got it all wrong? For a split second I think we're going to kiss and it's going to be fireworks and rainbows and unicorns. I look into his eyes and we're staring at each other and my heart beats louder, faster. It's spinning off its axis, gravitating toward Xander. My gaze drifts up, grazing his big hazel eyes. And his single curl that won't be tamed. And his perfect smile you know he wore braces for in high school. I want him so bad. I want to change my surname and believe in the social construct that there is "The One," and he's right in front of me.

And then we kiss.

It's like a kiss that's always meant to have happened. Like the whole entire universe rearranged itself for this moment to happen. It's slow. It's sexy. It's love. Love and chemistry. Xander presses his entire body into me, and I press back. My hands cup his face. It's practically game over for me. I'm done. Call me Mrs. Miller.

I end up in his bed that night. Rules be damned.

The next morning, I hear Xander in the kitchen. And I know I need to leave *now* before he sees me. Because I know if I see him, I will stay. And I can't.

I remember patient zero from my mom's book: my dad. And how fucked everything was after The Cheating. And I know I must protect my heart at any cost.

My head is having a drunken brawl with my heart. My heart thinks my rules are fucking stupid. My head thinks my heart is fucking stupid. See what I mean when I say *drunken brawl*? The eloquence. My heart tells me to go into the kitchen and just see him. My head tells me to avoid contact at all costs. My heart tells me we could work. My head runs off statistics about divorce. My heart tells me what we have is beyond math. My head tells my heart how we would end up cheating on each other. My heart hurts. My head wins.

So I search his room, high and low, for my own T-shirt and come up short. That's when I see his crumpled-up T-shirt lying on the floor. And so I take the opportunity.

I pull it over my head, refusing to let his sweet and salty scent convince me to stay, and I get on my hands and knees and crawl.

When I get home, Emily gives me shit for rocking up in his T-shirt. Shame on her. But me staying in it as we get high and I eat our body weight in ice cream? Shame on me.

It gives her the ammunition she needs to make inferences that I have to deny for weeks. *He did a number on you, Ash.*

He did no such thing.

* * *

I watch as Xander pulls the T-shirt off the rack—the exact fucking T-shirt I stole; does he know?—and holds it up against my body. It's oversized. Just like his original.

"It's perfect," he says, before walking toward the cash register. I trail behind him. Oh, he definitely knows. But if he's not going to bring it up, neither will I.

"Are you alumni?" The undergrad at the register asks before blushing as Xander throws her his best charming smile.

"Sure am," he says, his curls curling hard. "Want to look me up?"

"No, you're good," she says, through a nervous laugh. Of course he's good. After purchasing his T-shirt with a 10 percent discount, we head out the doors toward Wilson Plaza. With every step, I can't help but see the T-shirt swinging in the clear plastic bag. It taunts me.

"Why did we come here?" I say, opting to converse with an actual human being and not an inanimate object.

"It's where I met you," he says like it's obvious. Then he gives me a half smile. "And since you never really gave me a chance to get to know you then, I figured I'd take you back to the beginning for a do-over."

"Don't worry. You'll get a front-row seat of my upbringing at the wedding," I say, sucking the air between my teeth. "Get ready to cringe." It's supposed to be a joke, but the delivery is sharp around the edges.

"Hey." Xander gives my shoulder a squeeze. "I'll be a great date. Promise. I can't salsa for shit, but I'm not a bad slow dancer usually."

"Just no ditching me for a hot bridesmaid," I say.

"I would never," Xander says, shocked that I'd suggest he go against the plus one code. I stare at him a moment. "Hey, remember. I'm not one of your Bone It hookups. I got your back."

And this time, I actually believe him.

"In that case, I feel the need to confess," I say, slowing down until Xander stops walking and turns to face me, giving me his undivided attention.

"I stole your T-shirt that night," I say, tilting my chin to the bag. "I'm sorry."

A wide smirk spreads across Xander's face before he hands the bag over to me. "I figured you'd need a replacement after eleven years."

"You knew?" I say, reaching into the bag and running my hand over the soft cotton. Just like I remembered.

"The entire time," he says. He knew and he never once used it against me when he had multiple opportunities since the sleep study began. Because he is not like the others. And I know it.

I take the T-shirt out of the bag and throw it on over my tank top.

"How do I look?" I say, my eyes drifting up to meet his big hazel ones.

"You're incredible," he says, exactly like he did all those years ago. The tone of his voice is low and slow. And I know this is an important moment. A defining moment.

Because it's the moment I realize . . .

I like Xander Miller.

I like him a fucking *lot*.

I don't know how long I've been staring at him, but Xander finally says, "Are you having a stroke?"

And yeah. Maybe I am.

CHAPTER TWENTY-FOUR

I was supposed to be making Xander breakfast at my apartment. My way of apologizing, albeit eleven years too late. Or it's my way of congratulating him, for the five hours of sleep he got at the study last night. I haven't decided yet. But it doesn't matter.

Because I grab onto a fistful of hair and pull him toward me.

He throws me a megawatt smile, flashing his sunburst hazel eyes. And it's over for me.

He mutters something I can't make out right before we kiss, but I don't have the capacity to figure it out because he lets out a groan when our lips meet and I lose all sense of control.

I open my mouth and invite him in, and he doesn't waste a second. It's all teeth and tongues and hands everywhere.

It's three weeks of fucking with each other.

It's the memory of that night from eleven years ago.

It's how he feels right now.

Waves of want flood my body. And finally, I get to have him.

Xander's hands that have been roaming up and down my back cup my face as he presses his entire body into me.

"Ashleigh." Xander moans my name in my mouth before his tongue finds mine again. He tastes like candy. He feels so needy. He smells so fresh. Like brand-new.

And yet, when he bites my bottom lip—a move he did eleven years ago that had me mauling him for more—and a groan escapes me, I know the history we have is guiding us.

Old and new. An elite combination for getting off.

One of his hands finds my back and pulls me flush against his body. He's fucking hard already. The pressure of him straining against my stomach feels delicious. He finally breaks contact with my mouth to scrape his teeth along my jawline to my ear.

"Look what you do to me," Xander says, voice hoarse in my ear. The hot air from his breath travels the length of my body, from my ear to the pulsing between my thighs. The admission that he's on the verge of losing it from a kiss makes me ache for him.

"You already know what you do to me," I say back, as he sucks on the sweet spot between my neck and collarbone. There's going to be a mark there later. But right now, my remark is enough for Xander to reach his hand up underneath my T-shirt, his warm hands splaying across my back, holding me in place as he walks us backward, toward my bedroom.

Then his mouth is back on mine, and I tilt my head to give him full access. It sends him wild as he pushes me up against wall and devours my mouth.

With my back anchored in place by the wall behind me, his hands return to roaming my entire body. Mapping it like a trea-sure. He starts making his way up my stomach, his fingers now flirting with the lace of my bra.

Bed Chemistry

Just when I think he's about to abandon my bra and I'm about to chastise him for being a tease, he reaches the hem of my T-shirt and pulls it up.

The rich cotton of the UCLA LAW T-shirt I've been wearing since yesterday lands softly on the floor.

Xander leans back to drink me in. My checkered cotton shorts. My black lace bra.

"You're so beautiful," he says, his thumb rubbing my already swollen lip before he brushes the hair out of my face.

"You are," I say, and that's enough to end our mutual admiration because his lips are back on me. This time, he goes straight for my neck and starts trailing wet kisses to my collarbone.

His hands make their way to my back, expertly working the bra clasp. He hooks his fingers under the straps and slides them down my arms, leaving a trail of goosebumps in their place.

I watch as his eyes roam every inch of my exposed skin, unwilling to settle for just a piece of me. When he looks up at me through the curls, with his eyes dark and wide and a slight half smile on his lips, he says, "Even better than I remembered."

And with those words, I feel my temperature rising.

My bra now discarded on the floor along with my T-shirt, Xander wastes no time with his thumb and finger working one of my nipples while his tongue licks and sucks and bites the other one.

I moan as the sensation explodes throughout my body.

My hands fling to his hair, twisting and pulling, his curls the perfect length to tug and pull at. My back bows off the wall, riding the fine line between pleasure and pain.

"So perfect," he mutters, breaking contact before taking my nipple into his mouth again.

I am so fucking wet.

I grab a fistful of his hair by the scuff of his neck and drag him up to my mouth.

His tongue finds mine.

I finally regain the use of my limbs and push us off the wall, walking him backward, to my bedroom.

We trip over something on the floor, and break apart laughing for a second before Xander starts tugging at the elastic waistband of my shorts while I try to pull off his T-shirt, abandoning the mission to the bedroom.

A moment later I'm standing in my panties as I run my hands down his chest to the hem of his jeans.

He lets out a low sigh as I start to unbuckle his belt. Flushed and frustrated, I fumble the buckle until Xander's hands are on top of mine, helping me.

Then, he's naked.

My hooded eyes watch as he strokes himself. I suck air between my teeth in anticipation, but before I can reach my hands out, he tuts. "Not yet."

I drag his body back onto mine and attempt to redirect us to the kitchen bench, but he lifts me up and continues carrying me to the bedroom.

"For the last three weeks, I've been tortured by a bed. Do you know what it's like to share a bed with you every single night and not be able to have you?" His voice is rough like gravel, his pupils blown out. He doesn't stop walking me into my bedroom. "It's excruciating. We are doing this. In. Your. Bed."

His mouth meets mine, demanding and impatient, as he mercifully guides me onto the bed, his body following mine onto the soft surface. The heat from his body sends every nerve cell burning for him.

Bed Chemistry

Xander breaks from my mouth and trails kisses down my sternum, his fingers tracing lazy circles until he stops and looks up at me, a glint of mischief in his eyes. He hooks his fingers into my panties and slides them down my legs, and the anticipation of what's to come sends me feral.

I run my hands through his curls before bringing his face down to my stomach, but he doesn't need any encouragement as he starts tracing his tongue.

Lower.

Lower.

Lower.

At the last moment he reroutes his lips to where my thigh and hip meet.

I bite down on my bottom lip to stop myself from laughing, but the fun is quickly replaced with frustration when he jumps to my other thigh. "Don't stop," I say, pleading.

"Just savoring every mouthful," he says, holding his lips an inch from my skin. It sends a shiver all the way up my leg. Oh, he knows exactly what he's doing.

With one hand splayed on my stomach, holding me down, and the other one gripping my thigh, I feel his teeth and tongue scrape down.

Down.

Down.

Down.

His lips are on me.

There.

There.

There.

He starts gently. A trace of his lips. A hint of his tongue. The faintest hit of his breath.

It drives me insane until he finally opens his mouth and makes full contact.

At first, it's slow and drawn out. He takes his time, like this is his favorite thing to do in the entire world. Like I'm his last meal. Like he could stay in this moment forever.

I let out a moan, and I have nothing else to do but sink into it. No more thinking. Just feeling.

I relish in the build-up. Not wanting to rush. Not wanting it to be over. Not wanting it to end.

The hand Xander was using to keep my thighs wide lets go and his fingers swipe over me, getting drenched in the process before they're inside me, curling against my inner walls. The perfect spot.

Yes.

Yes.

Yes.

And right when I'm on the edge, he whispers, without losing contact, "Come for me."

The effect of pulling the pressure back sends an orgasm rippling through me—an ember turning into a wildfire. When I scream his name, Xander takes me fully into his mouth, coaxing out another wave of orgasms, one after the other.

Multiple. You don't get that from Bone It.

As I come back down, I can't help but let out a squeal. "Xander Miller," I say, laughing deliriously. "How?" It's all I can manage.

He hasn't come up yet so I dare to look down at him, and he's gazing up at me, grinning. "It's all you," he says, licking his lips like he just discovered his favorite flavor. Or that he's tasted it again after being deprived of it for eleven years. Either way, he looks euphoric, and *I'm* the one who just came over and over again.

"It's all you," I whisper back. And before I can freak out at that admission, he starts kissing me again. The taste of me on him is so fucking hot.

And then he's kneeling over me, stroking himself. "Condom?"

"Bedside table," I say, turning around to crawl up to the head of the bed, hearing a private moan from behind. I can't resist; I arch my back to turn around and look. Xander's eyes are on fire as he drinks me in from this angle.

His fingertips trace my naked spine before bracketing my hips. He leans down and kisses the dimples on either side of my lower back.

Then he looks back up at me, destroyed by the view.

"God, I want you in *every* way," he says, before lifting his body off the bed. I track his every movement as he walks to the bedside drawer. He rips a condom off the strip and in two seconds it's on. He's so close to being inside me and the anticipation turns me desperate.

He flips me onto my back and crawls slowly on top of me. There's a whisper in my ear that asks, "You still want this?"

There it is. An exit strategy. The disclaimer. We *can* stop. Just say the word.

The truth is, though, we can't stop. So I nod in desperate agreement.

"Tell me what you want," Xander says, not moving. Waiting for permission.

"I want you inside me," I say, almost whining.

And then he sinks into me and I feel him in *every* way.

My hands immediately find his shoulders, pulling his closer. The weight of his body on top of mine. The smell of his skin. The look in his eyes.

The curls blanketing out the world.

"Ashleigh." He says my name like a prayer as he slides a hand underneath my ass and pulls a leg up, angling deeper.

The position hits so good.

I look up and see the memory of him on top of me, his arms caging me, colliding with right now and—with the steady rhythm—I'm being nudged closer and closer to the edge.

I find his swallow tattoo and scrape my teeth over it before my lips travel up his arm where I lick at the sensitive spot on his skin between his shoulder and ear lobe.

"Fuck me," I murmur. It elicits a groan, sending Xander reeling.

Two words. One sentence. It changes everything.

Xander sits up on his knees, both hands holding my thighs in place as he watches himself get repeatedly coated in my wetness.

"Ashleigh." Xander says my name like a promise as one of his hands travels up my thigh and he thumbs me. "You're so close."

This is a far cry from the orgasm he pulled out of me moments ago. This is frantic. And needy. And chaotic.

This position reaches places not even his fingers could hit.

"Xander," I say, whimpering. I'm completely drunk on this feeling. I'm out of my mind wasted on Xander.

I need to taste him. So I bring his mouth to mine, pleading.

Give me the medicine.

One of his hands moves up to my hair and I completely lose my mind.

I'm peaking. *Oh.*

I'm peaking. *My.*

I'm peaking. *God.*

I'm coming. Fucccckk.

I feel him chasing my orgasm with his own, as he drives and drives and drives.

And then he buries his head in my neck and stops.

"Ashleigh Hutchinson." He says my name like an oath as he kisses me one more time. This one is slow. And deep. And he lingers on my lips. Then he rests his head on my forehead for a moment, eyes crinkling in the corners with pleasure. "How?"

And, goddamn it, I feel myself smiling back.

How?

CHAPTER TWENTY-FIVE

I wrap my lips around my fork and stuff my mouth with the ultimate bite of eggs Benny. There's a bit of English muffin, bacon, poached egg, and the hollandaise sauce that Xander made. From scratch.

"Goddamn it," I say, through an unsolicited groan, conceding.

Xander quirks his eyebrow up at me as I swallow my bite. "I'm going to need you to say it out loud."

"I'm only going to say this once—and if you ever dare bring this up in front of Emily, I will deny—but this is the best eggs Benedict I've ever had," I say, watching him over the rim of my coffee cup.

He's shirtless. His hair is mussed. His face is relaxed.

Getting laid suits him. The ache between my legs reminds me it suits me, too.

There's no denying it. Xander is a sexual magician, and there's a small part of me that kicks myself for missing out on this if only I'd stayed eleven years ago.

The sex. The breakfast. The banter.

The comfortable silences. The uncontrollable laughter.

But the smug expression that spreads over Xander's face reminds me that he's the reason why my rules exist in the first place.

He makes me feel. And feelings are bad.

I did myself a solid when I commando crawled out eleven years ago, I remind myself.

"Knew it," Xander says, as he interlaces his fingers behind his head and leans back, like he's *the man*. I shake my head, trying to keep my mouth in a straight line, but I can't. He's the exact amount of ridiculous that reels me in.

"All right, calm down," I say through a laugh. "It's just breakfast." I say it before I even realize the double entendre that fills the silence between us. I hold my breath as I wait for Xander to reply.

He leans forward, eyebrows furrowed, elbows on the table. "This isn't just breakfast," he says, staring me down.

Fuck. I am not prepared to deal with the consequences of my actions. Not yet. My heart rate picks up at what he's suggesting.

"This is a victory for the ages," he says, mock serious. I bite my bottom lip at the banter, loosening immediately. The way Xander knows when to be serious and when to completely mess with me doesn't go unnoticed. It's like he can read me. It's like he knows me. It's like he—I don't know. He makes it easy to keep him around.

"You've been waiting to gloat for eleven years?" I say, teasing. "That's depressing."

"Depressing or strategic?"

"Deliciously depressing," I say, picking up my fork and holding it out as evidence for just how delicious his victory is.

"What can I say, I play the long game," he says, sincere now. I know exactly what he's implying. It doesn't matter what happened between our first night and an hour ago. He wants me more than just sex. And I am choosing to ignore it.

Xander drains the last of his coffee. I glance down at his plate. It's completely empty.

This could warrant the end.

And still, I have no desire to commando crawl out of here, even though the moment I finish chewing my mouthful would be the perfect timing for Xander to walk back out my door and leave.

Sure, I'll see him at the sleep study tonight. I just know it won't be awkward. Xander has had a front row seat to all of me over these past three weeks and he's still sitting here. With me.

By the end of the sleep study—if I want—we could be waving goodbye for good.

This could all be so civil.

And yet, we are beyond that.

His eyes flicker to my lips right before a smile spreads across his face.

I reach up to wipe my mouth. "Do I have egg jizz on my face?"

"Egg jizz?" Xander says, delighted at my description of hollandaise sauce. His whole face lights up. And I mentally draw the number next to my name, like I'm the one who's won by making him smile like that.

"That's what my one and only attempt at making hollandaise looked like," I say, scrunching up my nose.

"You know, that is a very accurate description," he says, still smiling. "But no, you do not have egg jizz on your face."

Bed Chemistry

"Then why are you staring at me?"

"I'm just in awe."

"What'd I do?" I say innocently as I trace my tongue along my lip just to watch his reaction.

"You know exactly what you did," he says, his eyes flashing dark like he's accessing a memory and it's not from eleven years ago. More like an hour ago.

Him, on top of me. His arms, caging me in. My teeth, scraping the skin of the small swallow tattoo on his bicep.

I scrape my teeth over my bottom lip, in the memory with him.

"What now?" Xander says, reminding me I don't have to conjure up a memory of him. He's right here. And he's not going anywhere. But there's a slight pitch in his voice. He wants to know if he's the one who should be commando crawling out of here.

"Now, we watch *Criminal Minds*," I say, getting up and walking around the table to stand directly in front of him. His hands wrap around my waist and he pulls me close, burrowing his face into the soft fabric of the UCLA LAW T-shirt I put back on. My hands gravitate toward his mop of curls and I rake my fingers through them.

I don't know why or how, but what we're doing right now feels more intimate than what we did in the elevator, against the apartment wall, and in my bedroom an hour ago.

"Yeah?" he says, as he looks up at me through his curls.

There he goes, again. Being considerate. Giving me an exit strategy. Letting me know I'm the one who gets to decide. It's especially touching considering I'm the one with the rules that seem to be bending, breaking, crumbling down whenever he's around.

Elizabeth McKenzie

I don't know why I don't send him home at this realization. I guess I'm not done with him just yet. So instead, I interlace my fingers with his and pull him toward the sofa. "Yeah."

When he sits on the sofa and opens his arms, I don't hesitate and melt into the comfiest grooves of his body.

I am definitely in trouble.

CHAPTER TWENTY-SIX

A gentle knock wakes me. Ben enters and stops in his tracks.

I look over at Xander and see him asleep for a moment before he yawns himself awake. "Good morning," Xander says with another yawn. He proceeds to stretch his body like he's been out like a light for a solid eight hours.

He looks different.

Like this is the first time I've seen him.

I thought waking up to his bed face when he slept a solid four hours was something else. But today, holy mother of hotness.

Xander is so relaxed even his curls seem to have relaxed into a soft wave. All the furrows and lines that used to be etched into his face have melted. The red that once rimmed his hazel eyes— gone. The hard edge to his manner, replaced with a softness. The threat of a smile on his lips . . . permanent.

I know, without a doubt, that this person right here, is peak Xander Miller.

Xander Miller on a solid night's sleep.

It sets a dull yearning between my ribs.

Xander reaches over and lifts my hand to his mouth, dragging a kiss over my knuckles. The act has me hyperfocused on his lips and his fingers, turning the seemingly innocent kiss into something deeper.

Hotter.

There's a loud cough, interrupting us. We both look at Ben, who for the first time is smiling while interrupting us.

"Xander, you slept for a total of seven hours. That's your new record," Ben says, ready to replace his previous announcement to the Guinness World Records with this one.

I turn to look at Xander. A smile spreads across his face. His hardened features rearrange themselves in front of me. Relaxed, comfortable—happy, even.

"How?" I say, not taking my eyes off Xander even while I talk to Ben.

"I'd say somewhere between his cognitive behavioral therapy sessions and his new sleep habits," Ben says, flipping through his charts, even though he clearly already knew the answer. "And you," he adds.

"Me? How did *I* help Xander fall asleep?" I haven't had coffee yet. I can't be expected to have a filter.

"You know, coming here with me, being a supportive girlfriend," Xander says, cutting Ben off before he can answer. Right. Play along, I remind myself.

Ben nods. "I'm sure that's part of it. It also likely has something to do with the feeling of safety Xander has around you. His cortisol levels lower significantly as the night goes along."

I nod. It's all I can manage.

I tune out the rest of whatever Ben is yammering on about. *He feels safe around you.*

The funny thing is, after yesterday, I feel safe around Xander too.

"Thanks, Ben," Xander says.

As we leave the sleep study, Xander takes my hand and leads me out. We walk in silence until we get to his car, where he spins me around to face him. Then he puts his hands on his knees, crouching down so my whole world is Xander and his curls, and says, "You good?"

Am I good? I'll be good when we skate right over the feelings and get this banter bandwagon back together. Not let a silly little comment from Ben ruin a good thing.

We fuck real good.

And Xander now sleeps real good.

So I look up at him and let a smartass smirk grow across my face. "All you needed was a good lay for a good night's sleep," I say, joking.

His eyes narrow on me for a moment before his lips curl up at the ends. "I've had plenty of great lays over the years."

Ouch.

Why the fuck did that hurt? An image of Scarlett flutters behind my eyelids. She's on her knees, doing things to Xander that I like doing. Jealousy burns through my body.

Ignore it.

Xander stands to his full height and rubs his hands through his hair, but his curls aren't playing. They stick up everywhere.

Neither of us speaks for a moment.

Are we fighting?

"Ash," he says, caving first, the smartass replaced with softness. "I needed you," he says, serious like the heart attack I feel I'm about to have.

Feelings.

Safety.

Need.

Nope. The words spur me on.

"You needed a warm body," I say, trying to joke my way out of this.

"Really?" Xander's eyebrows shoot up, unimpressed with me. "Don't do that."

What? I've been honest the entire time about my rules.

"Do what?"

"Don't reduce whatever this is"—he points between us—"to a warm body."

"Xander, we're fake dating. You know that, right?" I implore him to agree with me. That the only real thing about what we have is the orgasms. "It's not real." I just stare at him.

Then he leans forward like he's about to pop the car door for me like he always does, but instead, his lips crash into mine. He pushes me hard up against the car door, demanding. My lips part and I willingly let him in. His fingers find my hair and he grabs the back of my neck. I tilt my head back, giving him access to all of me.

Showing him just how much I need him.

He pushes his hips into me. And the combination of the cool metal of his car door and the heat coming off his body has me feeling hot and cold and horny all over.

I moan. And that's enough for him to pull back.

"Tell me that was fake," he says, his voice rough like gravel. His fingers gently slide over my swollen lip.

Proof.

I stare at him. Not answering. Because how I feel in this moment isn't fake. But I'm not about to tell him that.

* * *

"EMILY!" I scream at my reflection in absolute horror.

I drop my kohl jet-black eyeliner into the bathroom sink and spin around as she comes running in. It's ten AM and I'm sweating like I've just taken a hot yoga class—which I would never *ever* do. Because no one needs to sweat that much. But here I am, taking boob sweat to the next level.

I've spent the last forty minutes trying to mimic Taylor Swift levels of winged eyeliner perfection, and in a dangerous game of trying to get flawless symmetry, the line got wildly out of control, and here I am looking more like the newest member of KISS about to embark on their "farewell" tour. *The no really, we mean it, we're never playing again (jokes we'll be back when the money runs out) tour.*

Em appears in the doorway of the bathroom and her eyes dart around my face, surveying the situation. Her expression tells me all I need to know. I'm a mess.

"I was gone three minutes," she says, shaking her head. "How is this even possible?"

I'm nervous, okay. Not that I say it out loud. The truth is, I've been a nervous fucking wreck since the realization hit me sometime between fucking Xander and snuggling him.

I don't just *like* Xander Miller. I have a *debilitating crush* on Xander Miller.

And I haven't told Em any of this.

And so I just sit, unnaturally still, on my hands so I don't fidget. Avoiding eye contact at all costs.

I'm completely and utterly obsessed with Xander, who I am constantly doing things with that not only break my rules but are illegal to my lifestyle.

I am a criminal.

If my mom found out, I'd be shunned. No, I'd be donated to science. How did a Hutchinson contract *feels*?

And on top of that, while I may have dabbled in acting to secure my spot inside the sleep study, for the past seven days, I have acted *professionally*, pretending Xander doesn't take up every single all-consuming thought. I have acted *competently*, like Xander doesn't light me up like a pinball machine every time he smiles at me. I have acted *skillfully*, as though Xander doesn't make my heart beat wildly out of control.

And now, I must maintain this level of mastery while I get Em to fix my face for the wedding.

The wedding that is happening today.

Today being the day I thought maybe, just maybe, I could master the winged eyeliner look. When will I learn that a high-stakes makeup situation is not the time to even try?

The intensity of the situation also means I now need to redo my hair—and the clock is ticking. Xander is picking me up in an hour and my hair, which forty minutes ago had a casual wave that was anything but casual to create, is now limp and sticking to my face.

Em grabs a handful of cotton tips from the medicine cabinet behind the sink.

"Close your eyes," she says.

I do as she says. Em is the queen of winged eyeliner, which is funny because I'm the one who studied advanced geometry as part of my science degree before majoring in chemistry. Em took the concepts *I* learned and applied them to real life, very important world-changing situations—like matching winged eyeliner. She could probably start a TikTok channel dedicated to winged eyeliner and be famous in forty-eight hours, she's that good.

I smell the citrus tang of the mimosa on her breath as she gets to work, dragging, dabbing, and drawing the cotton tip over my eyelids. So we had a few cocktails. What's a wedding without a breakfast mimosa?

"Are you okay?" Em says. Before I can even formulate a response because how does one answer such a loaded question, she continues.

"I know it's some upside-down shit that your dad's getting married."

Oh. Right. *That's* what she thinks I'm worried about.

I fling my eyes open, and there's a kindness in hers, letting me know she's here and she's not going anywhere. Truthfully, I haven't had an opportunity to think about Dad getting married. Not when Xander is consuming my every thought.

When I don't say anything, Em's face splits into a shit-eating grin. She's onto me. "You *boned* him," she says, just straight-up calling me out. Her eyes sparkling with excitement at this realization.

I have never lied to Em before in my entire life. Sure, I've omitted information. Like how Xander and I have been *boning* for the past week. But now faced with having to lie, I can't. Instead of telling the truth, I reach for my half-drunk breakfast mimosa, my sustenance, and take a sip, avoiding saying anything else.

This acts as confirmation.

"You *like* him," she says.

I don't know what to say, so I offer a noncommittal *ppffftttt*.

This pathetic attempt at brushing her off is all she needs. "Holy shit, you *like* like him."

All I can do is blink at her rapidly as my heart answers with a single resounding *yes*.

"Ash?" she says, softer this time. So as not to spook the girl who stopped talking because she felt too many things and thought she was going to explode. I put my hand on my knee to stop it from bouncing, but she continues. "Do you want to *love* him?"

"No. I don't," I say, firm. I desperately do not want to love him. And that is the truth. Sure, I can admit I like Xander. But hearing her use the L word out loud?

I am biologically programmed to reject it.

Am I willing to accept this crush? A stupid hormonal thing? Yes. But love? Impossible.

"I haven't seen you this distracted since, well," she stops midthought like she's trying to remember, and I send a prayer up that she has no fucking clue. To no avail. "Since you came home from that one night with Xander," she says.

Her eyes are pinned on mine like she's daring me to argue with facts. And so I take that dare.

"Em, you told me that I didn't have to do anything with these feelings," I say, trying to remind her that she's known me for fifteen years and that track record should count for something. "Once the sleep study wraps up, this will all fizzle out to nothing."

She opens her mouth to argue and I shake my head at her, cutting her off. "Because feelings are always fleeting." And then I stare at her and wait for what she always does. Moves on from the conversation.

And just like that, Em lets out a heavy sigh. "You used waterproof eyeliner," she says, groaning. "Now close your eyes while I scrub a layer of skin off to fix this, Gene Simmons." I win. Although, it doesn't feel like a victory.

"Am I supposed to take offense to that? The dude spits blood, breathes fire, and tongues thin air while playing the bass for KISS, and has enough energy to slay groupies into the thousands? Thank you," I say, taking it as a compliment, and do as I'm told, grateful for the change in topic.

"You're welcome," Em says, and I can feel a fluffy makeup brush circling the corner of my eyelids. There are butterflies in my stomach as Em's words wash over me. The mere suggestion that I want anything to do with loving Xander puts me on edge.

"We'll finish with Dragon Girl," Em says, reaching for my favorite red lip pencil from NARS.

I do that thing where you partially open your mouth in a semi-relaxed fashion that is anything but relaxed, all so Em can draw on my lips.

I watch as Em steps back and examines her work. Her eyes roam my entire face before breaking out into a wide grin. "Done." The woman works quickly.

I look at myself in the mirror. I could cry. I won't, because I will not ruin Em's art, but not only did she manage to one-up Taylor Swift's winged eyeliner look, she also added a smoky eye and outlined my lips, and still somehow managed to not make me look like a clown.

"I look so fucking hot," I say, turning to Em, who's staring at her handiwork. "Thank you."

"That's all you, Ash," Em says, as she starts putting my brushes away. "When will you learn that the right ones *never* walk away?" Em squeezes my arm.

"Not true, but thanks for the pep talk," I say palming off her compliment. She's my best friend. She's supposed to say shit like that. "And thanks for being there. Always."

"Always."

* * *

At exactly eleven AM, my intercom buzzes. Shit. Xander's here.

I let him up and study myself in the mirror one last time. Em did good. I'm wearing the blood-orange puffed-sleeve deep

V neck, exposed back, cut above the knees dress Em bought for me. She did real fucking good.

I grab my clutch and head to the door. I open it just as Xander raises his hand to knock.

His hand is frozen midair while he takes in the sight of me. I don't care because I'm staring at him.

He's wearing a suit. It's a three-piece light-blue linen complete with white shirt. His hair is styled back into a coif and perhaps for the first time in his entire life, his curls are staying put. It's like they rallied together and decided they were going to play as a team today. And they're winning. All I can think is, why isn't there a "men wearing suits" category on Porn Hub?

Damn. Am I breathless?

It's only then that I realize I've got my hand on my own heart like a lovestruck teenager at a One Direction concert. *Get it together, Ash.*

We finally make eye contact.

And when Xander smiles, the edge I felt about the line I'm dancing on, about liking him, melts into goo. I start to relax, and I wish I could blame something else, anything else, but I know it's the effect of his smile.

His sweet, sexy smile.

Em's words echo in my head like a goddamn yogi mantra. *You want to love him.*

CHAPTER TWENTY-SEVEN

Dad is not fucking around with this wedding. It's at an estate, in the middle of nowhere, with a marquee, and a wedding planner. Nothing like an expensive-ass wedding to try and prove to everyone that your second marriage is "The One." We get it. You believe in love. Again. And she's worth it.

After pulling up in the mammoth driveway with manicured hedges, being escorted through the marble hallway of the estate and out the back to the sprawling white marquee set against tall green trees, and doing a quick scan for Mom, who isn't here, we skip the waitstaff who're delivering bubbles and make our way to the bar to order something a little stronger.

There's a lot of shit I could say about my dad. The lying. The cheating. The not making an effort with me. I mean, I could go on for days about the decisions that have led him to this moment and the kind of surface-level relationship he decided was okay to have with his one and only daughter—but I won't. Not today, at least. Because the bar at his wedding is off the hook.

For something that's basically a tent, it's six-star luxury. The twinkle lights turn the entire wall of every single type of alcohol and liquor you could imagine into a sparkling invitation. Leaning in to get a look, there's nothing that's "house" about the choices. They're all top shelf. The glassware is French and crystal clear. The bartender spins a cocktail shaker in his hands, inviting us to ask for anything we want. Anything at all.

"I bet his margarita would blow our heads off," I say to Xander, without realizing the trip down memory lane that's imminent on the other end of this drink.

I look over at him. I have to admit, he's the picture-perfect wedding date with his three-piece suit perfectly tailored to show off his broad shoulders. He even bought me a matching corsage. All reds and oranges. And he's got the same flowers peeking out of his pocket. I mean, he went all out. He pulled out all the stops to be here with me.

"I'm down," he says, his lips tipping up at the ends.

"Two margaritas," I say to the bartender before I turn to take in the scene around us. On top of the real trees, there's garland everywhere—hanging from the tent, wrapped around the chairs, on top of tables. So my new stepmom is apparently a plant lady? Got it. It does look beautiful. And the afternoon sun streaming through the real trees makes everything look golden.

"Okay, give me the rundown. Who's the annoying uncle we need to avoid? What's the family gossip? Who are we *not* talking to?" Xander asks, and I can't help but laugh.

"They're all irrelevant. Except my mother." I reach for my freshly made margarita and study it. Perfection. The perfect green-yellow that not even Pantone can identify. "She's going to eat you alive. Bottom's up," I say, taking my first sip. Xander joins me.

"Fuck, that's good," he says, in a low groan that's borderline inappropriate. I take three more big gulps, giving the bite of tequila and freshness of the limes a chance to wash away the memory threatening to flutter behind my eyelids. "I'm not worried about your mother."

This earns Xander another laugh from me. I admire his cockiness. We'll see . . .

A moment later I look down at my glass and besides the melting ice, it's empty. Well, damn. That went down too smoothly. I'm going to have to keep track. One down. I lift one foot off the floor to test myself out. In my block heels, an absolute essential for a garden wedding, I'm sturdy. I look over at Xander, whose glass has paused at his mouth. I watch as he takes a sip and swallows. Drinking from a glass has no business being this sexy. And yet all evidence points to sexy. My gaze travels up the thick column of his throat, tracing the lines my tongue has licked in the past up to his lips.

It's my turn to gulp.

I order two more margaritas and wait for Xander to take another sip of his first one before reaching over and lifting the bottom of the glass, tilting it so he finishes it in one go. Then I grab his now empty glass, put it on the bar, and pick up the freshly made ones.

"Here," I say, handing him one. "Let's go explore." And just like that, Xander reaches for my hand and guides me toward the estate.

As we walk, I watch Xander take a sip of his margarita and not spill any down his shirt. Meanwhile, every time I want a sip, I take a quick pause and sip. I know what my strengths are, and they do not include walking and drinking without spilling. And you know what? Xander stops with me. Never letting go of my hand.

"I haven't had one of these in ages," Xander says, taking another effortless sip as we continue to walk across the perfectly manicured lawn. "It's really everything you'd want in a drink."

"Is it?" I muse. I stop to take another much-needed sip. Silently I add, *And they taste like you.*

"Yeah, I mean it's got just the right amount of kick." He steals a glance my way, and there's a smirk resting on his lips. Like he's not talking about the margarita anymore. I snap my head straight to avoid further eye contact.

"There's a little sweetness." His voice softens at this. Like he's in a memory that I have no business knowing. Do not look at him.

"And a touch of salt to keep things *interesting*." I cave on this last line, looking at Xander, whose glass is paused at his mouth. The glass itself is sparkling clean, and yet as he winks and takes a sip, my mind is filth.

"You just don't come across that kind of perfect every day," he says so casually he should be lying down.

"So you're saying a margarita is strong but refreshing, classic but versatile, and always a good time?" I say like I'm the Patron Saint of Tequila. Like I'm definitely talking about the margarita only. And not Xander.

"The best time," he replies.

"Mental note: Xander likes margaritas," I say. It's all I can manage at the realization that this is it. The end is approaching. And I should be excited. Jumping for joy. In twenty-four hours, our sleep study will be wrapped up too. Rent will be paid. And I'll have the rest of summer to spend with Emily on the tennis court. Happy days.

I'm able to resume our exploration of the venue when Xander stops and puts his drink on the grass. When he stands up and stares, my eyebrow cocks up at him. One step forward and he's officially entered my personal space. On instinct, I sling my arms over his shoulders and run my hands through the curls at the nape of his neck.

His hands gravitate to my arms, softly stroking them. I stare into his chest and I can see it rising and falling. My heartbeat joins in. Faster. Louder.

My gaze drifts up, grazing over his big hazel eyes. And his single curl that won't be tamed. And he kisses me.

Delicately. Lovingly.

And despite my best efforts not to, I'm transported back in time. To our first kiss. Where he tastes like limes and a future filled with possibilities. Then, things turn desperate. And that hint of salt comes through with bite. It sends an electrical current along every single nerve in my body.

Until my parents flash before my eyes like a wet fucking blanket, killing the mood and reminding me why this doesn't work. It never fucking does.

So I pull back.

"Come on," I say, pulling Xander around the corner of the estate. And just like that the entire wedding disappears. It's like we've stepped into someone's private and very expensive backyard. There's an entire decking situation with a lounge set that leads into the kitchen bustling with people. Oh, and there's a freaking pool.

I walk up to an empty lounge chair and flop down, crossing my legs because this dress sits above the knee and therefore deep lounging is a high-risk flashing situation. I finish my drink and look out over the pool that's so inviting in the heat. That's drink two, down.

"When we met, you were studying chemistry. Why?" Xander says as he gracefully takes a seat next to me. Oh, so it wasn't just me that was transported back to our first kiss. Nostalgia is a hell of a drug.

"You know why. Chemistry is the coolest," I say, looking at him with a raised eyebrow. "You've had a couple of lessons now."

Instead of chasing that innuendo down a path I don't know I can come back from, especially being so secluded out here, he doubles down on the question. "Why did you want to *teach* it?"

This time every ounce of attention is on me. My skin prickles as his eyes focus only on me. I look down at my glass. The ice is drowning itself as it melts. I take a sip, hoping for a little more courage.

"So my students would always know they had at least one person who was betting on them," I say, averting my gaze to the pool. "I know what it feels like when your parents are preoccupied with a different fight every night and all you want is help with your homework. All you need is someone who's invested in you." I get up and straighten out my dress, making sure it's sitting exactly as it should. "Come on."

"You constantly surprise me, Hutch," he says.

"It's the touch of salt that keeps things interesting," I offer, trying to U-turn our way out of this serious conversation.

"Nah, it's the little sweetness," he says with full sincerity. Then he holds my gaze until he can see that I believe him.

I smile at him as he holds out his elbow for me to hook in. We slowly make our way back to the wedding. More people have arrived since our wander. I'm always baffled at how people can have hundreds of guests at their wedding. How do you even know this many people? If this was my wedding—hypothetically, I know I'm never getting married—our invitation list would be me, the groom, Em, and the parents. That's it. Right now, with the amount of people milling around, I feel like I'm at a festival.

It all seems so unnecessary.

"How many people would you have at your wedding?" I ask. My eyes widen after the words are out. Now, I don't date, but I sure as shit know you don't go shooting your mouth off about *marriage* at a fucking wedding.

"At least four times bigger than this," he says, deadpan.

"As if. You're getting married at city hall." I poke my finger into his chest.

He immediately places his hand over mine, over his heart, and tilts his head to the side. "Oh yeah," he says, teasing. "How do you know?"

"I know you," I say because it's the only thing I can say to win this argument. And yet, he positively beams.

And somehow, I know, he's won.

* * *

"Congratulations, Dad," I say as I go in for a hug, daughterly love on full display.

People are congregating haphazardly around the newlyweds, trying to find their time to jump in and congratulate them before they're whisked off for professional photos, leaving us to our own devices with an open bar and waitstaff roaming around with trays of canapés.

"Thanks, kid," my dad says, embracing me. There's no denying it: Dad loves this woman. The poster boy for lying, cheating, and leaving is *in love*. I am utterly humiliated for him and his pathetic display as Keeley, my new stepmom, walked down the aisle. For shame.

I pull back, plastering a fake as fuck smile on my face and immediately feel Keeley staring at me.

"Ash, I've heard so much about you," she says, reaching out and giving me a massive hug. *Unlikely*, I think.

"Congratulations, *Stepmom*," I say, emphasizing *stepmom* to be inclusive. I mean, she does appear to be around the same age as my dad, so the title checks out. I internally eyeroll. My inner monologue has the snark of a bratty teenager. There's no need to cause her any grief. I still don't think she'll be here by Christmas. Being in love never helped my dad stay faithful before.

Tears well up in her eyes. She laughs at herself and dabs her eyes, which is the maid of honor's cue to swoop in and start patting her face with a tissue. That's my cue to bounce.

Xander and I were ushered to the front to sit with the family. By the time the seats were filled, my mom was a few rows back and it was Xander and me up front. The only daughter and her date. We sat through the whole ceremony, side by side, touching, my body settling into his. It was more comfort than chemistry, which I'm still trying to wrap my head around. How can I want to rip his clothes off one moment and need deep comfort the next?

There's nothing in Mom's book about that.

When they were about to say, "I do," I bit down on my lip to stop myself from laughing at the absurdity of it all. That's when Xander leaned in and whispered into the shell of my ear, "Do I need to distract you?" His breath felt like he was peppering kisses from my ear all the way to my lips. That shut me up enough to get me through to the official declaration of husband and wife. *You may now kiss the bride. Barf.*

Now Keeley's eyes are leaking and her maid of honor has executed an evacuation order to the bridal suite for a touch up with the makeup artist. I look out over the crowd and see Mom.

Holding hands with a man. Young. Polished. Smile rehearsed. He looks like she handpicked him from a catalog.

I watch as she touches his collar. She's acting like she's on a date. What the fuck is the bestselling author of a book that's essentially a legal injunction against dating doing parading a plus-one at a wedding? That deserves a no-holds-barred eye roll.

"Thirsty?" I say to Xander, who's watching me like a hawk.

"Parched," he says.

We grab two more margaritas—what number is that?—and raise our glasses. "Cheers," I say.

Xander cheers me back and then looks serious. "You okay?" he asks. "With this whole thing?"

"The ceremony? A bit excessive. The vows? Cliché," I say through a laugh. But Xander doesn't join in. He just watches me. "Oh, and the declarations about loving each other through sickness and health? Bullshit."

"You still think he'll cheat?" he asks. Again. Like watching this overly produced performance has changed my mind. No, I do not believe in a thing called love now that Dad's remarried. I see a pattern.

"I know he will," I say, determined.

"I disagree," he says, catching me by surprise. The guy who offered to distract me during said ceremony has opinions.

I study him. He means it.

"How can you know after watching a staged production?" I say, like we've just been watching an Andrew Lloyd Webber number.

"I felt it," he says.

"Felt what?"

"The love. It's real," he says.

"Okay," I say, not convinced.

I pause, deciding whether I'm going to argue instead of brushing it off. Xander looks like he's got more to say. "You're the expert." I sigh. "That's your official diagnosis of this *union of two people*, Romeo?"

"There's definitely yearning," Xander says, his eyes darting all over my face.

"You think he thinks about her constantly?" I say, the skepticism coming through thick.

"I think he craves spending time with her whenever they're apart," Xander says, eyes locking onto mine. And somehow the way he's looking at me, I get the distinct feeling we're not talking about my dad anymore. I watch him swallow. "I think she has such an intense feeling of joy when she's with him that she can also feel a bit unsure, because it feels so strong."

I do not.

"I bet she's dynamite in the sack," I say, going for a redirect.

"Is that what's happening between us?" Xander says, ignoring my attempt to put a visual in his head he can't come back from. "Just sex?"

The words hang between us, almost contradictory, considering we've been doing a lot more than "just sex" over the past few weeks. A slow, queasy roll starts in my stomach and I wish I could blame the margarita. I really do. But I know I'd be lying to myself. Because I didn't spend my college years training my insides to withstand copious amounts of cheap alcohol to not stomach the best margarita of my life.

"Hello, darling," my mom purrs, interrupting the game of truth or dare—hold the dare—we were playing. She holds my shoulders before going in for a two-cheek kiss and then moving onto more important matters like greeting Xander, also known as the very first male specimen I've ever introduced to her. She grabs him by the biceps and looks him up and down. "Aren't you gorgeous," she says, by way of greeting.

"That's because you can see your reflection in my sunglasses," Xander says, sending the compliment right back to her, and she eats it up. She's wearing a gold sequin wrap dress, hair big and curly, and makeup natural. She does look gorgeous.

Clearly she's not going to introduce herself. "Mom, this is Xander," I say. "Xander, this is my mom, Hillary."

Xander gives her the megawatt smile that makes grown-ass women melt.

I look around for her date, who's nowhere to be seen. Getting drinks, I presume. "Where's your date?" I ask, interrupting this introduction.

"He's not my date," she says.

"If not your date, why date-shaped?" I say. Mom stares at me like I'm speaking gibberish. I try again, using words she'll most definitely understand. "Unless you brought a fuck buddy to a wedding?"

"Ashleigh, watch your tone," Mom says, warning me.

More wedding guests I don't know have congregated around us. Like without the bride and groom, the next of kin is where the party's at.

"Beautiful ceremony," Mom says to no one in particular. I stare at her. Is she high right now? "Love is such a gift."

And with that comment, a laugh slips out of me. I can't control it. And so I laugh again. Because if I don't, I'm going to lose it.

"What's so funny?" Mom says, tilting her head at me.

"What a joke," I say, disdain dripping through every vowel and consonant.

"What do you mean?" There's an edge to her voice. Another warning. But the therapist in her can't help herself.

"Love is a scam," I say, quoting her back to herself. I believe it was from one particular night after they tried to "make it work" only for Mom to find a gold necklace that Dad bought. And it wasn't for her. Funny story, that quote ended up on the giant-ass billboard along the 101 when the Netflix series premiered.

"Oh honey, what do you know about love?" she says, shaking her head. Then she turns to Xander and says, "Can you believe Ashleigh has never brought a romantic partner home to meet her mother? You'd think she was incapable of love."

I don't hear the laugh that escapes her mouth. She's just a pantomime as the roar in my ears drowns her out. My breathing shallows. Before I am completely flooded by anger, I feel hands snaking down my forearm and weaving around my fingers. I look up and see Xander, looking down at me. Grounding me.

He clenches his jaw before turning to face my mother. "Hillary, I forgot to congratulate you on the success of your book, *Dating, Mating, and Masturbating*," he says. I know that tone.

"Thank you," she says, clutching her heart, completely forgetting that she just shattered her only daughter's self-esteem with her previous remark.

"I thought it was an interesting take on love, sex, and intimacy," he goes on. I snap my head to him. He actually *read* the book?

"You read the book," she says, impressed.

"I did," he says, calm like a sniper. And I can clock the moment in her eyes when she realizes this is not a compliment anymore. A complaint, more like. "Pity it wasn't thoroughly researched."

I watch as Mom's eyes dart around like Xander is airing her dirty laundry. Dirty laundry she put in an international bestselling book. And a reality series. And a social media account followed by millions. And a page-a-day desk calendar . . .

"Anecdotal evidence is subjective, unverified, and statistically insignificant. I mean, it looks good on the shelf in Barnes & Noble, but it's bullshit," he says, lawyer cold.

"Excuse me?" Mom's brows shoot up, like she misheard. Nah, more like she's giving him one chance to take it back.

"Your book claims love and lust are mutually exclusive, but neuroscience proves they coexist—you just have to set the right conditions," he says, cold as ice. "Your book is an autobiography at best. And a marketing scam at worst."

Mom simply stares at Xander. And I stare at Xander.

She's stumped. I'm in awe.

Then he delivers the final blow. "Why do you think Ash has never brought a romantic partner to meet her mother?" It's exactly like how I imagine he'd ask the jury to come to the most logical conclusion. *If the glove doesn't fit, you must acquit.*

That must be the final straw because Mom finally finds her voice. "Ah, I see . . . you're in the lust phase." There's a dismissive laugh as she delivers this. Her eyes skate down the length of my arm, where I'm holding onto Xander. And disgust creeps over her face. "Very common, but let's talk about what happens after the dopamine wears off."

"Oxytocin is what happens," Xander says to her without missing a beat. My heart rate starts to thunder at this love confession riddled with chemical theory. But he doesn't stop. "Love doesn't mean losing the spark. It means keeping it alive."

Then, he looks down at me like I'm the only person in the world and says, "This isn't lust turning into love, Ash. It's both. It's all of you."

Oh, fuck.

Fucking fuck.

No.

I try to look away, but I feel his hand on my chin. I stare at his frown, avoiding eye contact at all costs. Then he doubles down to make sure I can't play the miscommunication card. "I feel everything for you."

I shake my head at him. Repeatedly. Hoping the repetition will calm my nervous system down.

"I *want* you, Ashleigh. God, I fucking *want* you," he says, and there's a rich quality to it that cuts through the hum of the wedding as it fades into the background. Hillary who?

"No," I whisper. I'm a Hutchinson.

"And I *love* you."

"No." We don't do love and lust.

"Yes."

"*No.*" Even if I wanted to. I force myself to look at him, willing myself not to break. His eyes lock on mine. My heart beats so wildly out of control I think it's going to throw itself up out of my body and flop around on the ground like a fish out of water. It's official. He's staring at me. And I'm staring at him. And what we have here is a stare off. I count my breath.

One.

Two.

Three.

There is no way I'm losing this stare off. Not after his love confession. I refuse to acknowledge it.

"Let me love you," Xander says, again, losing the stare off. Again. I start to shake my head, to argue again, but he continues. "Things have changed."

"What's changed?"

"Everything, Ash. You know it. Everything's changed," he says, imploring me to . . . what? Agree with him? The only thing that's changed is that we fucked. A lot. And I enjoyed using his body like a pillow. A lot.

Still, I don't dare say any of this out loud.

"Your rules are officially outdated by new evidence," he says. The evidence being Xander. And his big, beautiful heart. Again, I do not say this out loud. "That's kind of the point of science, isn't it?"

"You don't know what you're talking about," I say, looking past him to really make sure he knows I'm brushing him off. But the truth is, he's right. He's standing there, real and honest, and when he says it's all of me, a little more of my certainty crumbles. Because I know he means it.

"Do *you* anymore?"

My eyes snap back to him. How did I not realize how close he was standing to me until now? His face is inches from mine. An invisible string ties us together, tugging at my heart. But here's the thing about letting go of rules. You don't just lose the logic. You lose the protection it gives you. So no, I'm not ready to admit it yet.

Because if I'm wrong about him, it won't just hurt.

It'll ruin me.

"So just to recap. You don't have any feelings for me, and you, Ashleigh Hutchinson, will never, ever be in a relationship or settle down?" he says, staring into my soul.

"Correct," I breathe out.

"Great. I guess you're right then, nothing's changed," Xander says, stepping back, and his face crumples. He looks irreversibly broken. And the immediate regret I feel now that he's put distance between us is palpable. "I've got to go." He shakes his head like he's shaking off *me*.

"They always leave." Mom's voice floats back into my reality and I tear my eyes away from Xander to see an almost regretful look on her face for a split second before she says, "You dodged a bullet, darling."

"Just stop," I say to her, while looking back at Xander—but he's gone.

CHAPTER TWENTY-EIGHT

Well, this is fucking bullshit.

I am sitting next to Xander in our sleep study bed that somehow has shrunken from what felt like a king-size mattress where I couldn't get enough of touching him to a single where I have to consciously be aware of every tiny movement so we *don't* touch.

After Xander left, I hung around the alcove where I awkwardly had to share the outdoor space with one waiter who was vaping like his lungs depended on it. In that moment, I deeply appreciated the addictive nature of social media because that guy did not look at me once. He just sat there, scrolling and vaping until his alarm went off. Then he took one last hit, got up, almost walked into me, and said, "Oh" before leaving.

The perk of being invisible is that he didn't see me spiral over my confrontation with Xander. Brought to you be the capital L.

Love.

Fuck.

The whole point of commando crawling out the door without so much as a "thanks for the orgasms" was so we could avoid *this*.

Whose idea was it to fuck around with feelings and find out while I'm contractually attached to Xander for the next twelve hours? Em. I blame Em. That's what friends are for.

I should be at home with Em. Talking shit about Xander. Drinking my body weight in margaritas. Celebrating the fact that I dodged the drama. I should *not* be here, discovering that if you concentrate hard enough, you can unlock the superpower to feel the air around every hair on your arm.

The side effect of this superpower is that when you think about said arm hair for too long, it starts to feel itchy. And scratching my elbow has me inadvertently touching Xander, who is keeping it very professional. He doesn't make a disgusted sound when our arms brush. Like my presence isn't even an inconvenience. Meanwhile, it feels like every single cell has gravitated toward my arm hairs hoping to cop a feel.

He was already at the sleep study when I arrived, which naturally means he's established the upper hand, thus causing me to second-guess every single breath I take.

My body feels so loud and obvious.

And like undesirable number one.

And yet . . .

God, I fucking want you, Ash. And I love you.

My brain glitches out replaying his love confession, sending my body hot and cold. I mean, what the fuck was I supposed to do with that? I'm a Hutchinson.

We don't find The One. We find family. And we find lovers. And they aren't ever the same person. And we're better off for it. We're *happy*.

Did I Google the neuroscience of love and lust in the back-seat of the Uber on the way here? Yes. For I am a fact-loving teacher who can't ignore science. And sure, Xander got me on a technicality. Because while love and lust are distinct they're also interconnected, meaning his love confession is probably true.

He wants me.

And he loves me.

But me? Hi. I'm the asshole. It's me. And this is exactly why doctors don't want you to Google anything. It's always cancer.

The temperature in the room drops significantly.

I don't know if it's the air conditioner kicking into high gear or if it's because I'm just a cold-hearted bitch, but I need to get under these blankets. The only problem is, Xander's lying on top of them, next to me, with music in his ears. Pretending I don't exist. Which is actually fucking perfect.

He offered a quick head tilt when I walked in. You know, the kind of greeting you give someone you haven't seen in years in the freezer aisle of Trader Joe's. The gesture that means you do not want, under any circumstances, to encourage any more conversation.

I try to pull the sheets back to climb under, but Xander is rock solid. That hard, muscular body weighs a ton. I'm basically half-under, which isn't good enough for the current state I'm in. I need to be swaddled by this sheet.

I muster as much strength as I can for one final yank, and I honestly don't know what I was expecting. Like yanking this hard was going to have the tablecloth effect, just slipping straight out from underneath Xander's body and onto mine.

Again, I am not a physics teacher, and yet even I know that was never going to happen. Desperate times, and all that.

I end up throwing myself off the bed, landing square on my ass. I look up at the ceiling, annoyed as all fuck. I swear to God, if I can get through tonight, the final night of our sleep study, I will—I cut myself off. I don't need to be making any more deals with Xander. Or with the devil. And sure as shit not God.

A moment later, I catch the sight of the curls before I even see his face. They're just hanging over the mattress. Then, his hazel eyes appear. They dance with mischief. And I ignore the fact that my heart leaps. I can't look away. So instead, I brace for impact. Then, I see his smart mouth. He holds it in a straight line and just when I think I'm out of the woods, he has the audacity to unleash a smirk.

Then, he pulls out one of his earbuds before saying through a laugh, "You good, Hutchinson?"

"I'm just great," I say, through gritted teeth. Obviously, I'm not fucking great. And I'm not talking about the bruise on my ass bone that's already starting to form.

His eyes dance over my face, just drinking me in. I removed all the makeup from the wedding. My hair is in a high ponytail. And I'm wearing *his* pajamas. Captain America boxers and all. It kind of became my uniform when we were—for lack of a better word—together. In theory, I should feel defenseless. But I don't.

Then, his eyes linger on my shoulder, where his T-shirt has slipped, exposing my bra, and his eyes flare like I'm a slut from the twenties exposing too much skin.

Now it's his turn to shake it off. I see him blink away that thought, but too late. It's now stuck in my head. He scrapes his teeth over his bottom lip. Of course he does. Nothing like being distracted by filthy thoughts about those lips scraping over my inner thigh when you need to *focus* on the fact that what we had is over. Fleeting and finished.

He stretches one arm out for the assist. And I stare at it like he's grown a new appendage.

"You want to help me?" I say, sarcasm coming in thick. I don't believe it. *I hurt you.*

"Yes, I do," he says, so clear it can't be misinterpreted. *I love you.*

"This isn't some prank?" I say. *Why would you?*

"No," he says. *I'm not like the others.*

I need to put an end to this emotional whatever-the-fuck. So I reach out for Xander's hand and he pulls me up.

And my lips crash into his. Hard. Hot. Heavy. *Stop talking.*

His tongue responds, dining out on mine like it's his last supper. I can feel him being sucked back into my orbit. He hauls me into his lap without breaking contact. My heart rate picks up and this time, I go with it. I let it beat wildly out of control. For Xander.

But the heart rate monitor starts going off. And it's over just as quickly as it began.

We just stare at each other, gasping for air, unwilling to move on from this moment. His eyes search mine, looking for an answer. Looking for everything he's wanted.

Looking for all of me.

And yet, I falter. Again. And he sees it. Sees me holding back. So he pulls away.

"I can't do this with you anymore." His words have the same effect as taking a cold shower.

"I'm sorry," I say, crawling off him. Because of course I ended up in his lap straddling him.

"It's okay. I can't force you feel anything for me," he says, accepting his fate. He returns the earbud back to his ear and settles back in.

Funny thing is, that's exactly what he's doing.

Making me feel everything.

There's a knock on the door, and Ben enters the room. It only takes him a moment to look between us before he says, "Is everything okay?"

Yep. Just fucking great.

CHAPTER TWENTY-NINE

We're back in Dr. Waitley's office. For the last time. Sitting next to each other. For the last time. Pretending to be a couple. For the last time.

Thank fuck.

I need my own bed. I need to sleep like a starfish and hog all the blankets and wake up in the morning feeling marvelous.

As we wait in uncomfortable silence, I sneak a look at Xander.

His jaw is locked. The dark circles under his eyes are back. His curls don't have the strength to look professionally mussed. He proceeds to cross his arms over his chest.

He looks like I feel. Exhausted.

No denying it.

We both didn't sleep last night.

There was a moment in the middle of the night where he whispered, "Are you awake?" to which I said, "Yes," and he said, "Can I snuggle you?" to which I said, "Yes."

I didn't realize his palm splaying across my stomach as he big spooned the shit out of me was going to feel so . . . lonely.

Like physically, we were connected. But that was it.

Before I have the opportunity to dissect that little tidbit, Dr. Waitley walks in with a clipboard, pages flipped over the top, like she just discovered the answer to Xander's insomnia.

I reach over to Xander. One last time.

His fingers intertwine with mine. One last time.

He offers me a short smile. We're in this together. Until the very end.

"It's interesting," Dr. Waitley starts as she takes a seat. "Your overall trajectory has you clocking in seven solid hours. Exactly like Ash." She beams for a beat.

"That's incredible," I say, just as her smile fades.

"Except last night."

I press my lips together. I glance at Xander. He mirrors my strained expression. It's obvious we've returned to our roots. Fighting. And I honestly don't have the strength for another impromptu therapy session. The trajectory shows Xander should be sleeping fine once I'm out of his life, so please just deliver the paycheck.

"We recommend Xander continues with his cognitive behavioral therapy," she says, flipping the chart closed and adding it to the pile on her desk. "But based on what we observed during the study, we saw a marked improvement in sleep onset and duration." And then she finally lets herself smile. "We're optimistic. If he's able to replicate similar conditions at home, there's every reason to believe that progress will continue."

"Thank you so much," I say, and it's the most genuine thing that's come out of my mouth since I've met this woman.

Xander squeezes my hand and I look over at him. *Thank you.*

Bed Chemistry

I squeeze it right back. *You're welcome.*

Then, the strangest thing happens. A slow-burning warmth spreads all throughout my heart. Not sparks, like chemistry. Like a golden hum. It's such an intense feeling of joy, I almost alert them to call the paramedics.

Instead, Dr. Waitley hands over a white envelope.

Signed, sealed, delivered. The money's mine.

Out in the parking lot, Xander and I don't linger.

We wrap up our goodbyes with an ill-timed handshake from me turned crushing hug from him.

Then we go our separate ways.

And that's when the yearning starts.

* * *

At home, I slam the front door behind me, sliding all the way down so I'm sitting in the darkness of my apartment, trying to process what the fuck just happened.

I mean, I know we just wrapped up the sleep study, but that's not what I'm thinking about. Every time I blink, I see Xander. And his dumb face.

Xander and his dumb curls, laughing. Xander and his dumb mouth beaming. Xander and his dumb eyes pinning me with a look so intense he might die if he doesn't have me right then and there.

And because I'm a sadist, I texted him on the way home. I kept it light, but of course, we can read each other like a book now, so it was heavy with everything I wasn't saying.

Thank you for the bonus. Read: *I miss you.*

Thank you for helping me sleep. Read: *I miss you too.*

You heading for a surf to celebrate? Read: *Can't we just, you know, fuck around?*

Heading to the office. Need to play catch-up. Read: *I'm sorry. I can't do that with you anymore.*

Oh, you working on getting a murdering bitch off on a technicality? Read: *Nothing has to change.*

Lol. Something like that. Read: *Everything's changed.*

Have fun. Read: *Damn.*

Three dots appear. Then they disappear.

My finger hovers over his contact name for a moment; I'm *thisclose* to just calling him. But to do what, exactly? Beg him to keep sleeping with me with no strings attached? He wants me and he loves me. He's right. Everything has changed. And that is the nail in the coffin of my conversations with Xander.

"Fuck!" I shout into the darkness.

"Ash?" I freeze at the sound of my name coming from the other side of the door. I haven't moved since I got home. I haven't even turned on the light. "You in there?" It's Em.

"No," I say, half-heartedly. I don't want to deal with the aftermath of Xander with the human embodiment of love.

"I have weed and Ben & Jerry's," she says, and it's not lost on me that she is throwing back to the last time I walked away from Xander, eleven years ago. Reminding me she's always been there. Through it all.

I sigh, reaching up to the doorknob and turning it without actually getting up off the floor. The door swings open and Em stands in front of me.

She looks down at me with a sweet smile, and without a witty remark about me sitting on the floor of my apartment in the dark. I love her. Why is it so easy for me to say it to her? Because she's family.

Then she reaches her hand out for me, and I take it, hoisting myself off the floor.

Bed Chemistry

I turn the light on and Em walks past me, making a beeline straight for the kitchen, rattling in the cutlery draw for two spoons.

I head straight for the couch. A moment later she sits next to me, pulling out a cute pink-and-orange tin with the word *Houseplant* embossed on it.

"You got Seth Rogen's weed?" I say, surprised. "Damn, you fancy."

"We've come a long way from our broke university days," Em says, opening the one called Pancake Ice. She already pre-rolled a joint.

"You mean you didn't have to go into Bong Jovi's dank dorm room for a baggy?"

"Free delivery," Em says, handing it to me. "Times have changed."

Nothing has to change.

Everything's changed.

I bring the joint to my lips while Em flicks the lighter, and I cough on the inhale like a fucking amateur.

I look over at Em, who holds my gaze a moment before we burst out laughing. Tears slip down my face and I convince myself it's because of the THC. But I'm not so sure.

"I love you," I say to Em as she takes a hit. She's much more badass than me, holding her own.

"I love you too," she says, turning on the TV. "You know, you could marry me, take my surname, and change the prophecy." She navigates to Netflix to find *Criminal Minds*, and we're greeted with the biggest jump scare of our lives: my mother's face. Her show is getting the promotional push thanks to a "Five Year Reunion" special attached to it.

We both scream. And then fall into fits of laughing again.

I don't know if it's Seth Rogen's weed, the fact that Xander is gone, or Em's proposal, but something in me snaps at seeing my mother's over-the-top veneers sitting inside a bullshit smile even I can see straight through. It's her eyes—they're the dead giveaway.

She's *not* fucking happy.

* * *

I need to talk to my mom. You don't watch (and rewatch) 324 episodes of *Criminal Minds* without learning that in order to catch a serial killer, you need to understand how they think. And since Mom wrote the fucking manifesto-turned-reality-TV show on what happens when you ask one person to be "all" for you, she's the one to give me answers.

In the formal living room of Mom's apartment, I wait. And wait. And wait. Don't let the word *formal* throw you. It's the only room in her apartment that feels like home to me. I've come to know the comfiest grooves in the chesterfield armchair I'm currently reclining in as I wait.

Sitting opposite me is her assistant, Annie. I use the term *sitting* loosely. She's more perched on the edge of the sofa, waiting for Mom to summon her at any moment.

"Annie!" Right on cue, my mother's voice punctures the silence. Annie is up before I can blink, which tells me she must have a killer squat at the gym, and leaves.

I pull out my phone and mindlessly scroll through my messages, landing on the text chain from Xander. His last message reads: Lol. Something like that. The subtext: *Everything's changed.* Fuck, it stings. Like a metaphorical knife has weaseled its way into my heart and is staying put. It's part of my body now. I have to live with it. And the pain. I have a thought that maybe I should just bail. That this conversation is too hard to have anyway. But the rejection message drives the knife in further, making my heart ache. I need Mom to comfort me, to tell me I did the right thing, to soothe this pain.

"Mom!" I scream after the waiting goes on just a few minutes too long. You can put the kid in a formal room, but you can't make her act like a grownup.

"I'm here, I'm here," she says as she rounds the corner, wearing head-to-toe athleisure. The boxy oversized T-shirt has big black letters that spell out IVY PARK. Of course she's wearing Beyoncé's brand. And of course she got the one item of clothing that shouts the brand at you from fifty yards away.

"Well, this is an unexpected visit," she says as she leans in for the double kiss. After remembering the shit she pulled at the wedding, I offer her nothing. "I have cake!"

And just like that, Annie appears around the corner with a small slice of thick white icing around three layers of *something*. And a teeny fork.

Great. Wedding cake. Arguably the most disgusting cake available to eat.

This day just keeps getting worse. I almost ask Annie to wrap it up in foil so I can rage eat the gross cake in the comfort of my own home when I remember why I'm here. Also, Annie has already disappeared.

"I need to talk to you about you and Dad," I say, surprised at how little my voice sounds. What the fuck is wrong with me? I'm supposed to be pissed off. Not regressing to a tween who's walking on eggshells around her emotionally unavailable mother.

"Oh," she says, like I've caught her off guard. It's only a moment, and by the time she takes a seat in the opposite armchair, she's composed. The whole scene reminds me of a therapy session. Which probably isn't far off the mark for today's impromptu conversation.

"Sure, what do you want to talk about?" she says, crossing one leg over the other like she's getting comfortable. There isn't anything comfortable about sitting with one leg crossed over the other. *Stop stalling, Ash.* Fuck. Okay, here goes. I take a shallow breath. The only kind my body will let me take.

"When I caught Dad cheating, I was devastated," I say, stopping, hoping she'll jump in. But she didn't become a *New York Times* bestselling author, international therapist sensation, star lecturer, and now TV host by not being good at her job. She holds the space and waits for me to continue.

"But you fucking lost it. All hell broke loose," I say. I feel like my core is shaking. Like it's been holding this conversation in for fifteen years and finally, I get to let it all out.

Again, she doesn't speak. Holding the space. I rush ahead, filling it in.

"I *listened* as you told me you loved Dad with your whole heart while simultaneously cursing his name." The shaking from my core spreads to my heart.

"I *watched* when you forgave him over and over again because sex is fleeting only to throw him out of the house after another affair." The shaking spreads to my lungs.

"I *took it to heart* when you wrote an entire book declaring that you don't have intimate relations with the people you love like it was sanctimony," I say, the shaking now spreading to my voice.

"That's why I walked out on Xander eleven years ago. That's why I walked out on him today. Your book, based on your volatile relationship with Dad, became my rules." I didn't realize I'd raised my voice at the end.

And then it hits me.

"And now he's gone," I whisper.

All because I walked out on him again.

Before I can control myself, I burst into tears.

"Oh, Ash." My mom breaks from playing therapist, gets up off the chair, and hugs me.

I don't know how long I cry for, but eventually, the tears subside. I pull back and look at Mom. To my surprise, she's distraught. It's enough to make me catch my breath. I've never seen her look perturbed. Not once.

"Ash, when your father cheated on me, I was absolutely devastated too. The only way I could get through the heartbreak was to write," she says, sighing. "And so I wrote the stupid book."

"The *stupid* book?" I say, my eyes wide at the confession. "Your bestselling *stupid* book that left millions of women worldwide 'uncapable of love'? Are you kidding me?"

I register the shock on her face as I quote the words she used to describe me at the wedding.

"I'm sorry, I didn't expect it to take off like it did. I wrote it from a place of hurt, and somehow it turned into a movement. I had no control over it."

"You didn't have any *control* over selling your book to a streaming network show for millions more?" I shout, the last of the tears vanishing.

"The TV show escalated quickly," she says, wincing. "I never wanted the book to be an anthem for how anyone—especially my daughter—chooses to live and love."

Are you shitting me?

"Hate to break it to you, Mom," I say, as my reality seems to shatter around me. I narrow my eyes. "It wasn't just my anthem. It dictated my life."

My mom has the decency to look down at the floor. But I'm not finished yet. "You know, your words made women everywhere so certain that the person they *do* actually love will leave, cheat, abandon, or hurt them that they don't even bother letting them in—like never *truly* let them in." My voice cracks on that last one, my heart flashing to all I've kept from Xander. And all he's revealed to me.

"I'm sorry, that was not my intention," Mom says slowly.

"So, you *don't* believe your own bullshit? Love and lust *can* coexist? One person *can* be it all?" I say, my frustration growing. She looks genuinely upset. But I don't care. I'm so angry.

"You father was my everything," she says, and this time her voice wobbles, like admitting that out loud is a pain she hasn't felt in fifteen years.

And there we have it. Even with the cheating and the heartbreak, he was the one person who was her all, and yet, it all ended in heartbreak, so who cares? She was right.

"Was it worth it?" I ask, but I know the answer.

I want to smack myself upside the head. I'm so embarrassed. Here I was, thinking I'd gamed the system. The system Mom told me was broken. I was never going to be heartbroken because I was never going to let anyone in. But the system isn't broken. It was never broken. It was all a lie. Fuck.

You either get heartbroken by walking away from the love of your life, or you take a chance on love—so why not have all-encompassing love? Even for a little bit.

"I'd do it all again if I could," she says, and silent tears roll down my cheeks.

Bed Chemistry

I stare at her, still trying to comprehend that I took my parents' relationship and built an entire lifestyle based off it to protect myself. I studied chemistry so I could rationally explain every feeling with science. I set the rules to see every guy worth sleeping with as an instant douche so I could remove emotion.

And it was all a complete and utter joke.

CHAPTER THIRTY

I hit the ball with such frustration it lands smack bang in the crotch of our tennis coach, Cody.

"Fuck!" He clutches his manhood as he goes down. All we see is his sandy-blond hair as he curls up in a ball. "You've got a serve on you," he says, wheezing from the ground.

"You weren't using those anyway, right?" I say, calling out from our side of the tennis court. Oh, I am in a mood.

And because Cody didn't wake up and choose violence today, he raises a thumb up, but he's more like rolling around on the court, withering in pain than A-okay. I turn my back on him and walk back to the baseline.

"Let me get you some water," Em calls out, then grabs me by the arm and pulls me toward our water bottles on the edge of the court. Oh great, now Em's in a mood, too. This'll be fun.

"Was that necessary?" Em hisses. She was planning on asking him for drinks—and most likely more—after our lesson.

"I'm sure you'll still be able to play with his balls later," I say, dismissing her. I reach for my water bottle, but she slaps it out of my hand before I take a sip. Before I can chastise her, she beats me to it.

"What the fuck is going on?" Em says, standing with her hands on her hips. I stare at my water bottle that rolls from left to right until it finally stops. Then, I look at her, and her face morphs from pissed-off to concerned. "What happened between you and Xander?"

She picks up my water bottle and hands it to me.

I take a sip then tell her everything.

Every kiss. Every laugh. Every snuggle.

The wedding. Xander's confession. Me walking off on him. Again.

And most importantly, I tell her about Mom admitting her entire book is a fucking hoax.

When I'm done, Em is silent. And then she lets out a whistle. "Holy shit. You just had a reckoning with your rules."

I nod. "I mean, part of me still thinks I was onto something back then. That I wasn't entirely wrong. That my mom wasn't entirely wrong. Because I haven't had my heart broken in eleven years. So I must have done something right—"

"Really?" Em says, interrupting me. "You think you haven't been walking around with a broken heart?" Sarcasm drips off every word. I proceed to ignore the subtext.

"Until now," I say. "No."

"Bullshit."

"Excuse me?"

"You are full of shit," Em says, enunciating every word. "You've heard me say this in one form or another over the years, but I'm going to say it again."

Oh fuck, here we go.

"Your parents' relationship was so brutal that you decided love means war. And now you're blowing yourself up to stay true to some thought formed when your brain wasn't even fully formed. You're willing to ignore love, real love, because of that?"

"Who said anything about love?" I say, pumping the brakes on this conversation.

"You're joking, right?" Em says, eyebrows raised.

"I'm dead-ass serious."

"You're in love with Xander," Em says.

"What?" My heart squeezes so hard I almost join Cody on the ground.

"*Love.* You know, a profoundly tender, passionate affection, often mingled with sexual desire, for another person," Em says, and I wouldn't be surprised if that's the actual definition in the dictionary. Fucking English teacher.

"I didn't think that was possible," I say.

"Of course you didn't. You've been spoon-fed bullshit by your mother for the past fifteen years," she says. Well, that is one thing we can agree on.

"Love is not just possible. True love can last a lifetime," Em says.

I let the words wash over me.

Eleven years isn't a lifetime, but it has felt like forever.

Holy shit.

"I'm in love with Xander," I say, blinking.

And our first night together comes flooding back, all encompassing.

The heat coming off Xander's body, fanning the flames I feel inside. The moment I put my hand on his heart to feel his heartbeat. Fast but steady. Like he's never been so sure of anything in his entire life. He was all in. All. In.

I blink, and there are tears in my eyes. Because the truth is, in that moment, I was all in too. But here I am eleven years later, with a fuck-ton of excuses, half in. Only half in with anyone. Only ever half in with Xander. And this hurts the most. The fact I was only brave enough to give Xander half of me.

My heart shudders.

* * *

Let me tell you, finding out you're in love with someone is the worst. Actually, scrap that. Finding out you're in love with someone you hurt is the actual fucking worst.

That's why I'm rotting on the couch.

No *Criminal Minds*. Just moping.

After Emily nursed Cody's crotch back to health with an assortment of cold compresses, he bounced right back, completing our first lesson. And before Em slinked off to drinks with him, she pulled me aside to double, triple, quadruple check I was okay.

When I asked her why I wouldn't be okay, she said she'd called my name like ten times. Turns out, being in love is a full-time job. A massive distraction. An obsession. An addiction.

Still, I gave her my blessing to go get dicked down by Cody and made my way home.

"You're going to get him back," she'd called over her shoulder, trying to reassure me.

And that's exactly what I'm *not* doing. Because there's a small doubt that's crept up now that my dumbass heart is involved.

It was over then. And it's over now.

A knock on the door jolts me out of my mope. If this is Mom, coming with more wedding cake as a way to make amends, I'm going to lose it.

I drag my feet to the door and fling it open with an air of irritation, only to see Xander standing there.

"Hey," he says. His voice comes out rough. My breath hitches at the strain in his voice.

I rake my eyes over him. He's got on his classic white T-shirt, bare forearms, ripped jeans, curls curling in a way that makes my stomach bottom out. I'm aware I haven't said anything.

Why is he here?

Is he here to get *me* back?

A sliver of hope weasels its way into my chest, and I have to clutch my hands to physically stop myself from reaching for my heart to massage it away. Impossible. I'm the one who walked away. Not once. Twice.

And he was the one who put it all on the line. Not once. Twice.

What's that clichéd saying? Fool me once, shame on you. Fool me twice, shame on me.

No, he's not here to get me back. Xander Miller is many things. Funny. Freakishly smart. And kind. He is not a masochist. And yet, all evidence points to him being one, standing at my door.

"Can I come in?" he says, waiting for me to respond.

In my mind, I lean forward and run my hands through his curls all the way to the base of his neck, where I grab onto a fistful of hair and pull him toward me.

I want to hold him. Forever.

Love him forever.

"Ash?" Xander says, reminding me that I have yet to respond.

"Yes," I breathe out, blinking. He walks past me, giving me a whiff of his so fresh and so clean cucumber scent. And I immediately crave burying my face into his neck.

Nope. No. Get it together, Ash.

I watch as he shrugs his satchel bag off his broad shoulder, throwing it on the floor near the kitchen bench. And that's when I notice a stack of papers in his hand.

He turns to me, and I see it in his eyes.

He's not here to win me back. He's got that ruthless determination look, the one I saw back in the café, when he caught me playing the penis game with Emily and he was in the middle of a court case.

"I know how to get your job back," he says, his tone cool and calculated. All business.

The eye contact alone has me squirming inside. I want to grab his hand, drag him to the bedroom, push *him* against the wall, and drop to my knees, watching his eyes grow dark.

"Ash," he says, pleading like I projected that image right into his brain.

"Mmmm," I say, almost breathless. My gaze drags down his body.

"No," he says, reading my mind. His words have the same effect as taking a cold shower. And this is why I wanted to massage that sliver of hope right out of my heart.

It was over then. And it's over now.

Because you don't reject someone twice and live to tell the happily ever after.

God, I'm so fucking embarrassed.

"No, I know. Of course," I choke out, scurrying behind the kitchen counter and making myself busy getting him a glass of water. "Thirsty?" I say, handing him the glass, desperate to not talk about just how much we're not doing anything with each other ever again.

"I can win your case for wrongful termination," he says, already moving on from the fact that there is no "us." He opens the cream folder with purpose, but I can't take my eyes off his face. "Because you were fired due to discrimination, we'll file a report with the Equal Employment Opportunity Commission."

He finally looks up at me, and heat creeps up my neck. Discrimination?

I want to vomit. I'm going to be the poster child for sexually empowered women who are secretly lovesick over their lawyers.

I don't know what to say at this point, so I just say, "Okay" to let him know I heard him.

Xander studies me a moment before continuing. "I had my team request footage from the security cameras on campus. The . . . incident happened off school property." He stumbles on *incident*—which is professional speak for *ass-grab*—but composes himself quickly. "You're in the clear."

I internally freak the fuck out. I thought he was looking into it. I didn't realize he'd set the wheels in motion. That he'd reached out to the school. That this is *happening*.

He takes my silence as acceptance and continues. Turns out, lawyers have a lot to say.

"We'll need to prep you for a deposition," he says, clasping his hands together. "It's basically your verbal testimony. We'll do it in my office conference room, but don't let the chill nature fool you."

"There is nothing chill about you right now," I blurt out. I had kept my running commentary of the situation to myself up until this point. You know, all business. No feelings.

Now, I watch as my uncontrolled comment sends Xander raking his teeth over his bottom lip before releasing it into a smile. God, it's the first smile I've seen since he walked in. And it melts the tension I didn't realize was hanging between us.

He softens ever so slightly while keeping his cool, calm, and collected lawyer on retainer.

"What I mean is that all the answers you give during a deposition are sworn testimony and admissible at trial."

My eyes widen. "Trial?" I say, that sick feeling in my stomach returning. People will ask me about my sex life, and I'll have to air my laundry list of rules and men and sexual encounters in front of the court of law to be judged.

No fucking way. I am not that strong.

Like I'm having this conversation out loud, Xander slowly walks up to me. I put down the glass of water—which was serving as a prop anyway—before he reaches me. That cold tension we had between us when he first arrived is now replaced with anticipation.

He puts his hands firmly on my shoulders and directs me to sit.

When I'm seated and he's sure I'm not a flight risk, he takes a seat next to me.

"We won't go to trial. The school will settle. But we need to light a fire under their asses by filing a formal complaint in court," he says, leaning in. He's aiming for comfort, and I can't resist. I lean in ever so slightly, and every surface possible from my ankle to shoulder is now gently touching him. The amount of control going into keeping this touch so light there could be plausible deniability is intense—but worth it. That entire side of my body lights up like a Christmas tree.

I want to twist my fingers around his. I want to trace my finger along his love line and read his future and tell him I'm in it.

I stare ahead, afraid I'll project that directly into his brain.

I'm sorry. I can't do that with you anymore. His testimony echoes through my mind.

Shut it down, Ash.

Xander's arm moves, and I look down to watch the thick chords of his forearms as he slides the cream folder over to me. "Here's everything you need to prepare for the deposition."

I let my eyes snake up the intricate details of his tattoo, up his forearm and past his bicep that disappears behind his T-shirt. I keep traveling up his neck. The neck I've dragged my mouth over. Past his lips and into his eyes.

His gaze flicks to my mouth before looking at the folder as he flips it open.

Inside are sheets of paper. But in the corner is his business card with *Friday, 4* PM stamped on it.

He points to it. "Don't be late." I watch as that same hand reaches back for his jaw and he scratches it.

We lock eyes a moment longer. "You're really going to get my job back, aren't you?"

He gives me a barely there smile. "Yes."

It's all business. No feelings.

Exactly the way I *used* to like things.

CHAPTER THIRTY-ONE

"There is no way in hell that man is getting my job back," I say to Em, flinging the paperwork in her face. "Have you seen this?"

"Relax," Em says, chilled like she's had enough orgasms to tranquilize a horse. I blame Cody for that. Because of course the one time I bring the theatrics to our friendship she doesn't even react.

I thrust the papers I've been waving around into her face and she finally takes them, and begins reading.

"Name, address, occupation," she says, unbothered. Yeah, so was I when I read over the initial introductory questions.

"Keep reading," I say, pacing.

"Are there any details of the case you find unclear?" she says, as she reads down past the deposition preparation questions. "Uh, yeah. Why the fuck you got fired in the first place? Please explain." The sarcasm dripping from her comment eases the stress that's been building since Xander arrived all cold-blooded, but it's momentary when I hear the "oh" drop out of her mouth.

She's arrived at *Tips for Preparing*. Number six.

Watch out for conclusions disguised as yes/no questions.

Her eyes widen as she reads from the paper. "'So you don't do romantic relationships beyond one night, but you couldn't wait until you got home, off school property, to attempt to satisfy your needs?' What the fuck is this?"

"That is the kind of question I can expect when they try to paint me like a fucking perve who shouldn't be allowed around children," I say, shaking my head. "I can't do it. I'd rather move than have them take my fucking dignity."

"You're not moving," Em says, stating facts.

"I'll try a different school," I say, agreeing that me threatening to move was a little unbelievable.

"As if Principal Holland didn't handle that the moment the paperwork was filed. He's a fucking asshole."

"It says here that you can answer the question in sections. No, you don't do relationships. Yes, of course you waited until you were home. Just tell the truth," Em says.

"I can't even answer the first part of that truthfully, under oath. Do I do relationships beyond a one-night stand? Well, Your Honor, I want to. Just the person I want to do it with, who is sitting opposite me right now—for the record—I rejected not once, but twice, so I'm torn. Maybe I do. Maybe I don't," I say, trailing off. I do not have the capacity to deal with this deposition after discovering that my rule was based on a bunch of bullshit and that the last eleven years of my life were built on a lie.

"Ash, I know you're freaking out," Em says, reaching out to me with her hand, but I don't take it.

"I'm sorry, you've had a lifetime of love to get used to. But this is new and awkward and weird for me, and my heart is beating wildly out of my chest," I say, my words tumbling out.

"Oh, Bambi," Em says, getting up and refusing to take no for an answer as she goes in to hug me.

"I don't understand how anyone is supposed to feel like this," I say, sagging into her. I can literally feel the confidence leeching from my body.

"You can do this," Em says, holding me.

I don't bother arguing with her. Before Xander came back into my life like a fucking hurricane, I was a confident woman who knew exactly what she wanted. And now I'm cowering to the idea of having to speak my truth, under oath, that will be kept on record, in a court of law.

I mean, sure, love and chemistry *can* coexist. But it doesn't mean it's for me. Because of my stupid fucking rules. I made that abundantly clear to Xander.

My rules might have been built on bullshit, but they have served me well for eleven years.

Until now, I've never wavered in my confidence. Never questioned myself. And I sure as hell never, *ever* moped.

What happened?

Xander happened.

Well, fuck that.

I'll figure out how to get my job back, but I'm not doing it with Xander's help. I've never relied on a man for anything more than one night before, and I'm not going to start now. In fact, that's probably the best place to start.

I let go of Em and stand tall in front of her. A smile grows over her face. "Oh hey, where've you been?" she says, acknowledging that the Ash she's come to know and love is standing before her, and not some spiraling mess.

Mad, I can do. Angry, yep, I love that for me.

But not shrinking into a ball and wanting the world to swallow me whole. That just isn't me. "Sorry, took a brief detour. I'm back now," I say, reaching for my phone and swiping to my apps.

"Fuck yes," she says, placing the paperwork on the kitchen bench. "You are going to nail this."

I ignore her as the app loads on my phone. Seconds later, there's an unmistakable chirp. A match. With a guy called Brad. My eyes scrape over the photo. He's wearing a fedora. And a deep V-neck T-shirt. It's a gym selfie. He's flexing his biceps. He's perfect. *Douche.*

I smile, accepting the match and the plan of meeting up on Friday afternoon. I look up at Em, mid-grin, and she's frowning at me.

"Well, I'm definitely going to nail Brad," I say, that mid-grin growing. "Ash is back."

I do a little shoulder shimmy as I make my way to my bedroom to get ready for our next tennis lesson. She follows me into the bedroom.

"Ash, that's not what I meant when I said you were back," she says, crossing her arms over her chest. "We need to prep for your deposition and plan your big romantic gesture to win Xander back, not fuck around with a rebound." She's scowling at me now like she would a student.

"Fuck around with a rebound," I start chanting, just like she did when we were playing the "Fuck Xander" game that seems like forever ago. She doesn't join in. "Fuck around with a rebound!" I continue to chant.

"Win him back!" she chants over my voice. The problem with her being an English teacher is that her voice carries like she's in an amphitheater. I know I can't win, so I stop and wait for her to finish.

"You done?" I ask.

"Are you?" she says back.

"Yes, Em. It's over," I say, surprisingly calm at the definitive nature of this comment.

"It's not over until it's over," she says. I roll my eyes at her, trying to brush her off, but she doesn't let me.

I sigh. "You didn't see his cold eyes slicing into me. He rejected me," I say, serious now. I don't let myself linger in the rejection, afraid it'll be all consuming and have me slinking to the floor in a puddle of tears.

"Ash," Em says.

"It's over. Ash is back. And I don't need a guy to get me my job back," I say before walking past her toward the door, ready for the last month to be ancient fucking history.

* * *

I sit at the bar, ignoring the third message from Xander today asking how the deposition preparation is going.

It's not going anywhere, bro.

The more I thought about it, the more I convinced myself I'm not making a statement admissible in court about my rules and my relationships. I will not be the punching bag. That's my mother's job.

Plus, it's summer vacation. And I wasted four weeks with Xander. I'm not wasting another second responding to messages.

I flip my phone around because after spending the last two days avoiding Xander, I am *thisclose* to meeting Brad, and therefore I am *thisclose* to being thoroughly distracted for the next few hours.

My glass sits empty. The whiskey went down well. But when the bartender asks, I don't go for seconds. I'm not here to fake it.

"Ashleigh." A low, deep voice snags my attention. I turn to look at the man standing next to me. Before I can look up at his face, my eyes are drawn to the dark button-down shirt that's straining against his chest.

"You must be Brad," I say, eyes landing on his face. Brad is your stereotypical frat kind of hot. His perfect fade haircut oozes social status. The look in his eyes suggests he hasn't moved on from the competitive hookup culture of his frat days. And his deck shoes serve as a reminder that Brad is privileged.

All in all, he's a perfect hookup.

"What are you drinking?" I say, waiting for my skin to prickle with anticipation. I feel nothing.

"Bulletproof coffee," he says to the bartender, and I bite back a laugh. Looks like he grew out of the drinking culture from his frat days and now treats his body like a temple. "Empty calories, bro."

My eyes land on the bartender, who steals a glance at me like *what the fuck* before he turns back to the gym bro and says, "Where do you think you are?"

An hour later, we're sitting opposite each other in the coffee shop around the corner from his temple. The gym. Me with my cappuccino, Brad with his coffee with butter and coconut oil. He's on some intermittent fasting diet to help with his gym gains blah blah blah. I did not come to attend a seminar on using ketones as energy and how good it is even though the side effects include shitting yourself uncontrollably at random.

I'm kicking myself for not just letting him meet me at my apartment. I'm not on the app for four weeks and I'm rusty, matching with a man who insisted he buy me a drink first.

"So, are you ready to go?" I say, interjecting his spiel on how carbs are the devil. And how "science" has "literally" proved it. Yeah, where's the systematic review (with homogeneity) of case-control studies, buddy? Oh, you don't have that? It's all anecdotal? I'll stick to my milky coffee and trust my next fart.

"Almost," Brad says as he whips out a protein bar, offering it to me.

"Gross. I mean, no thank you," I say, bouncing my leg to keep me looking alive. I am literally dying of boredom. The complete and utter lack of chemistry is palpable.

"Do you eat burgers?" I say, as he tears into the protein bar and starts chewing excessively. I don't know why I wanted to poke the bear.

"Do you know how many calories are in the bun alone?" he says, shaking his head at me and my stupid question. He goes on to list the calories in the makeup of a Big Mac. Wow. How did this used to be foreplay for me?

My mind wanders to Xander and his sharp tongue and the infuriating fact that he had a comeback for everything.

Witty. Smart. Sarcastic. Deadpan.

Sincere. Kind. Sweet.

God, I want that mouth.

I berate myself for wanting something I can't have and refocus my attention on Brad and his chewing. I'm so turned off. And this makes me angry. Still, this can be salvaged. I can be leaving his apartment in an hour as chilled as Em was.

"Are we doing this?" I say out loud to Brad, but I'm actually asking myself. *Am I really doing this?* Am I really going to go home with this gym bro to try and fuck the feelings away?

"No, you're not," a low voice growls from behind me. It sends a shiver up my spine. I know that voice. I love that voice. Except, I can't love that voice.

I look up to see Xander standing there.

He's wearing a corporate suit without the jacket. His sleeves are rolled up, exposing his forearms, one of them decorated in his tattoos. His curls look like his hands have raked through them many times.

His anger is palpable.

"Get up, Ash," he says through gritted teeth, his hand resting on the back of my chair. I feel the brush of his knuckles on the back of my exposed neck and it sends shockwaves through my body.

"Woah, dude. You good?" Brad says, standing like doing bicep curls at the gym gives him an advantage. Xander finally acknowledges the guy I've been sitting with, sweeping his eyes up and down his body before shaking his head and turning back to me.

"Bone It? Really, Ash?" he says, deadpan. I bite my lip to stop myself from smiling at his amusement. I still haven't said a single thing to Xander rocking up to ruin my hookup. I mean, how can I since I'm mentally undressing him?

"Is this some lovers spat?" Brad says, drawing my attention away from Xander for a moment.

"No," I say, throwing as much disgust in the tone as I can muster.

"Yes," Xander says at the same time. I snap my head back to him, frowning.

"No," I say again.

"Get up, we have a deposition," he says, not taking the hint that when I said no, that was me, having the final say.

He's staring at me. And I'm staring at him. And what we have here is a stare off. I count my breath.

One.

Two.

Three.

There is no way I'm losing this stare off. Not after he rejected me. I would never let myself live it down.

"I'm out of here," Brad says before I hear the scraping of the chair against the floor. I still don't take my eyes off Xander until Brad comments, "No stars."

This comment halts our staring content. "It's not fucking Uber, you douche," Xander says, spitting the words out. Brad, to his credit, which is already in the red, doesn't respond as the door swings closed behind him.

When Brad is long gone, Xander turns back to me and I cave under his expression.

"I don't want to," I say, sounding more like a distraught teenager than the kind of woman who doesn't give a fuck. "I'm not doing it."

"Yes the fuck you are," he says, harsh on every consonant. "Let's go."

I reluctantly stand because if there's one thing I know, it's that you can't win an argument against a damn fucking lawyer.

CHAPTER THIRTY-TWO

Xander directs me to sit in one of the swivel chairs surrounding the mahogany table in the boardroom of his office. Hanging on the beige walls are three large gold frames, each with a portrait of an old white dude. They're painted like they're fucking royalty.

We'd walked past the whimsical older lady who looks like she's been the receptionist since prehistoric times, and who's also the mother figure of the office and knows everyone's secrets. A knowing smile had passed over her face as she said, "Boardroom one is ready for you." Xander had thrown her a grateful smile.

Clearly he has only one thing on his mind: his fucking job.

Or is this his pro bono work?

Great, I'm his charity case.

And now, I'm standing in boardroom one, which reminds me a lot of Principal Holland's office. I wouldn't be surprised if this is where Xander's corporate clients come to circle jerk about how successful they are.

Still, with two other lawyers sitting in the boardroom, I do what Xander says and take a seat. I gave up my right to resist when I left the café with him—willingly—even if I was dragging my feet the entire way up to level thirty-four.

I'm introduced to both lawyers, and one of them, Liam, takes a seat next to me. He emits a warmth that makes me wonder if we're going to do good cop/bad cop.

I briefly glanced over the deposition preparation papers before deciding I'd get my job back myself. Good cop/bad cop was one of the tactics lawyers are prone to using to elicit responses.

I look at Xander, who stalks around the table and takes a seat opposite me.

He's seeing red.

"So you're definitely the bad cop," I say, cocking my eyebrow. A laugh escapes from the lawyer sitting next to him. Jake, I think it was. I'm assuming his role is to be the court reporter in this scenario because he starts typing. I feel a small victory, but it only lasts a second before Xander's straight-set face blooms into a mischievous smirk.

"Why, am I destroying your focus?" He volleys this quip like he didn't even have to think up a witty comeback. It's just there. On the tip of his tongue. My body heats up as he raises one eyebrow, challenging me.

Yes, you're destroying my focus, but no way I'm admitting that to him.

He scrapes his teeth over his bottom lip, knowing exactly what he's doing, and immediately a core memory of Xander flutters behind my eyes.

Him, on top of me. His arms, caging me in. My teeth, scraping the skin of the small tattoo on his bicep.

I squeeze my eyes shut hard to cut off the image supply. When I reopen them, Xander's smirk hasn't left.

"Stop fucking with me," I say before I'm able to control myself. I watch in horror as Jake continues to type.

"What have you prepared?" Xander says, ignoring my request.

"What have I prepared?" I say, repeating his words with a lace of mockery. His eyes flare in irritation at this. Then, he leans back and crosses his arms, like I'm a total inconvenience.

What a fucking asshole.

"What is your educational background?" Liam says, his gentle voice cutting through the tension. "Let's start there." I can see Xander glaring at him, but he doesn't argue. Instead he sits back up straight and waits for my reply.

"I'm a chemistry teacher," I say, neutral. I'm thankful for the redirect.

"What do you know about love and chemistry?" Xander says, not letting up.

"Excuse me?" I say, letting his attitude get the better of me.

"Do I need to repeat the question?" he says. God, he's arrogant when he's in full lawyer mode. Fuck him.

"You want to know what I know?" I say, leaning forward, taking the bait.

"Well, I asked the question, didn't I?"

Exasperated at this little game he's playing, I let loose with my new theory. "While you can experience love without lust or lust without love, it's possible to experience both at the same time for the same person. In fact, studies have shown, contrary to popular belief, that lust and love *aren't* mutually exclusive." I'm practically shouting but now that the floodgates have opened, I don't stop. His lips part slightly, but nothing comes out.

"While lust is something that can hit you like a brick wall, lust is also something you can cultivate. Same with love. Lust and love can develop over time through shared experiences and self-disclosure," I say, the words tumbling out in full fucking confession for Jake to document forever. And yet, I have more to say because I can't seem to shut up.

"Lust developing over time. It happens to people. It's science. My experience, though? Love and lust—they *both* hit me the day I met you. I was just too scared, too heartbroken, too afraid to let you in," I say, shaking through my rage.

It's only after I stop that I realize what I've said.

I'm standing now. So is Xander.

I can almost hear his heart beating, it's so loud. Like maybe this is too much for him.

Then, without looking at Jake or Liam, he says to them, "Leave now."

They get up and leave without saying a word until it's just Xander and I staring each other down on opposite sides of the boardroom.

There's a slight frown. Concern. I see his Adam's apple bob up and down.

And all the rage dissipates. Fuck. He's shaken at this half-cooked love confession. The look on his face tells me I've got more to do if I have any chance of salvaging this. And there is a small chance, because he hasn't kicked me out of here yet.

"Xander, I've been a complete fucking dumbass," I say, walking my way around the boardroom table.

"Not going to argue with you."

"Not only am I in love with you. I've been in love with you for eleven years, I've just been too scared to *let* myself be in love with you," I say, coming around the oval table. There are now only five steps between us, and I hesitate.

"My one-night-only rule was a neat little party trick I used to protect my heart, but I kept it up for eleven years to keep every other guy at a distance because my heart belonged to you. Belongs to you," I go on, making it clear this isn't a thing of the past. This is now. "It always has."

He turns so he's facing me.

"I fell in love with you the moment you walked up to me at the quad," I say. I test the waters and take a step closer to him. He doesn't move.

"I've been in love with you from the moment we kissed," I say, taking another step closer. "I've been in love with from you the moment I commando crawled out of your place. I'm in love with you, Xander," I say. It's time for the grand finale here. Go big or go home. "I'm pretty sure I'll be in love with you forever." I'm now standing right in front of him.

Our breath mingles. I let my arms reach up and around his neck.

When he doesn't pull away, I step closer.

He lingers. Teasing me. The first time, he waited for me to kiss him.

This time, he kisses me.

This time, we're not slow. We're not gentle. We're not pretty. We're desperate. We're practically mauling each other. It's hot. It's heavy. My heart and my head, who've been fighting for eleven years, high five like they're two cops in a buddy action comedy who caught the bad guys. And for the first time in eleven years, I feel whole.

A knock on the door jolts us out of our impromptu make-out session. We break apart, laughing.

Liam pokes his head into the room. "So that was fucking terrible," he says, a wide smile on his face.

"The worst deposition I've ever seen," Xander says, agreeing with Liam.

"I'll schedule in another session," Liam says, his eyes darting between the two of us. "In a couple of days."

Liam closes the door.

Xander turns to look at me. A lazy, lingering smile rests on his face. That's when I notice the faint red-rimmed look around his eyes. "You tired?" I ask.

"I've never felt so alive," he counters.

And my heart fucking grows tenfold.

CHAPTER THIRTY-THREE

"Welcome back to another school year, Sherman Oaks Private. This is Principal Hutchinson, peace out." I release the intercom and spin around in a standard swivel chair in my office. I am fucking beaming.

Connie, our administrative assistant, stands next to me with a stack of papers, waiting for me to sign off on a new curriculum with a focus on mindset, well-being, and psychological safety.

My signature dances across the page, proud.

"The removalists will be here shortly," Connie says, grimacing as she takes in the walls of participation awards. "But I took the liberty of fixing this one."

She hands me my Best Chemistry Teacher award plaque with Principal Holland's name hacked off.

"Thank you, Connie," I say, smiling. She and I are going to get along just fine.

The school bell rings and I stand up. "See you tomorrow."

Bed Chemistry

I bolt out of the office, across the yard, and take up residence at the entrance gate. I might be the principal now, but I sure as shit am going to ask Aaron how Advanced Chemistry is going.

"Principal!" I turn toward the sound of the unmistakable teasing of my favorite class clown, Jonah. "So that's why you were called into the office at the end of last year?"

I point at Jonah as he approaches.

"Ms. Hutchinson," a female voice interrupts us. I swing my gaze to find myself face-to-face with a middle-aged woman who bears some resemblance to Jonah.

"Mom," Jonah scoffs. "It's *Principal* Hutchinson now."

She nods. "I'm sorry, Principal Hutchinson."

"Please, call me Ashleigh."

"Can *I* call you Ashleigh?" Jonah says, interrupting.

"It's Principal Ashleigh to you," I retort, my eyes crinkling.

"I wanted to thank you. You'll likely agree that Jonah is unique," she says, and I already appreciate his mom's choice of word. Not bad. Not difficult. Not disruptive. Unique. "But with your guidance and support, Jonah isn't just excelling at chemistry. His grades are up across the board."

"Jonah's a natural-born leader," I say, as warm as the afternoon sun.

Jonah's mom's eyes shine at this, like it's the first time someone other than herself has come to bat for her kid. And I couldn't be prouder that Sherman Oaks Private does that for Jonah. And not just him. Every kid that goes here.

"Keep up your grades, and the world's your oyster," I say to Jonah.

"I don't like oysters, Miss," Jonah says, before a wayward soccer ball meets his boot.

"It's an idiom. You'll learn about it with Ms. Emily in English," I call out but he's off. Playing. Being a kid.

I turn to his mother. "Seriously, you've got nothing to worry about with Jonah. He's doing just fine."

Thirty minutes later and with a final sweep of the now empty school, I cross through the gates and round the corner.

"Principal Hutchinson," a low, deep voice calls behind me. I know that voice. I love that voice. I spin around and that's when I see him.

Xander. Twenty feet away. In his corporate suit.

I'd be a dumbass if I didn't attempt to stop time for a minute just to take him in—his crisp white shirt rolled up his thick forearms. His dress pants pulling on his thighs.

"How'd it go?" he says, referring to the new curriculum. Fifteen feet away.

When I was asked by the school board what I'd do differently, besides teaching them how to make green fire for the *Wicked*-themed Halloweens or including simple syrup on the exam—you know, two very important life skills—I knew we needed to start helping these kids feel safe.

"We're taking it to the school district next week," I say.

"My girl, making a difference," he says, excited. Hearing him call me *his girl* gets me every time. Ten feet away.

He unconsciously ruffles his hair to shake off the day. The whole vision reminds me of what he looks like post-sex.

He catches me blatantly perving on him, and a smile creeps across my face. This makes him smile, and we're smiling at each other like a pair of dickheads who can't stop smiling. Xander smiling is a brilliant sight. The eighth wonder of the world. Ancient and modern combined. Five feet away.

Xander closes the last of the distance in a few steps and then he's cupping my face, kissing me deeply. "I fucking love you and your brilliant mind," Xander says into my mouth.

"And my body," I say.

"Mostly your body," Xander says, kissing my neck. I melt.

"Wait, what are you doing here? Weren't you supposed to be sleeping at your place tonight?" I say, breathless as he sucks on the sensitive spot on my collarbone. I berate myself for even asking. Who cares? He's here. I wrap my arms around his waist and lean in, feeling the hard lines of his body.

"Can't sleep," he says, winking. "Stay awake with me?"

Flirty Xander does things to my body that give teenagers with raging hormones a run for their money.

"And let Dr. Waitley down?" I say, fake indignant.

He looks down at me from behind his curls. The curls that could end wars. Who am I to deny the curls? Of course I will stay up with him.

I'll stay up with him for the rest of my life.

EPILOGUE

One year later

Operation proposal is a go. I read the text message from Em five steps ahead of Xander, on our way back to the apartment.

Now that I'm actually doing it, I'm excited as fuck. I've never been so sure of anything in my entire life. And I was the girl with the no falling in love rule for eleven years.

When I told Em I was going to propose, the Valley's very own Sandy from *Grease: The Musical* could not contain her theatrics. But I *am* a responsible principal now. So there was no raiding the school supplies for chemicals that have been classified as way too dangerous to use outside of the lab, even if the ideas were fucking dope.

No. It's glow in the dark paint on our brand-new bed.

Cute. And safe.

I feel Xander's arms snake around me, pulling my back into his chest. I pocket my phone quickly and tilt my neck, giving him access.

He presses kisses along my neck as we walk toward the door of our apartment. And suddenly the nerves are replaced with absolute certainty.

I want this man and his mouth forever.

When we reach the door he spins me around and pushes me against the frame, his mouth finding mine. "I can't wait to get you into our new bed," he breathes into my mouth, not breaking contact. One of his hands slides up my side and flirts with the underwire of my bra.

Proposal sex. I'm down.

Especially after we broke the old bed last week.

Why yes, I *am* excited to report that love and lust don't just coexist—they set each other on fucking fire.

His spare hand runs over the top button of my jeans and pops it open. The legend of the sexual magician lives on.

There's a loud *thunk* behind the door to the apartment that has Xander stopping in his tracks. And then we hear Em's muffled, "Shit."

Xander's eyes catch onto me. "Em?" he says, confused. I offer him a look that shows I also have absolutely no idea what Em is doing in the apartment.

Another loud *thunk* and Xander spins me around so he's standing between the door and me, all protective. I swallow a smile. He opens the door in seconds, eyes roaming for the threat.

"Em?" he calls out.

"In here," she says, panic rising in her voice. He takes off toward the bedroom. At this point, I'm trying to understand what could have possibly gone wrong.

Did Em smack her knee on the new bed frame? Stub her toe in the dark? Get paint on the carpet? I mean, the packaging said it was safe for ages three and up.

This proposal was supposed to be simple.

Glow in the dark fabric paint. Em writes *Marry Me?* on the sheets while we're out. She turns the lights off and waits.

It's a cute as fuck throwback to our time at the sleep study together.

"Ash?" Xander says from the bedroom, his voice raised in a question at the end.

"Coming," I say, as I round the corner only to be greeted by darkness.

On the bed, written in perfect cursive is *Marry Me?* Em pulled it off. She did it. Of course she did.

Nothing like the present to propose.

I spin around, looking for Xander, but I can't see him. Shit. I didn't think that part through.

I flick the lights on, and that's when I see him.

On one knee.

Holding out a ring.

"You really think you could beat me to this?" he says, smirking.

"Wait, you've been walking around with a ring?" I say, stealing a glance and—woah—it's a fucking rock. The perks of marrying a lawyer.

He shrugs, like it's the most normal thing in the world that he would propose to me on a regular Tuesday night.

"I'm in love with you, Ash. I've always been in love with you. I'll never stop loving you." He says it so matter of fact, like it's an undeniable truth about life. Like water is wet. Fire is hot. Gravity always wins.

And he's The One.

I join him down on my knees. He discards the (expensive) ring on the floor. I cup his face.

"Will you marry me?" Xander says.

"Yes," I whisper. "I will marry you."

He kisses me deeply.

Then he reaches down for the ring. I stand up. "Not yet."

I turn the lights off, sending us back into darkness.

Marry Me? glows in the dark one final time. My turn to ask.

"Will you marry me?"

"Abso-fucking-lutely I will." I hear Xander's voice hit the shell of my ear before I feel his chest press into my back. Then he's snaking his hand down my arm until he reaches my ring finger and I feel the cool metal slide against my skin.

He spins me around to kiss me.

It's a kiss that was always meant to happen. Like the whole entire universe rearranged itself for this very moment. It's slow. It's sexy. It's love.

Love and chemistry.

It's everything.

ACKNOWLEDGMENTS

First off, in the infamous words of Bella Swan, I am unconditionally and irrevocably in love with Xander Miller. I get that I conjured him out of thin air, so I guess, what I'm really saying is, I am unconditionally and irrevocably in love with myself. And my life. But that statement wouldn't be true if it wasn't for my people.

Let the gratitude begin.

To my agent, Elizabeth Rudnick. You welcomed me into your inbox with a few chaotic paragraphs and a very big dream, and somehow, you saw something worth fighting for. You requested the first fifty pages, then the full manuscript twenty-four hours later, and in that one act, you changed *everything*. Thank you for championing this story, for matching my (completely justified) obsession with Xander, and for believing in me when I was still figuring out how to believe in myself. I feel incredibly lucky to be doing this with you in my corner. Also, to the rest of the team at Gillian Mackenzie Agency.

Acknowledgments

Thank you to Jess Verdi, my editor. You saw the potential in a book that revolves entirely around one bed and then brilliantly suggested we up the spice. (Reader, you're welcome.) Editing with you has been an absolute joy. Your insight, care, and love for these characters made this book better in every way. To Thaisheemarie Fantauzzi Pérez, Rebecca Nelson, Dulce Botello and Mikaela Bender, Stephanie Manova, Megan Matti, and the entire team at Alcove Press, thank you for turning this story into something that exists in the real world (like, in bookstores!). And thank you to my copyeditor, Elizabeth Oliver, who helped tighten every comma and spelling of the word *T-shirt*, you are the unsung hero of this book.

To Sam at Ink and Laurel, for designing a cover that took my entire mood board around Xander's hair and making me scream into a pillow. In a good way.

To Melissa Cassera, you showed me what was possible. Your mentorship, friendship, and fierce encouragement cracked open a door I didn't think I was allowed to walk through. To Pilar Alessandra, you championed my work from the very first, very bad pilot. You saw the promise and made me believe in my voice. To Dawn Ius, you met up with me every week, read every scene, and helped me get this story across the finish line. Your encouragement carried me through. To Carrie Hutchinson, you're always on the other end of a panicked message—"Can you just run your eyes over this?"—and drop everything to do it for me.

To my parents, Duncan and Eva McKenzie, you've shown up for every dream I've ever had. No questions asked. Even when I wanted to be a singer in year seven, despite being, objectively, tone deaf. (I didn't know that at the time. Honestly? I still don't believe it. That's how unwavering your support has always been.) Thank you for believing in me, always.

Acknowledgments

Also . . . sorry not sorry that this book turned out so horny.

To my brother, Keith, and my sisters, Grace and Kathleen, thank you for always asking, "How's the book going?" even when you had no idea what I was talking about.

To my husband, Edwin Jungwirth, for choosing me, every single day. For being the kind of person who doesn't flinch when his wife says, "I'm going to be a writer," but instead replies, "FUCK YEAH," with a grin and a full heart. You've cheered me on through deadlines, drafts, spirals, plot holes, and the many nights I was physically present but mentally in Chapter 17. Thank you for loving me through all of it, and for reminding me that every good love story needs someone who says, "Of course you can." Hey. Look at us. We did it.

To Melvin, my soulmate dog. You died the same week I got the life-changing news I was going to be a published author. You were *literally, physically, emotionally* with me for every single word. I wish you were here to bark during the proofs. We belonged to each other. And I will miss you forever.

To Harry, my son. I started this book when I was pregnant with you. So technically, do you get a cut of my royalties? (We'll negotiate when you learn to read.)

To Jessica Tutton, for listening to every thought, spiral, meltdown, and mini triumph. You didn't just hear it. You *held* it. Thank you. To Clare Desira, for the on-the-fly coaching that reminded me to stop and actually *celebrate* this wild ride. To Kathy Loewenstern, you keep me sane and grounded. To Adrian Stephenson, your excitement is contagious, and you constantly remind me that this is supposed to be fun.

To the Syn Sisters: Yen, Ayesha, Farhanna, Lynne, Narelle, Helen, Sue, and Gabby. Thank you for letting me hijack every boozy lunch to talk about this book.

Acknowledgments

To the crew responsible for nailing Xander's hair (they voted unanimously for the "Golden" music video or Venice Film Fest), for securing tickets to Louis Tomlinson for me after I got PTSD getting Eras Tour tickets, and for screaming "Where Do Broken Hearts Go" with me: Jacky, Karis, Sam, Anna, Tahlia. Thank you.

To Mhairi McFarlane, your books were the reason I believed funny, emotional, whip-smart love stories could exist in one package. You lit the match. This book exists because your words came first.

To Mindy Kaling, watching *The Mindy Project* was the moment I thought, *Oh, I want to do this.* You were the reason I wrote my first pilot. You turned daydreaming into a career. Thank you for showing women like me that we can be funny *and* a boss bitch.

And finally, to you—the reader . . .

Thank you for opening your hearts (and wallets) to Ash and Xander.

My characters love fearlessly. They're passionate to a fault. Often spiralling, frequently messy, and occasionally walking five hundred miles in the wrong direction. But they always mean it.

If there's one motto I live by, it's this: **Always follow the voice you doubt**.

And, most importantly?

Just be delusional.